THE WOMAN WHO RAN FOR THE HILLS

CARMEN REID

B
Boldwood

First published in Great Britain in 2023 by Boldwood Books Ltd.

A CIP catalogue record for this book is available from the British Library.

Paperback ISBN 978-1-80162-809-9

Large Print ISBN 978-1-80162-810-5

Hardback ISBN 978-1-80162-808-2

Ebook ISBN 978-1-80162-812-9

Kindle ISBN 978-1-80162-811-2

Audio CD ISBN 978-1-80162-803-7

MP3 CD ISBN 978-1-80162-804-4

Digital audio download ISBN 978-1-80162-805-1

Boldwood Books Ltd
23 Bowerdean Street
London SW6 3TN
www.boldwoodbooks.com

For Diana, who just kept on believing in me and this story, especially when the chips were down.

1

LONDON, JANUARY

I'm in the back of the ambulance rattling towards the hospital when I make the big decision. Probably quite a lot of important decisions are made in the back of ambulances. I mean, it certainly focuses the mind, all that searing pain and panic, and the prospect of meeting serious-faced doctors, who are going to have to perform surgery, most likely this afternoon.

Generally, in ambulances, people are not thinking: Do I have any pasta sauce left? Did I put the bins out? Drat, I really need to cancel that app subscription before it renews.

No, in the back of the ambulance, it's either: I really wish I hadn't gone up that ladder/answered my phone on the treadmill/walked the dog when it was icy... or else it's big decisions time.

So, my decision is, I'm going to leave Jono.

Yes. I am.

Definitely.

Well, I sort of have to... it's the only thing I can do now to keep what's left of my dignity. I have to see the situation for what it is. And act accordingly.

I have worked for Jono for three years, as his legal secretary or 'right-hand woman', and for close to two of those years now, we've been having a relationship that our work colleagues don't know about and, for all of this time, I've been in love with Jono.

I've organised and smoothed out every one of his working days and in all the time away from work that we've been able to spend together, I've listened to him, loved him and soothed his soul. Because he's older than me, and separated with young teenagers, I've always had to share Jono with his demanding career, his boys, his elderly parents, his golf time and the regular demands from his former wife.

I've put up with the indignity of only getting him during the workday and then in the time he can find for me in his busy schedule of a life – when he's told the boys he's working late, or 'popping out for a pint with the team', even, shudder, 'servicing the car' one weekend. As his executive assistant, I've even sent some of these messages myself to sophisticated Sophie, the separated wife, mother to his two children.

So sorry, Jono won't be able to take the boys to the party on Friday evening because he's working late, but he's booked a taxi for them at 7 p.m. and he'll pick them up at 10.30 p.m.. Will this work for you all? Just let me know, Jennifer

Leaving me with less than three hours of Jono time, of which at least a third will be spent wondering if it's time for him to go yet.

For almost two years, I've put up with all our office-hours secrecy and all this sharing of his time because when I was with Jono – in the office, chatting on the park bench outside the office, making frantic love in my flat just ten minutes' walk from the office, or drinking the cool glass of wine together afterwards – I felt happy. Nine years older than me, wise, experienced, an excellent legal mind, a good storyteller, a handsome man, I enjoy everything about his company.

But he never wanted to make me 'official'. He doesn't like to think about Sophie and their two boys, Oliver and Charlie, age fifteen and thirteen, having to know about me, having to accept me. Occasionally, when we have talked about it, he says that this is, of course, something he plans to do in the future, when the children are older. He doesn't want to make them any more unhappy about the divorce. He's worked on too many divorce cases. He hates divorce. And says it is almost always quite amicable until 'the new woman' turns up and then it all goes to hell.

'Why don't we go on holiday?' I've been asking him. 'I want to go away with you. I want to spend a whole week with you and wake up with you every morning. Surely you can tell the boys that it's for work? Your demanding client? Or a conference? We'll go somewhere sensible, plausible... like Brussels, Zurich, or Frankfurt... no one would take their girlfriend to Frankfurt.'

Jono had promised to think about it, which gave me hope that I would get a taste of the sophisticated, grown-up life that I had all planned for us in the future. In my fantasy future, we would live in one of those beautiful old mansion flats in central London. Inside, everything would be perfect, if a touch old school, like Jono really. There would be lovely crockery and lamps; polished, satinwood antiques; an art deco cocktail bar with crystal glasses and an array of bottles; me, with my hair done, in a dress and expensive underwear, having a cocktail with Jono, then a visit to the theatre and a delightful time together in that luxurious, king-sized bed afterwards. No children, I couldn't really see children in this grown-up haven I was building – although I would aim to make friends with Oliver and Charlie and maybe even Sophie – no dogs, no cat, just me and Jono, looking after one another, devoted, enjoying our work and enjoying our lovely life together... travel, dinners, art galleries, love and passion. That was what I wanted for us. That was what I thought Johnathan wanted for us.

* * *

But now, this morning has happened.

It is still so raw and so painful that I don't want to think about it clearly. Plus, one of the ambulance crew is now fitting a mask over my nose and mouth and I don't think laughing gas has ever helped anyone to think more clearly.

I take a deep breath in and the events whirl about in my mind. It began, of course, when I answered the office phone and the woman at the other end said she was Sophie, and that I must be Jennifer, and she'd heard so much about me... For a moment, I paused, no idea what was going to come next. Was she going to scream at me? Or ask me out for a bonding lunch, maybe?

But instead, she sounded quite relaxed, almost breezy, as she said: 'I've left messages for Jono and tried to get through to him, but no reply. So, can you just make sure he definitely knows it's today, 3 p.m., at the Marylebone Hospital antenatal department for the second scan? Marylebone Hospital, antenatal department, 3 p.m.,' she'd repeated. 'Have you got that, Jennifer?' she'd asked. 'I really want him to be there.'

And as my stunned, make that whacked-sideways-with-a-bat, mind struggled to grasp the meaning of this hospital antenatal scan information, she'd added just to make it crystal clear to me: 'He'll have told you, of course. We're expecting twins. Who would have thought? Back together again and pregnant in our forties! We are thrilled. Absolutely thrilled.'

I'm a little blurry about the sequence of events that followed, but I do know I dropped the heavy, landline receiver. I remember the clang that it made on the desk. And then I interrupted Jono in a client meeting.

'So sorry... it's very urgent...' I said at the door, voice low and trembling, but urgent.

'Really? Are you sure?' he'd looked at me in dismay as he racked his mind for what could possibly be so urgent.

And then, in my little office room, I furiously whisper-shout at him. I am as angry, as enraged as anyone could possibly be while whispering to make sure his client and no one else in a nearby office can hear.

'That was your wife on the phone!' I whisper-screech, yes, turns out whisper-screeching is possible, if you're insanely angry, but also allergic to 'making a scene'.

He is utterly shocked and aghast. It's as if it's come as a monumental surprise to him that his lover, who is expecting him to commit to her in the very near future, might be quite unhappy to hear that he and his 'former-now-separated' wife are happily reunited and, in fact, planning to welcome in a whole new branch of the family.

He sits down, he stands up, he walks from one side of the office to the other.

'When did this happen?' I keep asking and when I say 'this' I mean the whole hideous scene: from Jono back with Sophie, to Sophie getting *pregnant* to antenatal scans. Yes, *scans*... this is a second scan... and *twins*... twins!!

'I was going to talk to you...' he keeps repeating.

Funnily enough, this information does nothing to calm me down, as I now spiral, thinking of recent short 'holidays' he's been on, supposedly with Oliver and Charlie, plus a smattering of 'golf weekends with the chums' when he's been completely unavailable on the phone. Then there's a torrent of other strange little memories that had me wondering momentarily and now they all make sense … his shirts smelling of Lenor and lavender ironing water, instead of the starch-heavy laundry service; his car not being at his 'Divorced Dad flat', on occasion, with no explanation…

I remember Jono putting a glass of water into my hand and my hand shaking hard. I remember getting up and rushing out of the room into the corridor, my footsteps ringing out on the hard limestone tiles. So, I'm rushing towards the lift. I just want to get out. The glass is still in my hand, shaking, spilling. I'm rushing, crying and my foot in my high, office pump skids out behind me and I crash to the ground… glass shattering, water spilling, bones and soft tissue landing hard, hard on those shiny, unforgiving tiles.

Pain in my chin and my face, where I've hit the floor and bitten into my lip. Burning pain in my elbows, which have been skinned on landing. But much worse, shooting, searing pain coming from my knee, which has taken the full impact first. My knee feels squishy, wrong, too far into the tiles. I don't want to move. I don't want anyone to move or to even touch me.

* * *

So, it will have to be over. Jono and I aren't going to have a mansion flat, or a cocktail bar, or a delightfully harmonious working relationship and passionate love life. It is over.

Instead, Jono has gone back to his wife and children, and he and Sophie are going to have twins. They'll probably buy a bigger house, right out of London. He'll focus even harder on his career to provide for all these children. Maybe he was trying to find the 'right' moment, whenever the hell that would be, to tell me it was all over for us and time for me to move on.

It hurts. It hurts and hurts.

I take another deep breath of the gas and find that it numbs my aching lip but has no affect on my emotional pain whatsoever.

What I wanted, what I had planned isn't going to happen now. I'm trying to let this sink in. I'm trying to get a handle on what this means. I'm thirty-nine years old... I'm a glorified PA, who lives in a rented flat, and is single all over again. Plus, I've shattered my kneecap. I might never be able to wear high heels again.

This was not the plan. This was so not the plan.

I can hear the ringing of my phone and I'm astonished that I've somehow managed to bring my phone and maybe even my handbag along with me into the ambulance.

I look at the paramedic and point.

'No, I wouldn't worry about that right now,' she says, 'anyone in the back of an ambulance is allowed to ignore phone calls.'

The phone rings twice again before the paramedic relents, passes me my handbag and lets me answer it.

'Someone's very worried about you, are they?' she asks as I take out my sleek silver mobile and she removes my mask.

Just as I expected, it's Jono.

'Hello,' I answer, not sure that I want to talk to him or even hear his voice.

'Are you at the hospital yet?' he asks.

'No, not yet. Still in the ambulance.'

'I am so sorry,' he says for about the one hundredth time.

'I don't think I want to talk right now,' I tell him.

'I understand, totally, and I wish I didn't have to ask you this,' he continues. 'I'm so sorry,' he repeats, 'but the file for this afternoon's case...'

I slump back against the strange plastic pillow under my head. And now I'm not dealing with Jono, I'm dealing with Jonathan Chesterton QC, and despite the drama going on in his personal life right now, he has a court case to get to this afternoon.

The papers he needs are in my top desk drawer I remember with relief. They are in order, absolutely organised, typed perfectly and held together the way he likes them with a small bulldog clip in the very top left-hand corner, in a cream-coloured file with a bold and easy-to-read label on the front and along the spine.

I tell him exactly where to find them. Then the paramedic takes the phone with her plastic-gloved hand, taps the end-call button and puts it back in my handbag.

'That's quite enough of that,' she says, 'no one in the back of an ambulance needs to explain themselves to their boss. And that's final.'

'Thanks,' I tell her.

Unfortunately, he is not just my boss, so it's all much more complicated. But I decide to take her advice and stop even trying to think about it all. I rest my head, look up at the ambulance ceiling and wonder what on earth I'm going to do now.

2

I'm propped on white pillows, a white sheet below, a white sheet above, and a white cotton blanket over the sheets. There's a thick white cast on my right leg all the way from mid-thigh to below the calf. I've demolished my right kneecap – *patella*, it turns out is the medical name – and I've had an operation to repair the damage.

'That's you off the dance floor for a few weeks,' joked one of the nurses as she helped me back into bed.

I'm going to need crutches or a walking frame for a couple of weeks, then a stick, then physio. Apparently, I should be 'as right as rain' in about two to three months, according to the brief chat I had with the surgeon, pre-op.

* * *

It's almost 7 p.m. now and I'm lying in my bed in this hospital ward feeling very strange. I'm not in pain, I've had too many drugs for that. But here I am, stuck in a hospital bed. When I got out of my own bed this morning, I could never have guessed at what this day had in store – news of Jono's *twins* and a knee operation. I feel nostalgic for this morning's me, drinking tea and eating... what did I have for breakfast, I wonder? Was it oatcakes and marmalade because there was no cereal left? Anyway, this morning's me listened to the radio, showered, put on a nice work outfit, did her hair, her eyes, applied red lipstick and had no idea how pear-shaped everything was about to go.

And there is no one here to see me, I realise, feeling more than a little sorry for myself. Every other bed has a visitor, but I'm on my own. My phone has run out of charge and I don't have a charger... or a toothbrush, or clean pants, pyjamas, or anything nice to eat or drink, and I've missed supper because I was recovering from the anaesthetic.

Earlier, I had to sign a consent form, giving details, names, addresses and contact information. The 'next of kin' question stopped me in my tracks.

My blue biro in my shaky hand hovered above it.

Who is my next of kin?

My mother died four years ago.

My Dad and I are not really close... we're not unfriendly though; in fact, we're really quite friendly. But I don't see him often and I couldn't imagine landing him with a call from a hospital informing him that I'm in Ward 22 having broken my knee.

There's my younger sister, Isla. She is next of kin. But we are, let's be honest, quite unfriendly. We've hardly spoken since Mum's funeral because things are painful and strained between us.

So that leaves Jono.

Even though I know I'm going to have to leave him, he is, for the time being, my next of kin. So, I filled in his name and his mobile number and asked them to please let him know I needed an operation, all the while thinking: when I leave Jono, whose name will I put in this space the next time I need a next of kin?

I live in London, a city of millions, and I no longer seem to be really close to anyone else. I've wrapped my life around Jono.

Then there is also the baby divide. Almost all my friends have children now and their lives have become so different from mine. Yes, there are one or two singletons, still trawling the London dating circuit. Oh my god... to avoid any kind of panic, I quickly squish down the thought of having to get back 'out there' to that terrible scene.

I mean... I do *see* people. I do spend time with and enjoy the company of a circle of friends: there are messy home dinners with the baby families and wine bar crawls with the singletons... but if I'm honest, it's been a long time since I felt truly close to anyone other than Jono.

Most of my time is spent with 'Jonathan' the barrister at work and out-of-office hours, Jono.

I look at the clock on the ward wall.

Six minutes past seven.

Seven minutes past seven.

Is my decision to leave him final?

Until today, I had thought he was my keeper, my forever. I had thought that one day, he would set up home with me and be truly mine.

I feel a tear slipping from the corner of my eye.

So, now what?

Is it really over, like I told him in a furious whisper-shout?

What if he swept in with a bouquet of wildly extravagant long-stemmed roses and a diamond ring and said he'd told Sophie he couldn't possibly go back, despite the imminent babies, and I was to marry him as soon as possible?

What if he arrived at my bedside with two flights to Brazil because he'd made enquiries and Brazil needs high-flying lawyers and I'm to come with him because we're starting a brand-new life together over there?

I realise, even as I imagine these scenarios, how unlikely they are. Jono is not the type of person to rush into romantic gestures or onto aeroplanes to Brazil.

What if he just turns up and sits by my bedside and looks at me deeply, intensely, the way he did that very first time we kissed against his office door and tells me: 'Jennifer, I'm here for you, don't worry about Sophie, don't worry about the new babies... I am yours. I love you and I want you to be mine forever. I know how much this means to you.'? OK, I'm obviously getting carried away now and muddling Jono up with the kind of hunky, yet totally emotionally attuned, men that Hollywood would have us believe are just hanging about in every coffee shop and supermarket.

No, I don't think I will ever hear Jono utter the words, 'I love you and I want you to be mine forever.' In fact, he's never once told me he loves me. Whenever I've said it to him, his reply has been: 'I care for you so very much.'

Yet again, I have failed to wake up and smell the proverbial cup of Columbian.

But... what if he came through for me with one big, sincere gesture... a promise of Paris, or New York, or even just a bottle of Champagne and, 'Let's try to work this out, because it's you I want to be with.'?

That, yes... *that* could still save the situation.

Another half an hour passes and I try not to mind that visiting time looks as if it's coming to an end and Jono hasn't appeared... of course, he hasn't. He's probably safely in the family bosom by now, showing the twins' antenatal scans to Oliver and Charlie.

But then, just as hope has totally left and I feel a tear of self-pity slip from my eye, the ward doors open and my heart skips a beat as

Jono walks in. He's still tall and handsome and this evening, he's buttoned up into his grey tailored overcoat. He looks around, spots me and approaches my bed. He's smiling, but I can read the anxiety in that smile... no wonder.

I smile back, feeling my heart thud in my chest.

As he reaches the bed, he takes hold of my hand and kisses it gently.

'Hello, Jennifer, how are you doing?' he asks.

'I've been better,' I say.

'How did the op go?'

'Pretty well apparently... just two to three months on crutches and a stick, then I'm good to go, apparently.'

'Good grief!' he exclaims, sounding alarmed. 'Is the kneecap—'

'Smashed,' I tell him. 'It's been replaced by something else... plastic, metal, I'm not sure.'

'Good grief...' he repeats, looking quite shocked.

'So, how did the scan go?' I ask crisply, as if this is a standard work-related enquiry. 'Are the twins doing well?'

At this, Jono sits down on the visitors' chair and buries his head deep into his hands.

'Jesus Christ,' he says now.

During our whisper-fight earlier, he told me that having another baby, or two, had not been his idea. In fact, Sophie had apparently completely 'sprung' this on him.

'But *twins*?' I'd demanded. 'Are you sure you haven't been doing IVF behind my back?'

'Of course not,' he'd insisted.

I'm waiting for him to say something, anything, that might give me some hope. I look at the side of the face I've kissed so many times. It's always so easy in the movies: guy does Unforgivable Thing, but quickly Realises His Mistake and Declares Undying

Love, or heroine has Moment of Blinding Insight and Breaks Free in dramatic scene to start New Life. But I love Jono and I hurt so much about this. He doesn't look as if he's about to do any undying love declaring, but I don't want to break free. I want to be with him. I love him. I even love that he still loves his wife and kids and doesn't want to hurt them, which isn't helpful, I admit.

He still doesn't say anything.

At his feet is a Waitrose carrier bag. He picks this up and sets it on the bedside table. This is not the kind of bag that would contain a dozen red roses, or Champagne, or commitment diamonds, or flight tickets, or any kind of dramatic gesture.

No.

It turns out to contain a carton of apple juice, a large bag of salt-and-vinegar crisps, salmon and watercress sandwiches and a yoghurt.

'I thought you might be hungry,' Jono says.

'Thanks,' I manage. Tears spill out over my cheeks, because usually crisps and my favourite type of sandwich would be fine, would be kind and thoughtful even. But not when you need roses, or diamonds or just some proof that I mean as much to him as he means to me... proof that there's still a hope he will choose me over his family.

'I'm so sorry,' he says. He hands me a clean tissue from my packet on the bedside table. I take it but feel it's a bit too small to soak up all my heartbreak.

We're going to break up now... I know it. I feel it. Here, in this nondescript hospital ward, me with my leg in plaster, surrounded by other ill or injured people.

'So, this is where we are...' he says finally.

And that's when I realise he doesn't want to be the one to say it has to end. Maybe he's thinking it can all carry on somehow...

Sophie at home with Oliver, Charlie and the twins... me in the office and the flat, available for whenever he needs me.

But the imminent twins have changed everything. Even if Jono now left Sophie again, we would probably have to look after the twins several days a week in some complicated joint custody agreement. I imagine a pair of toddlers rushing about my future flat, pulling bottles from the cocktail cabinet, mashing soggy biscuits into the Persian rugs. Sophie and the older children would loathe me. And my whole life would be heading off in a direction I never wanted.

'Would you like a sandwich?' Jono asks.

'No!'

'But you must be hungry, Jennifer. What about some crisps?'

'No. I don't want any bloody crisps,' I hiss. And then, somehow, I manage to blurt out: 'This is over between us, Jono.'

'I realise you must be very angry,' he says quietly.

'Yes, I'm pretty bloody furious,' I reply, voice low. 'I thought that one day we would be properly together... you know, have a home, build a life together.'

'So did I...' he says quickly. But I hear only the past tense. There's no moment of hope there.

'I'm sorry,' he says AGAIN and I could just scream. Sorry! Sorry!! Sorry just won't cover it as the future life I had planned with him is smashed up into pieces.

I try not to look at him. I try to think of all the possible disadvantages of staying with Jono that I can bring to mind... he's nearly a decade older than me, one day in the future I'd have been his carer not his other half. I'd have been clipping his toenails, cleaning his earwax, making appointments to have his hearing aid reviewed. And he is fussy... maybe he'll get more and more fussy as he ages, have quite the hissy fit if his supper isn't served exactly the way he likes it. And does he have to play golf for four hours every Sunday? I wonder if the twins will bring that to a halt.

I'll be fine... I'll be absolutely fine... I tell myself very quickly. I'll... go abroad... have a wild adventure... do something to get out of this horrible, sad situation.

'Jennifer?' Jono turns to look at me, he even reaches over and takes hold of my nearest hand. I still can't help hoping that this will be it – the grand declaration, the big promise, the choosing of me over them.

But, instead, Jono asks: 'Could you consider still being my PA?'

I pull my hand away as if I've been scalded.

'No! I bloody well could not,' I tell him. 'I'm resigning.'

And then I realise I am actually resigning, right now, as I say the words. Oh god. This mess just gets wider and deeper and uglier.

Slightly panicky, I add: 'And I'll need a decent severance package. You might want to tell the HR department to look into it.'

Maybe I'm even issuing a slight threat with those words. No one at work *knows* about us, even if they may have their suspicions.

'Of course, of course...' he says.

We exchange some other sad, defeated sentences about will I get home OK tomorrow and does Jono have things he might need to pick up from my flat and when would I want to come in and pack up my desk? Then I tell Jono he should go.

I watch him walk towards the ward door. I'm sure he'll turn to me just before he leaves and sure enough, he does. I read the look on his face as part sad, part baffled and part relieved.

And now what... now what... now what? That's the only question that rushes round my head all evening.

A nurse comes round with fresh painkillers later and I wonder if she has anything to help me sleep.

'I'm thinking maybe horse tranquilliser,' I tell her.

'Rough day?' the nurse asks.

'Let's just say it's been quite disappointing. Maybe it's just as well I broke my kneecap, otherwise I'd probably have kicked my *ex-*boyfriend very hard in the—'

'Jacksie?' she volunteers.

'Yeah.'

'There's still time,' she assures me, 'in a few days, you'll be a pro on the crutches and able to swing the good leg nice and hard.'

3

The next day, I'm taken home by ambulance, so that two paramedics can help me get up the three narrow flights of stairs to my top-floor flat. Built at the turn of the 1900s, there is no lift.

'Now, you do have someone checking on you, don't you?' one of them asks once I'm in the front door and they've clocked that this is a small, one-bedroomed place and I live here on my own.

'Yeah, of course, I'm going to be fine. And there's Amazon and Deliveroo for anything I might need,' I assure them, desperate to be home and on my own and temporarily ignoring all the problems that might come with not being able to put any weight on one leg for at least a full week.

They go down the stairs and one of them climbs all the way back up again with a wheeled Zimmer frame and a pair of crutches, so I can work out what suits me best. Until the cast comes off, I am to put NO weight on my leg. The doctor has been very clear about that.

'I didn't expect to be using one of these so soon,' I tell the paramedic as he wheels in the Zimmer.

'Best get your practice in early,' he jokes.

At first, it's a complete relief to be home. I flop onto the sofa and enjoy the calm, the quiet, the view from my window, the fact that no one is going to come up to me and take an unexpected blood sample. These are all positives. But it soon dawns on me that this is not going to be easy. It takes a full thirty minutes to negotiate doing a wee. When I Zimmer myself to the kitchen, I realise that, yes, I can make a cup of tea, but I will have to drink it standing at the sink as I can't carry it back with my crutches or my Zimmer. That is definitely a low moment.

Back at the sofa, I let the calm of the room soothe me as the events of the last two days settle around me.

So, I've split from Jono and left my job. How I feel about this seems to vary from moment to moment. I seem to swing from shocked and furious to devastated and lost and then back again. I really did love him, even if our relationship was built on many a compromise about his family, our work relationship, how much time he wanted to spend with me and many other things. I did love him. And all my plans have now evaporated because they were all centred around him. I feel alone and completely directionless and my knee has trapped me in my flat.

* * *

Three long days of pyjama grief go by. I do not answer any calls. I only eat toast and ice cream. I watch entire box sets – the more frivolous, the better. I reread some favourite old books and I wallow. Occasionally, I brush my teeth, carefully avoiding the healing gash inside my lip, but that's about all the self-care I can manage. I do not look in the mirror. I spend quite some time working out how to wash with a straight leg in a cast that can't get wet. In the end, I manage a brisk shower, holding my cast over the edge of the bath with the shower curtain draped carefully over the top of my thigh.

Then on day four, I wake up after a deep sleep and feel as if the weight on my chest has shifted a little. I feel quite significantly better and braver. There is some pale, wintry sunlight falling into the room and from the moment I open my eyes, I'm almost cheerful, definitely more energetic and ready to do something. I have my strange, lop-sided shower to keep the cast dry and, even though it takes almost forty minutes, for the first time since coming home from hospital, I get dressed.

I make strong coffee for breakfast. Once the mug is empty, I start hobbling about my small kitchen with a cleaning cloth and find I can't stop what I've started here. I deep clean, going so far as to wash down the fridge and the cupboards, and then sorting out all the jumble of supplies inside.

Vintage herbs and spices, untempting tins of beans and jars of crusty mustard all hit the bin and when I've finished every last cupboard and spice rack, I don't feel tired, just ready to tackle the next thing. So, in the bathroom, I wipe everything down as best I can with a cloth in one hand, a crutch in the other. I look through the open shelves and then the cupboard, briskly throwing out all unused tester pots, half-used tubes and old, dried-out bits of make-up.

In the sitting room, vigorous vacuuming, pillow plumping and dusting is out of the question with the cast, but I can sit and sift. So, I go through the bookcase and the DVDs, sorting out my keepers from my to-be-donated. I make a small, tempting pile of to-be-reads and put them on the coffee table, just an arm's reach from the sofa. Even the droopy pot plants get some water and attention and I hobble out to the tiny balcony to wipe down the table and chairs that haven't been used since late last summer.

Finally, I'm in the bedroom, opening up my wardrobe doors and looking at the carefully chosen things that clothe the life I've built for myself... up till now. Two-thirds of what's hanging here is sober lawyers' office wear: shapely pencil skirts, fitted shirts, cashmere cardigans, cropped jackets and all the office heels – pumps, boots, ankle boots, lace-up boots. There's nothing like having an office affair to make you pay close attention to your workwear and work shoes.

Then there is my underwear collection: expensive bras, silk and lace camisoles, slinky expensive slips and suspender belts, black lace body stockings... most of this has been bought by Jono... for Jono.

With determination, I haul one of the big suitcases out from under my bed and begin to pack it with every office skirt, office shoe and office jacket. Then, on top of that, I pile the hundreds of pounds' worth of bras, slips, suspenders and lacey, slithery things. I try to ignore the flashbacks that almost every one of them brings: the peach one, the blue... the cupless bra and Jono's reaction to me wearing that. Then I look carefully through the remaining clothes for anything else that has a strong association with him. There's the luxurious pink wool scarf he bought me for Christmas. That goes into the case, along with the perfume he loves and the blouse I know was the one I wore when we launched into our first kiss against his closed office door.

I shut the suitcase lid and even do up the buckles to make sure those clothes won't escape and I won't change my mind.

What's left in the wardrobe, apart from the blouses and cardigans, looks limp and under-funded: several well-worn pairs of jeans, some lacklustre jumpers, sweatshirts and T-shirts, then there's the flesh-coloured smalls – a tangle of tights, T-shirt bras and jaded microfibre pants; in the far corner, a smattering of evening and 'smart' dresses, although I can't think when I was last at a cocktail party, art gallery opening, or anything properly dressed up.

My social life has completely withered in the time that Jono has been my focus. For a long time, I did believe that this would all change and Jono would properly let go of his former family life and our life together could begin. But if I'm really, brutally honest with myself, maybe somewhere along the line, I stopped *believing* and began just *hoping*. Deep down, I knew the pull his children and former wife had on him and I must have known there was a risk he would go back... I'd just never wanted to really think about it.

As I push the case out into the cupboard in the hall because I don't want it in my bedroom, I realise with something of a jolt that maybe I wasn't as happy with Jono as I thought I was. Maybe I did all the running and the loving and the soothing and the organising... and maybe... I didn't get enough back.

* * *

'Oh bloody hell!' I say loudly, out loud. It's the first time I've used my voice for days and it feels hoarse and creaky.

'Bloody, bloody hell!' I repeat, louder now. 'Goodbye legal executive assistant Jennifer. And goodbye Jono and Jennifer.'

But now what?

I feel almost panicked... because the question is terrifying, overwhelming, but also exhilarating. So, I do what almost anyone would do when faced with a major life decision. I make more coffee, open up my laptop and google every single possibility I can imagine.

The search starts close to home:

Legal secretary jobs

and

men aged 40+

I drink more coffee, give my imagination free rein and the search moves further afield:

How to move to New York, Manhattan apartments to rent, US legal secretary jobs for English law secretaries, men, New York, aged 30+, US visas

Followed by:

Australian visas
Canadian visas
New Zealand visas

More coffee and now I'm onto:

volunteering in Africa/India

Maybe that's what I need to do, something completely totally different.

Up pops a suggestion to:

volunteer on horseback in South America!

This offer stops me in my tracks.

I try to imagine travelling to South America... when the furthest away I've ever been is a long weekend in New York. Hanging out with horses... something I haven't done since I was young when I had riding lessons twice a week and spent my summer holidays helping out at the local stables. I try to imagine having the chance to see the Andes and gallop across the Pampas... and hike to Machu Picchu. I'm scrolling through the pictures on the website... this really would be an adventure to jolt me out of my bubble of London heartbreak. And that's what people do in situations like this, isn't it? Tear up the rule book, go somewhere brand-new, have an adventure and realise there's so much more to life than waiting around for a man to make up his mind about which woman he wants to be with.

I glance down at my cast. Unfortunately, I'm several months away from mountain hikes and galloping across the Pampas.

So… what do I do until then?

4

Finally, the leg cast comes off and physio starts, with all its finickety little exercises, and then, at last, comes the day when I can sort of walk again with just a stick for support.

The next morning, when I see myself in the bathroom mirror in my jeans with my stick, looking close to my old self again, I decide that this is finally the day when I can get away.

With just a stick, I have one hand free to wheel a trolley case, so I can get the hell out of here. I have to get out of here. Apart from hospital trips, I've been staring at the walls for eleven days in a row, running over and over through all the emotions from tearful to terrified, from exhilarated to panicked.

I have to get out and get away.

And no, I may not have a plan, but I'm sure that if I can just get out of here with some belongings, I can make a plan. Or maybe a plan will come to me.

What the hell. Pack up, get out, think later.

I hobble on my stick to the bedroom, put a compact trolley case on the bed and quickly pack up everything in the clean, lean, post-Jono-purge wardrobe. It's no big job to pack up my toiletries and make-up either, because they have also been streamlined during my days of searching around the flat for something to do.

Feeling almost shaky and tearful now, I look in every room, wondering if there's anything else I want to take. A book or two here, a DVD there, some photographs in frames, but really, there's nothing else that feels as if it has to come right now. I can organise a packing and storage situation when I'm further down the line with this whole 'total change and what I'm going to do next' situation.

Heavy photo albums, boxes of mementos, several shelves of books, the suitcase of office things, boots and more shoes... furniture... I'll worry about all that in a week or two, when I've worked out what on earth I'm doing next. But right now, I have to Get Out.

I take my stick, my coat and my suitcase and hurry out of the flat and out of the building as quickly as I can on my wonky knee. I'm walking towards the station with only the vaguest plan of going to stay with my friend Isobel who lives alone, with the luxury of a spare bedroom, beside the sea in Brighton.

She would take me in for a while. I've gone through a bad break-up with her help before. She prescribed long beach walks and endless nights out as my cure. So, a whirl of windswept, sandy, salty days and then feeling sick and lost in charmless pub toilets followed, along with thudding hangovers which did nothing to ease the heartache.

But she has a spare room, she is a big-hearted friend and she would probably let me stay for as long as I need. She's most likely at work, so I'll have to phone her and maybe meet her in her lunch break to collect keys.

* * *

I'm standing on the station platform scrolling for Isobel's number when I realise that moving into her spare room is not going to be enough.

I need a much bigger change. I need to get further away than Brighton. That's just 35 minutes on the train from London, from Jono, from my flat, my current life, from everything that's familiar and now completely spoiled. I need a sense of freedom, a new start... at least some fresh surroundings and new inspiration.

I look around the colourless train station. It's a dull, slate-grey day at the tail end of January and everything looks washed out, washed up and bare. Only when I pace further down the platform, letting trains come and go because I still don't know where to go next, do I see the advertising hoarding.

It's a vast billboard, maybe five metres wide, displaying the kind of luminous, fairytale image advertisers use to lure you away from reality and towards the fantasy life you'd much rather be leading.

Brown-green peaks are bathed in early sunrise, and the glassy water is silver under a bruised and brooding sky. It's an endless, timeless landscape and it stops me in my tracks... after so many years of being a Londoner, a city girl, I can't help thinking to myself – *that* is what I need to do. *There* is where I need to be, until I feel better, until I'm strong enough to venture out to New York's most glamorous bars and/or to volunteering on horseback in South America.

For the first time in my adult life, I think that it might be best to go home for a while. No, I *want* to go back home.

Maybe exactly what I need is to go back to the place that I am from.

5

Once I've made my decision, I immediately start to feel a little calmer and more composed. I stop hobbling up and down the platform with my stick and my trolley case and even find myself smiling at the poster.

Even though my mum has died and my dad is not exactly Father of the Year material, the best thing about my hometown is that it's wonderfully far away from London and completely different.

I know I'm bathing it in the warm glow of nostalgia, but it suddenly seems like the perfect place to go to now and I can't believe it's been so long since I've been back.

So, I board a train to Elephant and Castle and look up train times for the journey I now have in mind. It's still early, which means there's plenty of time to say the important, final goodbye and still get myself to King's Cross Station with plenty of time to spare.

* * *

I wheel my suitcase into Southwark Crown Court and put it through the X-ray machine. The two security guards at the door both know me well.

'Good grief, Jennifer, been in the wars, have you?' one of them asks as he sees my stick.

'You should have seen the state of the other guy,' I joke back and this gets a laugh.

'So, what's the bag for? Going on holiday, are you? Dropped in on us to say goodbye?' are the follow-up questions.

'Something like that.' I smile.

'Bring us back a souvenir, mind.'

'Of course.'

The cosy, old-fashioned barrister's office is empty, so I sit down for the last time at the desk I've used at least twice a week for three years, whenever I'm here in the court office. There's strangely nothing of mine here to collect. Back at the main office, I've left just a few pencils and biros, notebooks and papers, nothing I would miss.

When Jonathan strides in, he's energetic, focused, his wig in place and his black gown billowing out over his pinstripes. I see him before he sees me and I appreciate immediately all the things I fell in love with: Jono, handsome, serious, old-school, all manners, business and the dry side of charm.

'Oh... Jennifer... hello!'

He's surprised, of course, but manages a warm smile.

I smile back at him and realise I'm surprisingly calm. The sight of him hasn't flustered me because the billboard hills and the yellow-pink glow of the sunrise are still at the forefront of my mind.

'Sorry to appear out of the blue,' I begin, then wonder why I'm apologising. I'm not really sorry, well, maybe just a little bit for him, not least because it will be hard to find a legal secretary even half as good as me, what with my deep legal knowledge, efficient stapling system, colour-coded files, beautiful punctuation, spelling and flawless copy, I'm going to be class act to follow. Yes, he'll struggle to find as dedicated an assistant as me, let alone as dedicated a lover.

He doesn't take a seat, just hovers, not sure as to how long I'm planning to be here.

'I've come to say goodbye, Jono, because I've decided to go to Scotland,' I say.

'Oh!' his eyebrows shoot up.

'Yeah... I don't know how long I'll be there before I head off to something new, but I really need some time away... and a proper change.'

'Yes, of course.'

'You will give me a nice reference though? I'm counting on that. And the severance pay—'

'Jennifer... of course. And you know you can always come back. The door is open... to the job... to... playing a part in my life. Oh my goodness...' he sits down heavily now in the chair close to mine.

'My dear Jennifer,' he says finally and takes hold of my hand. 'I didn't mean to—'

I wonder what's coming next. What did he not mean to do? Fill me with hope and love for someone and something I couldn't have? Let another two years of my life pass without any commitment or longer plan? Waste my time? Break my heart? Make me feel like the lesser person in his life?

Because he has done all of these things.

'—Let this get so serious for both of us... and let you down,' he says.

'Well, you did,' I say, 'and please don't say sorry again, because I will honestly scream.'

His eyes find mine and hold my gaze. His smile is kind and

understanding. I know there's a fine human being underneath the suits, the wigs, robes, bluster and towering impatience.

Maybe I should be offended that he never wanted to get serious. But instead, I just let it pass. It's too late now. It's all too late.

I think of his children, Oliver and Charlie. In their mid-teens... I know so much about them. I've even ordered a good number of their birthday and Christmas gifts online. I always thought I would meet them one day. But now, it's not going to happen. And as for the twins... no, I can't even think about the twins.

'It's time for me to leave you,' I say simply.

'Yes, I understand,' he says finally. 'You need to think about yourself... think about what you want.'

I'm going to cry, of course. I feel the lump building in my throat and I quickly dab at my eyes and my nose. I'm just so supersensitive... a peeled grape, a boiled egg without the shell, a hermit crab exposed on the beach.

Jonathan offers me the clean white cloth handkerchief from his pocket, but I turn it down. He spots my suitcase standing beside the desk and asks: 'So, where are you going to in Scotland?'

'I'm going back home,' I say, swallowing down my tears and trying to hold it together.

'Back to Mum and Dad... that's a good idea. They'll take care of you while you decide what to do next. And you will stay in touch, won't you?'

'Yes...'

There's no point correcting him. I've worked with him for three years, been his lover for two, but he doesn't remember that my mother is dead, whereas I even know what kind of dog biscuits Daisy, his family Labrador, prefers. But let him go ahead and think I'm going to be scooped up by my loving parents in the plural.

'Oh, Jennifer, how am I going to manage without you?' he exclaims and I can hear the emotion catching in his throat.

This is one of the nicest things he's ever said to me and I will treasure it.

Then it's time for one last, long hug and goodbye.

Just as we part, the court clerk pops his head round door to announce: 'They'd like you to come back in, sir.'

As he turns to go, Jono says: 'I'll make sure you're paid for the next four months,' in a burst of generosity that leaves me speechless. Then with one final 'look after yourself,' out walks the man who –aside from my dad – I've had the longest relationship with in my life.

* * *

In the back of a very expensive taxi, I cry all the way to King's Cross.

I realise I'll have to cope with my crying fits the way people cope with the weather. They wear raincoats and carry brollies and acknowledge that it's pretty awful now, but it will clear up in twenty minutes or so and then there will be a sunnier spell to enjoy before the weather sets in again. I rummage through my handbag in search of a packet of tissues.

I get a little reckless with my money too. Usually I'm so careful, never overstepping my weekly spending allowance, carefully saving every month. But I've just dropped £50 on a taxi and now £134 on a *single* train ticket.

Single was important. No, I didn't want an open return, even though it didn't cost much more. I wanted to make the dramatic gesture.

And, oh my god, I need to phone the lettings agent and give notice on my flat. Clearly running away is not going to be quite as straightforward as I thought.

When I board the train, find a seat, get comfortable and settle down, it still doesn't feel real. I can't believe that I'm on this train, for the first time in three years.

In a few hours, I'll be back in Scotland.

By the end of today, I'll be back home.

I have no idea what this is going to be like.

6

There is some crying on the train, of course. We pull through north London and as places I've been to, streets and stations I remember all pass by the window, I am saying goodbye to it all.

I feel convinced that I won't come back to live in London. I've been an honorary Londoner for almost half of my life, but my relationship with this city is over. I don't know where I'm going to belong to next, but I hope St Andrews will be OK until I decide.

As the train heads north, in the gaps between thinking about London and St Andrews and myself, I find myself wondering about Jono's unexpected twins, letting the hurt into my mind in painful bursts. Will he have boy twins or girls, I wonder? Or one of each? And will they look like his handsome sons? I have, of course, been curious about his family and seen plenty of photos. Why did Jono not feel brave enough to tell me about all this before I found out?

The twins must have been conceived last October. I'm scrambling to think about what we did that month... then I remember that Jono was away on a trip to see a supposed 'client' for the best part of a week in France. Ha... I wonder if that was part of the big reconciliation between him and Sophie. And how many other meetings and overnights and weekends away had there been before then?

It makes all the time we spent together over November, December, Christmastime and January a total lie. I think about my carefully chosen and wrapped present to him and I feel a bit less sad and a bit angrier. Was he waiting for some kind of 'right time' to tell me? That would have been difficult.

I thought he really loved me. Maybe he did, in his way. Maybe he loves his wife, his children and me. Maybe he'll be sad that I've left him... or maybe he'll get over it pretty quickly and he, Sophie and his four children will live happily ever after.

At this thought, I sob so hard, I have to go and hide in the bathroom. Get it out, I urge myself as tears pour onto the wad of tissue in my hands. I mourn my loss, until finally, it's time to pull myself together again and keep going a little further on this new journey.

I blow my nose, wipe my eyes, splash my face with the trickle of lukewarm water from the train tap and emerge swollen eyed. I need to stop thinking about Jono all the time and try to think about me.

As we approach Doncaster, I buy a large cup of tea and stir sugar into it, still feeling shaken and fragile. But another two hours into the journey, as we pull out of Newcastle, my heavy heart begins to lift just a little. The crowd in the carriage has thinned out. There's room to stretch my cramped legs and gaze out of the window onto a new and soothing view. We're travelling through open countryside with gentle hills, hedges, trees, fields where sheep huddle together. The sky has cleared to a cold, marine-blue and here and there come glimpses of the coast and the wild North Sea smashing against black rocks and deserted strips of beach.

As we pass over the long bridge of elegant arches towards Berwick-upon-Tweed, I'm moved by the prettiness of the old stone houses against crisp blue sky and sea. My sadness tones down and I feel something close to enthusiasm.

Finally, a change. A new adventure. Not the same old, same old.

I head back to the bathroom, to soothe my blotchy face with more water and repair the damage with a proper make-up job.

The make-up helps. I'm building a layer of protection against the world with each dab of foundation, stroke of eye pencil and a coating of my favourite creamy lipstick. I'm still hurt and uncertain on the inside, but I don't have to look like that on the outside.

At some point in the future, it will be OK again, I tell myself. I'll build a new life and a new plan. I don't know how it's going to work out from here, or where I'm going to go, but at least I'm on a journey to something different.

I change trains in Edinburgh, pulling my bag along with me. On the vast rust-red drama of the Forth Rail Bridge, I stare out of the window looking for other landmarks, drinking in the view, remembering how empty and how savagely pretty this landscape can be.

I am not in London any more.

This is wildly different and I do feel the pull of home. I know these landscapes. They're still a part of me. I can almost feel the sharp sea wind outside, bracingly cold and clean, blowing just some of my little tragedy away.

This will be all right for a while, I think, as this slower train trundles through Markinch, then Cupar.

* * *

I pull out my phone because it's time, past the time, for me to make the phone call I've been putting off.

It rings for quite a while before I hear the familiar: 'Hello?'

'Hello, Dad... it's Jennifer.'

'Oh hello, Jennifer. Everything OK?'

Dad sounds surprised, of course, because we phone one another on Sunday evenings for a friendly round up of the week's events. We rarely feel the need to speak to each other outside the parameters of the Sunday evening call.

'Dad, I'm on my way to St Andrews,' I tell him. 'In fact, I'm going to be there in a couple of hours.'

'Oh goodness!'

He sounds surprised, maybe even a little taken aback with this news.

'I'm sorry it's such short notice... it's a bit last minute,' I add quickly. 'I've got an... ummm... unexpected holiday and I thought it might be nice to come up, see you, see the town again. I was going to book myself into a B&B,' I add quickly.

'A B&B? Well, up to you of course, Jennifer, but you're always welcome here. Always welcome.'

It's a relief to hear this. I don't think I'm ready to stay at the family home. I don't know if that's what Dad would want either. But I've no idea how long I'm going to be in town, or how much it will cost to stay for weeks in a guesthouse, so I'm glad he has immediately offered.

Let's see how it goes, I reassure myself.

'When do you get in?' he asks.

'About 6.30, I'll take the bus from Leuchars and...'

Suddenly it feels too much and I find myself on the verge of tears again. Arriving back without a plan, without anyone to welcome me on the platform, without even a booking for the night – what am I doing?

'Well, you'll come for dinner then?' he asks.

'Yes... that would be nice. Thanks, Dad.'

'Righto, I'll see you later then. You'll probably be here about 7.15. Bye then, Jennifer.'

And he hangs up, because he still has this idea that phone calls are an extravagance and conversations should be kept to the minimum.

'Bye...' I say to the phone. And already the whole escape to my brand-new life fantasy seems a little more difficult, because of course it's going to involve Dad and my hometown and maybe meeting people I used to know again and all the complications of finding somewhere to stay and paying the bills and...

Stop it, I warn myself. Let's take it one step at a time.

* * *

Finally, the train pulls into Leuchars Station with its big 'Leuchars for St Andrews' sign. My suitcase unloaded, my shoulders back, I cross the platform and walk to the connecting bus. We are a mixed crowd heading towards the most famous small town in Scotland. There are the locals in sensible, weatherproof anoraks, walking boots and woolly hats; a gaggle of maybe Chinese students in brightly coloured miniskirts, legwarmers and platform heeled shoes; golfers, of course, wearing diamond patterns and tweed, anxious about loading their golf bags into the bus; well-groomed continental tourists; students of the more hipster, bearded kind, and me.

Homecoming memories flood in on me: arriving back as a student, bringing various boyfriends home to meet the parents, the grey and stormy day, over four years ago now, when Dad met me here and we drove home, wordless, because my mother had died and neither of us knew how to begin to cope with it.

To visitors, St Andrews is one of the prettiest small towns in Scotland: home of the golf bunker, the Prince William and Catherine Middleton romance, the windswept town beaches and ancient university. To me, it's the claustrophobic hometown I felt compelled to get away from as soon as I could: first to university in Edinburgh, then to bright lights, big city London.

* * *

It's already too dark to see the countryside passing the bus window, but as soon as we reach the town, the streetlights reveal the pretty terraces and squares with old, grey-stone townhouses, cosy teashops, golfing shops and pubs, but with enough of a smattering of real life to keep it from being totally chocolate boxy. There are shoe shops here, too, chain stores and charity concessions in among the art galleries and estate agents.

I can't help thinking that it looks nicer than I remember. But maybe I'm ready to like it more, to fall under its spell even.

I watch a girl, probably a student, walk along, hair streaming in the wind, in boho sheepskin boots with buckles, a Victorian-style tweed coat and layers of multi-coloured scarf draped around her neck.

As soon as I step off the bus, I remember why sheepskin, tweed, swathes of wool and practical mountaineering anoraks are so important in this town, especially in the winter. A smattering of rain and the wild east wind, damp from the sea, whips at my head, stripping me of make-up and hair-smoothing efforts in one brutal gust. In my inadequate London clothes, I'm immediately chilled to the bone. I should have remembered.

This place! Memories and emotions whirl round me like the icy sea air, the wind hard on my face like a welcome home slap.

I may have my reasons to come back now, but I also still have good reasons to stay away.

7

I considered walking the 15 minutes to my dad's house, but it feels too cold and raw to be outside even for that long, plus I have to consider my fragile knee. So, instead I join the queue for taxis and soon I'm getting out in Grove Park, feeling a little overwhelmed with memories and nostalgia.

Despite the early evening darkness, I can see that the street looks exactly the same. It's a tidy suburban crescent with neat lawns and hedges and the chalet-style homes, all sloping roofs and dormer windows, that everyone wanted back in the 1970s.

It all looks much smaller now, of course, and I remember my teenage self, just about dying with boredom and longing for a world that was anywhere but here.

In the time since Mum died, I've only been back for brief, overnight visits. The truth is, I've avoided coming 'home' because I don't have the kind of family life that cosy sitcoms are made of. I rarely speak to my younger sister, who lives a few miles out of town, and I'm on friendly terms but not very close to my dad. If I'm going to be really honest, I wasn't as close to my mother as I could have been either. They were old-fashioned parents, reserved, traditional, and not very involved with us. As a teenager, I got out of the habit of confiding in them and into the habit of hiding my real life from them.

Once in a while I ask myself if I'm a bad daughter because I don't visit my dad very often and I leave family Christmases and other daughterly duties to my sister. And really, the answer is – yes.

I should try harder.

My dad isn't perfect, but he's getting older and probably frailer and I should make more of an effort.

I take a deep breath and let it out slowly, watching the taxi drive away.

This could be a chance to start afresh with my dad, to try to enjoy spending some time with him. I bump my suitcase up the four large concrete steps to the front door of my old family home and ring the bell. I can hear music, or maybe the TV on at full volume, so I ring again.

The noise quietens down and within a few moments, the door opens and I set eyes on my dad. I realised in the cab that it's been eight months since I last saw him in person, so I'm a little taken aback at this older, thinner and more stooped version of the dad I had in my head. Age seems to progress like growth spurts, nothing for a while, then a leap forward. When I look at him, I see not just his old face, but I remember the much younger version of this face too.

Dad looks genuinely pleased to see me and I realise I'm pleased too.

'Jennifer, hello there! How nice of you to come and visit, come in, come on in.' His voice is warm and familiar.

'Hello, Dad.' I lean in and hug him. He used to be five foot ten, an inch or so above me, but he seems to have shrunk down to my height and his shoulders feel slight and bony when I put my hands on them.

'I'll put my bag and coat in the hall, if that's all right?' I ask stepping in, closing the door and realising there's a smell to this hallway – carpet, biscuits, a hint of furniture spray – that I recognise immediately and suddenly there are tears in my eyes. There are things I've missed... and I didn't even know.

'Of course, of course... so, have you decided to stay here then?' he asks.

'Em... let me have a little think about that,' I counter, not wanting to rush this decision. Maybe we should see how dinner goes first, I think to myself.

'You're looking well,' he says, peering at me through a pair of sturdy, silver rimmed bi-focals, 'a little older of course, but that happens to the best of us.'

'You're looking a bit thin,' I tell him off. 'I hope you're eating as well as drinking.'

If you could get all of your daily nutrition from the lemons in a G&T, Dad would be covered.

'I'm eating very well I can assure you. Remind me what's happened to your leg?' he asks, clocking my walking stick.

'Tripped over... bashed up my knee,' I tell him airily, not wanting it to be a big thing. 'It's mending nicely.'

'Oh yes, well, that's a relief,' he says. 'Hamish took a tumble on the golf course last week and tore every ligament in his leg. It all gets a lot more serious at our age. Now, come on through and tell me all the latest news.'

I follow him into the sitting room, my feet sinking into the thick carpeting and I wonder what I'll tell him and what I'll leave out. In my experience, parents, especially Dads, never want the unfiltered truth. They want the edited highlights; the bits that make you – and by association them – look as successful and together as possible. Your hurts and disappointments need to be shared carefully, because they hurt and disappoint your parents too.

It's stiflingly warm in the room, all the radiators are blazing and the gas fire is turned up high.

Elvis is crooning from the stereo and the decor is exactly as it always is, cream walls, pale-green carpet, a full set of matching John Lewis furniture: one sofa, two armchairs, a fitted bookcase, coffee table, sideboard and large TV on a dedicated TV bench. My framed sixth-form photo is still perched in the bookcase, along with a full complement of other family photographs. I don't give them more than a glance, knowing what I'll see there – the carefully edited highlights of our family history, the greatest hits, the PR spin; photos of my sister and I when we were young, my parents' wedding photo, my sister's graduation photo, wedding photo and many photos of her two children as babies. I don't want to be reminded that I'm not fitting the family narrative here of graduate, get married and procreate, so instead, I look at the watery paintings of assorted landscapes that have hung on these walls for as long as I can remember.

There's a much stronger smell of furniture polish in this room, undercut with the juniper scent of gin.

Dad's armchair, opposite the TV, has a side table charged with a vast crystal tumbler loaded with his favourite drink, made with plenty of ice and a slice.

'Sit down, Jennifer, get comfortable and I'll make you one of these,' Dad points to his drink, 'then you can tell me all the latest. How's the job going? How's London life?'

I'm still on painkillers and not long off antibiotics. So, I probably shouldn't have anything to drink at all. But it's been an astonishingly long day; so long that I can't quite believe that less than 12 hours have passed since I walked out of my home, said goodbye to Jono and my job, and simply walked out of my life with a little trolley bag and arrived here.

I feel as if weeks and weeks have gone by. I feel as if I'm on another continent on the other side of the world, or as if I've travelled back in time to my past and all the mistakes of my present have disappeared, or at least been put on hold.

So yes, thank you very much, a G&T, with ice and a slice, sounds just about perfect. In fact, I'm going to need a large one.

'I'll make it, Dad, you have a seat,' I offer.

'Oh no, no,' he insists. 'You rest that knee of yours. The day I can't mix up a G&T is the day you know I'm a goner.'

It's hardly a cheery thought, but I can't help raising a smile.

I listen to him clink and clank about the kitchen for a few minutes then he comes back in and hands me one of his mighty crystal tumblers. His own has of course been 'freshened up.'

'Cheers,' he says, holding up his glass, 'it's good to see you.'

'Cheers,' I hold my glass up too. Our eyes meet and we smile, then I take a big gulp, gag, and realise my dad can't mix drinks. He's mistaken the gin for the tonic and vice versa.

'So... strong...' I gasp.

'Not at all,' he insists, taking a seat. 'Drink up, it'll put hairs on your chest.'

Not really what I wanted, but...

I last ate a finger of KitKat at 4 p.m.. In fact, that may have been my entire calorie consumption all day. So, the gin is carried on a whoosh of bubbles straight to my head. Literally two minutes later, I feel woozy, over-relaxed and befuddled.

And over the next half an hour, I hear myself blurting out much more about my current situation to Dad than I perhaps meant to.

'I've left my job...'

'I just don't want to be in London any more...'

'I really need a change... I might go abroad for a bit.'

And finally, once I've broken open another pack of pocket tissues: 'I've broken up with someone because I thought it was serious and we would spend our lives together... but he... well, I suppose, in a nutshell, he didn't...'

I tell Dad quite a bit, but not everything. I don't mention that Jono was my boss, or that he had been separated but has now gone back to his wife, who is also pregnant with twins, because Dad would very likely tut and disapprove. Plus, it feels just too painful to think about that right now, let alone share.

I hear my dad sigh. I don't look over at him because I imagine he's shaking his head. This is another one of my 'serious' relationships that has gone up in smoke. I'm reluctant to count them. Nope, definitely don't want to count them...

My mum and dad met when they were seventeen and eighteen respectively. They did what people seemed to do in the not-even-very-distant past: they got to know each other slightly, got engaged and then married and spent the next thirty-odd years together.

I don't remember any big dramas. I don't think anyone had an affair, or even stormed out for a few days. Maybe there were a few sharp words and lingering disagreements, but mainly, I remember gentle harmony and understated love.

What is the matter with me and the people I've chosen? We've never made it past the two-year mark.

Maybe like shoes, sweaters, alarm clocks and wine glasses, love affairs just aren't made to last the way they used to be.

'I've come up here...' I pause and gulp at what is now my second G&T, 'because I really need a change. And I need to take a break.' A few tears slip out as I say this.

And that's the truth. I need to step out of my life. Take a holiday from myself. And work out where to go from here.

'Oh dear, oh dear...' Dad claps his hand against his slim thigh. 'Poor old Jennifer, that's a bit of a sad story.'

And I have a clear memory of him saying exactly those words whenever we cried when we were small.

We...

And now I'm thinking about my little sister, Isla: small and cute, bright as a button. Before we grew so far apart.

Dark-brown hair, green-brown eyes, dimples and mischief. A slightly too short bob with a too short fringe and everything a little squint. Mum never cut our hair, so maybe it was because Isla wriggled too much at the hairdresser.

'Dear, oh dear,' Dad repeats and he pats my hand kindly.

'Ah well...' I say, sinking back into the sofa, 'mustn't grumble.'

Listen to me... *mustn't grumble*? Am I now seventy-two as well? This is the gin talking. I want to grumble. I want to grumble non-stop for quite some time.

'Isn't the internet marvellous?' Dad asks next.

'Ummm... yes... I suppose so,' I reply, not sure how this follows in response to my personal tragedy.

'I can be here at...' he looks at his watch, 'my goodness, 7.35? Is that the time? Good grief, it'll be over by now.'

'What will?'

'This is the wonder of the internet, I can be talking to you at 7.35 and meanwhile, there's a horse running for me all the way over in Kentucky and I better tune in and find out how he's going.'

There's nothing for me to do but sit and drain my gin, which just about makes my eyes go blurry, while my dad faffs and curses at some ancient old monitor wondering why he can't call up the results of this afternoon's racing in Kentucky.

So that's it, I think sulkily. That's my relationship disaster and major life crisis all done and dusted. No need to discuss further. He's moved smoothly on to the racing.

That's my dad.

I realise he's still a little childish, even in his seventies, which isn't what you want in a dad, but on the upside, he lives happily for the moment. He probably won't ask me anything about my heartache again and, you know, maybe that might be a huge relief, as I won't have to talk about it.

I'm roused from my gin stupor by his question: 'So, why not stay here with your old dad for a bit?'

'Well... no, I don't want to impose, Dad. I thought I'd book into a B&B for a few nights and then get somewhere organised a bit longer term,' I tell him.

Dad shakes his head: 'I think you should stay here, Jennifer. Save yourself the money. The town has got ridiculously expensive: tourists from the four corners of the globe these days all over the place. And all year round. Be my guest for as long as you like. Move in, have your old room. You're more than welcome.'

I had planned to turn this offer down. Moving in seemed too much, too soon, for me and for Dad.

But now... he's looking at me expectantly. I haven't seen him for such a long time. I should try to get to know him again. Try to get on with him better. OK, to some extent, the gin has dulled my capacity for reasoning against this. But realistically, I'm still paying rent for my flat, I can't afford a B&B for longer than a few weeks at the most... and *renting* a place of my own here? Is that what I want to do? Not yet, because I have no idea how long I'm going to stay.

So would it be so bad to stay here? Just until I get myself sorted... make the new plans... decide where to go next.

Elvis is crooning in my ear, telling me that he 'Can't Help Falling in Love', G&T is lapping at my brain and I think maybe it would be OK to say yes... for now.

'Dad, it's very kind of you to offer, really, really kind, but don't you think it would be too much trouble?'

'Now, now,' he replies warmly, 'I won't hear a no. How will you be trouble? Make me the odd dinner, buy me an occasional bottle of gin and we'll get along just fine. Anyway, what will people say if I'm here with all my empty bedrooms and you're holed up in a B&B?'

Ah. Well, probably no worse than what they would say if they knew he was using the world wide web to bet on horses on the other side of the Atlantic.

Does he get up early, I wonder, to bet on races in Australia? And what about the Middle East? Can you bet on the horses 24/7 thanks to the www?

'I've got plenty of space here,' he says, waving his hands expansively. 'The least I can do is help to put a roof over your head while you sort yourself out. You're a clever girl, Jennifer, you always were. You'll pull yourself together. All right? Is that agreed?'

'That's very kind, Dad. I'll stay for just a little bit – if you're sure it's OK.'

'Yes, totally sure,' he insists.

'I'll share the bills, and it won't be for long,' I add.

'That's very generous... and stay for as long as you like,' he says and pats my hand again.

I sag back into the sofa, a little limp with relief.

So, that's settled then. I will stay here, just for a bit, sort myself out and get to know my dad again. Then, when I move out, it will be to something good and exciting and new, and in the meantime, my brand-new friends: gin and tonic will make it all bearable.

'I'll make myself very useful round here,' I say, or possibly slur. 'I'll cook, clean and do whatever's needed.'

'Oh, well, that's very kind, but I've got most of that covered,' Dad says with a cheery grin.

It's not much later when I hear a key turning in the lock.

'Someone seems to be at the door...' I tell him, as he curses at his computer.

'Well, there's some good news,' he says, rubbing his hands together. 'That will be *her* now.'

A smile of happiness breaks across his face.

Her? What kind of *her* is turning up at my dad's house after 8 p.m. with her very own key?

8

The front door opens then closes with a bang. There's a cheery call of: 'Hello, handsome! Have you missed me?' and as Dad gets to his feet, the sitting room door opens and a woman I vaguely recognise, mid-sixties maybe, petite with a pert figure, blonde hair and pink lipstick walks into the room and kisses my old, cardigan-wearing Dad just a little *too close to the mouth*.

'Hello, Joanie, you'll remember my daughter, Jennifer. Jennifer, this is Joan Swanson, you'll remember Joan and Jim...'

I have a vague memory of a house with a lot of leather sofas and two younger boys who used to let us *watch* them play with their Scalextrix track whenever we went round. We were never allowed to actually have a go at the precious cars.

'Jim passed away a few years ago,' Dad adds, which might explain why Joan is kissing him.

'Hello, Joan, nice to see you,' I say and hold out my hand. I have tried to get up, but the knee and the G&Ts have made this too difficult. 'Sore knee, sorry,' I say, pointing at my knee and my stick.

She shakes my hand with her soft white hand tipped with Barbie pink nails.

'Hello, Jennifer, what a lovely surprise to see you.'

'Joan very kindly cooks for me a few evenings a week,' Dad explains, still beaming, still unable to take his eyes from her, 'she's quite something in the kitchen.'

Joan beams back at him then pats him fondly on the arm.

'So, what are we having tonight, Joanie?'

'Shepherd's pie,' she replies.

'Superb. You'd like a bit of that, wouldn't you, Jennifer? Is there a little to spare for Jennifer?'

'She can have my portion; I'll have a wee piece of toast when I get home. Not feeling very hungry tonight anyway.'

I protest, but Joan won't hear of it. Then she goes back into the hallway and returns with a casserole dish. Maybe because I'm just about floored with gin and tonic, the mashed potato topping and the strangely homely smell of mince is incredibly tempting.

'That looks amazing, thank you very much. Shall I get some plates?' I offer.

Joan looks me up and down, as if to assess my plate-fetching skills.

'No,' she says, 'don't worry, rest that knee. I know where everything is.'

She returns from the kitchen with plates loaded with shepherd's pie and an alarming heap of coleslaw, plus knives and forks. She sets them down on the coffee table and just for a little tiny moment I think: 'How lovely to be old and mollycoddled.' But I blame the gin.

'Jennifer's split up with her boyfriend, left her job, and is moving back to St Andrews for a while,' my dad explains to Joan as she settles into an armchair.

'Oh dear,' she says and shakes her head. 'Mark, my youngest, you'll remember him? He got divorced last year and *she...*'

mentioned with a grimace, 'took the house, the kids, the car, the dog, the savings account, everything.'

I suddenly have an image of Mark – sandy curls, a striped T-shirt with a navy-blue collar, placing his little red car carefully back onto the track and I wonder what he did to deserve his wife taking the house, the kids, the car, the dog and everything. And the thought that little curly haired boys grow up to be men whose marriages crumble and collapse is a weight of sadness on my chest.

'That's a shame,' I say, but it doesn't seem adequate.

'Yes...' Joan says, and again, it doesn't seem adequate.

'Jennifer's going to stay here,' Dad goes on, 'until she's decided what to do next. She's a legal secretary, remember? She worked for some barrister chappie in London.'

'Jonathan Chesterton' I say, realising I don't want to hear one of London's most respected legal minds, and my ex-lover, being referred to as a 'chappie'.

'The St Andrews Players did *Legally Blonde* the musical just before Christmas,' Joan says, as if this follows on quite logically. 'It was an absolute hoot, especially watching Pamela's son, Tony, from the garage. *Is he gay or European?* I think we all know, Pamela.'

Joan dissolves into cackles of laughter and I find myself joining in, because I'm pretty much drunk and exhausted.

Dad gets up, makes Joan a drink and 'freshens' ours up again.

I eat my shepherd's pie and sip at water now that the gin seems to have made my lips feel numb. Just for tonight, I tell myself, I can't take this amount of booze every night. I'm somewhere between aghast and impressed at how much drink my father can handle. He's sitting up, wielding a knife and fork, carrying on a totally coherent conversation and he's had about five times more than me.

* * *

Afterwards, I insist on washing up and stagger about the kitchen, trying not to break things, then to my relief, we make the switch from bucketfuls of gin to bucketfuls of tea.

Not long after 10 p.m., Joan gets up and says it's time for her to leave. This involves kissing Dad on the lips again and giggling in a way that makes me look away.

'Goodnight, Jennifer,' she says, coming over to give me a hug. 'It's so lovely that you've come to see your old dad. He'll appreciate that. Always lovely to have the family home again.' Our eyes meet and I'm surprised to see that hers seem to be welling up. But with a blink of her heavily mascara-ed lashes, the teariness is gone.

Once she's left, it's finally time for me to head upstairs and face my old bedroom.

'I've had a long day,' I tell Dad, 'thanks very much for dinner and for putting me up.'

'No trouble at all,' he says.

'I'm going to take my stuff upstairs and get to bed.'

'Yes of course... night, night, Jennifer, you'll sleep well. The sea air.'

Night, night – something he must have said to me thousands of times as I was growing up. We exchange a look and I'm hit with a rush of déjà vu.

As I step into the hall, I can't quite believe that I'm back here and that I'm going to stay for a while. It's been so long, and yet this house feels so familiar, so under my skin. I know every step in every direction, every quirk of every door handle and in my current fragile state, this is soothing, despite the kaleidoscope of memories, good and bad, appearing before me at every turn.

I collect my suitcase and my handbag and carry them up the carpeted staircase towards my old bedroom, passing the door to Isla's old room on my left. Usually, it's quite easy not to think of Isla at all. But back at the family home, it's going to be much harder.

I try to concentrate on the room in front of me now. This is my room, but not as it was when I lived here. Several years after I moved out, Dad and the decorator decided to have it entirely clad in swirly, pastel-blue wallpaper, the ceiling included.

A small double bed was installed, instantly halving the size of the room. But my white wardrobe is still there and the white desk with its desk lamp and rickety office chair where I studied for my school exams. There's a framed film poster on the wall that has been in that same place forever. A selection of my old books remain lined up on a bookshelf and a flimsy-looking rail supports a pair of even flimsier blue curtains.

I park my bags, open the wardrobe door and see that it's empty apart from a jangle of wire hangers, an old-fashioned hairbrush and, inexplicably, a half-used tube of haemorrhoid cream. I shut the door quickly and sit down on the edge of the saggy bed. As I take another look around this blue box, inspired by a bad hotel bathroom, but neat and dust-free, maybe thanks to Joan, and I'm sorely tempted to have another cry.

Instead, I stand up, open the cupboard doors again and busy myself with some unpacking. My inner matron insists briskly that this room will look fine when I've got my own things set out. I'll put a low-watt bulb in the desk lamp; I'll pack away this horrible bedspread and get a lovely squashy duvet and pillow with new bed linen. I'll arrange my necklaces and make-up on the bookcase, put up some lovely artwork and it will all be fine.

Fine!

This is just temporary. Just for now. It's part of the process. Step one, chapter one, act one, scene one. It will get better soon.

I'll be somewhere better, doing something interesting, exciting, fabulous... soon.

Meanwhile, this is going to be fine. I insist, blinking back tears.

I head through the hallway to the carpeted bathroom with the cappuccino-coloured suite, which has had no makeover since the 1980s, dodge more Anusol tubes, brush my teeth and wee.

In my pyjamas, I climb into bed, feel a crushing lump in my throat and turn out the light, then I wipe a 90 per cent gin tear from the end of my nose and wonder if I can possibly sleep.

The orange streetlamp light shines into the room through a gap in the bargain-basement curtains. I close my eyes and try to ignore it, then decide I can't ignore it, I'll have to get up and pull the curtains closer together.

I haul myself out of bed, trip hard over my suitcase, claw at the curtains for support and manage not to fall onto my recovering knee but I do bring the entire curtain rail clattering down.

I'm too exhausted, overwrought and full of gin to do anything about it. So, I get into bed, close my eyes against the now much brighter orange glare and wish I could just sleep, but instead my mind has to play: Jen & Jono – the edited highlights – while Adele sings a heartbreaker in the background and more tears slide down my nose.

9

When I wake up, I register pastel-blue swirling wallpaper above my head, remember where I am and feel panicky.

It's all true.

I haven't dreamt any of it.

I am back at my dad's house, my family home; I'm in my childhood bedroom. All the details of my new reality percolate back into my mind as I wake up fully. I'm here. I'm not in London. I have really left my job and my home and Jono... and Jono and his once-but-no-longer-former wife are still expecting twins.

I wish I could stay asleep and forget about all of it for just a little longer.

Instead, I try to sit up, then realise my head is hammering, my throat is completely dry and I feel sick.

I fumble for my watch and see it's almost 9 a.m.. Time to get up. Time to wash, drink water and try to patch myself up for the day ahead. The first day of this new back-in-the-hometown reality.

Once I've drunk some water, showered, drunk more water and dressed, I pad around the silent house. There's no sign of Dad and I assume he's still sleeping off his lorry load of gin. Mental note to self: never, ever attempt to drink three of his super-strength gins again.

I make a horrible cup of tea, with a teabag that turns the water mahogany brown within seconds, I drink half of it with a shaking hand and feel the need to get outside. Fresh air... fresh coffee... that will make me feel better, won't it?

But at the thought of coffee, I feel sick all over again.

I settle for putting my coat and boots on over my joggy bottoms and sweatshirt combo, then, along with my stick, go out of the kitchen door and into the garden. The old wooden bench I expected to see is still there, so I sit down, drink the terrible tea and wonder what to do with all this newfound time on my hands.

After considering some simple options: a hobble to the beach, a hobble to the high street, or a plain old cup of coffee in the nearest café – it turns out that I want to do absolutely nothing. I just want to stay here because I'm still too fragile. Imagine if I met someone I used to know and had to explain what I was doing here?

I immediately think of those star pupils and golden girls that were in my year at school and trying to answer their questions: 'Yes... I'm up here for a bit, yes... staying with my dad... well, I was working as a legal secretary, but I'm taking a break and no... no "significant other" and no children...' I can't bear the thought of that. There are reasons I don't live in my hometown... there were reasons to get away to London. Now that I'm back, I want to protect myself from having to explain anything to anyone I might once have known.

* * *

The knee still feels too weak for long walks anyway. So, for the next few days, I tell Dad and then Joan that my leg is still healing and I move between the sofa, my bed and the bench in the back garden, resting, sleeping or trying to distract myself from everything.

First, I try the television, and at the start, there is some solace in watching people hunting for antiques, or cottages abroad. But then I start to imagine a TV presenter trying to solve my life problems for me. Until I can practically hear Kirstie Allsop telling me: 'So, Jennifer, finding you a new career and a new man is going to be a pretty steep challenge and you may have to rethink your wish list, but let's roll up our sleeves and see what we can come up with.'

From the sofa at Dad's, everything feels like too much effort. Getting dressed is difficult enough. The idea of finding a new job, a new home, a new partner, a new life, and going through all of that all over again, is so overwhelming that I stay on the sofa, duvet wrapped around me, day after day.

By the second week of this, Dad and Joan are obviously worrying about me and begin to suggest little trips in the car, and going out for afternoon tea, then they hint at making a doctor's appointment to see how it's going with the knee and 'everything'. But I say no to all their offers and mutter vague promises of 'maybe tomorrow' and 'I'll be better soon'.

One evening, when I switch my mobile on to delete the messages that have accumulated from Jono, the phone rings, flashing his name at me and almost out of boredom, I pick up. When I hear his surprised voice – 'Jennifer, hello, is that actually you?' – I'm overcome with a powerful burst of both hurt and anger.

'Yes? WHAT IS IT?' I fairly rage down the line at him, once I've moved to my bedroom for privacy. 'Why are you still phoning me?'

'I want to make sure you're OK. And... well, I wasn't expecting you to answer.'

'Well, guess what? I wasn't expecting you to make your wife pregnant with twins!' I shout back.

Hearing his voice has made me reel, and I don't want to just politely go away... I want him to know how much this hurts... oh god, I don't know what I want.

'Jennifer, you know how sorry I am,' and he does sound terribly sorry, 'but maybe this is for the best, for both of us.'

I close my eyes.

'How are you getting on up there?' he asks when the silence goes on too long.

'I'm fine and I'm being looked after, but I don't really want to hear from you, please. It's too painful.'

'I understand. I just wanted to make sure you were OK, as you never replied to any messages.'

I take a breath and realise there is one question I want to ask: 'Did you love me, Jono? At all?'

'Of course I did, Jennifer. How can you ask me that?'

'But you never said...'

'I didn't want to make any promises I might not be able to keep.'

'So maybe you always thought your family would be more important...' I summarise.

'Maybe... maybe... but that's not how I felt... a lot of the time. I felt and I still feel a great deal of love for you,' he says carefully, ever the lawyer.

'Me. You. Too...' I manage, 'but you'll have to leave me now, to get over you and get on with other things.'

'If that's what you want. But I'm here. I want to make sure you're OK. You can be in touch whenever you want.'

'Yeah...' my voice has fallen to a scratch whisper with the lump in my throat, 'I'll be fine...' I say, no idea if I believe that. 'You'll be fine,' I add, sure of that, 'hopefully we'll both be fine...'

I'm lying on a clapped-out bed in my elderly dad's house, cutting the ties on the life I used to live. I feel scared and alone and terribly uncertain about what will happen next. But I know that I want to do this, however hard it is. I need to do this. So, I dab at my tears and my snot with the corner of the duvet.

'I wish...' I begin, but I'm not sure what I wish for. I wish he'd properly left his family for me and that we could have begun to build a life together, but maybe that was never going to have worked for him... too much of a family man at heart. Anyway... never mind, it's over now.

'I may have to message you now and then with questions for work... there's a new assistant starting and it will take time...'

Too right it will, I can't help thinking.

'But is there anything I can do for you?' he asks now. 'Anything I can help with?'

I realise there are loose ends I need to tie up. My organiser side comes back into action, the checklist, tick-box, details head.

'I'll organise a removals company to pack up the flat and transport the boxes up here,' I tell him, trying to sound as brisk and efficient as I can. 'When they're done... could you go in and make sure everything's OK, then hand the keys back to the estate agent?'

'Yes, of course,' he says.

I picture the walls bare of my art and my photos... the anonymous beige sofa without my rug and cushions, the empty bookcase and the bedroom without my bedding, lamps and rug... and without Jono in my bed, ever again.

There will be no trace left of our time together. Nothing left of us.

'Jono?'

'Yes?'

'Promise me that when they're born, you'll spend plenty of time with your twins. You'll take time off, help to look after them and be a really good dad...' I'm crying again.

'Yes...' he agrees.

And then it's time to say goodbye.

'If you need anything... I'm here,' he says.

Once I've hung up, I cry for a long time. But when I finally finish crying, I wash my face and know that I need to be brave and believe that I have made the right decision. It's up to me to put myself together again and find a new path for myself.

* * *

A week later, my boxes arrive and I find I don't care at all about the contents. Coats, boots, kitchen things, boxes of old letters, photos and memorabilia, boxes full of stuff... I tell the removals men to stack them up in the spare bedroom, which already has a box collection of its own. I don't want to unpack or look at anything, apart from my box of books. So, I spend one enjoyable afternoon going through my collection and whittling it down into the books I've read and want to keep, and the interesting ones that are still to-be-read. I sort through my cookbooks too, wiping down the covers and unfolding turned down pages.

Then I start to do a thing I've never done before – I begin to read through the cookbooks. So now, I finally have a way to peacefully pass my sofa and chilly garden bench hours, reading my cookbooks. I'm too tired and too sad to actually cook, but the thought of the meals I will make and the cakes I will bake in the future, when I'm feeling better, does help. Yes, I find myself thinking with a little rush of optimism, in the rosy future, there will be the roasting of a harissa-flavoured chicken, and candles blown out on a perfectly risen buttermilk cake at a noisy birthday party with friends, and the sharing of a homemade Christmas pudding with whoever is at my Christmas gathering in the future.

It will not be me, all lonely and sad and wondering what on earth to do next, forever. And when the time comes, I will be able to make a perfect Madeira loaf and rosemary-flavoured breadsticks.

At night, I lie quiet and alone in my childhood bedroom. The room where I had such big and shiny dreams about my wonderful future, the room where I swotted to get my grades to get into Edinburgh University, the bed where I dreamed of being a civil rights lawyer, fighting injustice on a daily basis before heading home to my dashing husband and adorable children.

But this is also the room that has contained my heartbreaks, past and present. Every time I walk into this room, it hits me again – I've gone from 'brief blaze of glory' to 'big fat fail'. Over and over, I try to work out why and try to plot at least the first step or two back in the right direction.

And then finally, there comes just an ordinary sort of day, almost two whole weeks since the arrival of the boxes, when I wake up, look at the swirly blue wallpaper and feel that the sadness weighs a little less on me this morning and I've got some real, positive energy back.

Today really is the first day, I decide. I will do all the exercises the physio has given me for my rehab programme and then, with my stick, I will walk carefully into town for the first time since I arrived and see what's happening out there in little ol' St Andrews.

10

After a shower, I take time in front of the mirror to dry my long, dark below-the-shoulder hair straight and, for the first time in weeks, I carefully apply make-up – the full armour: foundation, eyeliner, shadow, mascara, blush, bronzer and lipstick. It's a bright, dry day, so there's not much danger of my efforts being blown or washed away. Then I take my favourite jeans from the wardrobe and the cute suede ankle boots with the very walkable heel. On top goes an emerald-green jumper with a fashionable label that has a little edge to it. All this sadness and grieving has left me thinner, so there's an unexpected bonus, and as I pull on my long woollen coat and luxurious scarf, I check myself over in the hall mirror. I think I look surprisingly OK.

There's no sign of my dad, who likes to sleep in. So, I decide I'll head into town, even though it's early, and maybe sit in a café and enjoy a breakfast latte and a croissant. I have an image of myself looking terribly Parisian: alone but contemplative, engrossed in serious thoughts, with a perfect application of cherry-coloured lipstick.

I close the front door behind me and set off towards the high street for the first time since I've arrived. The sky is a light, newly rinsed blue, the air is fresh with the tang of the sea and it feels good to be outside, breathing clean air and having somewhere to go once again. I have a particular café in mind, one I remember from past visits to the town.

As I make for the high street, I look around, viewing the town as a tourist, enjoying all its picturesque prettiness, but avoiding direct eye contact with passers-by.

St Andrews may be an international tourist and golf destination, it may have a student population in the thousands, but beneath that, it's still a small Scottish town where everyone knows many people and usually a little too much about each other. There's a dangerous moment when I think I pass an old friend of my mother's, a busy, over-talkative friend who I'm not ready to meet. But I dip my chin down into my scarf, walk on and she doesn't stop and turn.

I can see the café and there seems to be a huddle of people outside it. I check my watch: 8.50 a.m. and wonder if they're waiting for it to open.

It's a mixed crowd: foreign tourists, a golfer or two, all waving their phones about, taking photos, videos and smiley selfies.

As I near the crowd, two things take me by surprise. One, there is a tour guide standing in front of the group claiming that the humble Northpoint Café is where Prince William used to meet his future wife, Kate, for coffee dates. The Northpoint? *Really*? I'd pictured much more glamorous locations like the Old Course Hotel. Surely, they must have gone there too.

The second surprising thing is that the tour guide is none other than Alison McBain, now Alison Watson, who was my best friend at school. I haven't seen her for a good few years now, but I recognise her straight away, in her sensible waterproof coat, with an overgrown fringe and the kind of bright lipstick and hooped earrings she was always very fond of in her twenties.

I stand at the edge of the crowd for a moment, listening and not wanting to interrupt her in full flow.

'This simple little café was where the future King and Queen of Great Britain would meet up,' she tells her audience. 'Apparently Kate, the skinny little pin, liked a skimmed milk cappuccino while William would scoff bacon and egg rolls washed down with cups of—'

Casting her eye about the crowd, she suddenly spots me, looks astonished and loses her thread.

'—ummm... cups of... you know... tea. Please, feel free to go in and have a look, order a coffee if you like. I'll just be one moment.'

As the tourists begin to make their way into the café, she rushes over to me: 'Jen?! That is you, isn't it?! Oh my goodness! What a total surprise... How are you doing? And what's happened? Why do you have a walking stick? How long are you here?' she asks, taking hold of my arm and looking up at me with a beaming smile. 'And can I just say, you're looking completely, freaking fabulous. Whatever you're doing is totally working.'

This makes me laugh as I say: 'Hello, Alison! How are you? Oh... this... broke my kneecap, but it's healing up nicely.' And then we hug and break apart and both smile very happily at one another.

I take in this face that I used to know so well. Despite the time that's passed and the distance, she does not feel like a stranger – the way I might have expected – because I have so many memories of her as my really good friend. I haven't seen her for... well, not since my Mum's funeral, so it must be four years... the toddler on her knee back then is probably at school now.

'It's so lovely to see you!' she says, her voice warm and genuine and I'm flooded with the thought that it's lovely to see her too. 'So, are you up for a visit? Is your dad OK?' she asks.

And just like that I feel almost teary and a little overcome to see her. We were such close friends through awkward teenage times, and I think it would probably be incredibly nice to get to know her again. But I also don't want to give too much about myself away.

I realise she's waiting for an answer to her questions as I notice the changes that the years have made to her face. She looks so like her mother. I realise with a start that I must have known Mrs McBain when she was this age.

'Dad's really well,' I reply. 'Yeah... I'm visiting... staying with him, in fact... for a while.' My answers feel half-baked. 'I've decided to give London a rest... and I... I needed a change of scene.'

'But that's so exciting!' she says with a big smile.

No, not really. Moving back in with your parent is the universal sign that everything's gone wrong in your life. I find I'm dreading any further questions about my current set up.

Alison maybe senses my reluctance, so she says: 'So your dad's doing well, that's great.'

'Yes, fit as a fiddle... a fiddle steeped in gin,' I add.

She gives a big laugh at this, a sound that is still so familiar, I feel properly sorry I've not had her in my life for so long.

'I'm up here for a while,' I tell her. 'I'd love to catch up. Are you at work just now?'

The last I remember, Alison was in sales and marketing for a small whisky distillery. She's also – as far as I know – married to a farmer, so probably busy with their farm too.

'No, well... yes, I have this little part-time job,' she replies, 'alongside the main one. And I'll have to get back in there to my flock, but it's lovely to see you, Jen, you haven't changed at all.'

I so have, I think. I have changed in all kinds of ways, both inside and out. A lot of life has happened since we were seventeen-year-olds, giggling over gossip in the back of the bus to the 'big shops' in Dundee.

'I'd love to catch up. So much to catch up on!' she adds. 'Why don't you come out to the farm on Saturday? West Cadder? You'll remember how to get there. Come in the afternoon, just phone me when you're setting off. We're still in the phone book, under Watson. Wattie won't hear of going ex-directory... I think it's to make sure any long-lost relatives can always contact us if they feel the urge to give away any money... or more likely, to come and claim it – knowing our luck!'

This makes me smile. No swapping mobile numbers, no LinkedIn, no WhatsApp – they're in the phone book... under Watson.

'OK, see you on Saturday,' I tell her. 'Can't wait!'

* * *

And then it's time for me to walk on, find a different café and sit there sipping at a large foamy coffee. I can't help stealing glances at the table beside mine, where two beautiful girls are sitting, ruffling their blonde hair, jangling their bracelets, the files open in front of them completely ignored, as they chat high speed in a language which sounds Eastern European.

And yes, Alison McBain and I used to be like this: intense friends with almost everything in common. When I first moved away from St Andrews to go to university in Edinburgh, she was the person I would meet in the pub every single time I came back.

But then I came back and she got married and was busy with her new family, so we drifted, then lost touch. More easily done then. Now there are people I'd gladly lose touch with, but instead I'm looking at photos of their dog and their breakfast smoothies on a daily basis.

I bring my phone out of my bag but give my social media sites a miss. I'm not ready to handle that yet. I'm dreading the updates...

changing my job status on LinkedIn to...? On sabbatical? Changing my location to St Andrews with a new profile pic? No, I'm not ready to do any of those things and invite all those questions from the people I know at work, in London and elsewhere.

I can barely answer my own questions at the moment, let alone anyone else's.

Instead, I google 'jobs in St Andrews' and scroll through what's on offer. Not a huge selection: care home assistant, council gardener, café manager and waiting staff. I think about each one carefully, picture myself doing the work. I could stay here for a few months, live with Dad, work at something temporary. Part-time even... give myself some time to think.

Once my coffee is drained, I decide to go to the newsagents I spotted further on along the street, so I can do that old-fashioned thing of buying the local paper and finding out more about what's going on in the town. As I walk, I check the people I pass a little more carefully because I'm not in London any more, so the chance of bumping into someone I know, or used to know, is suddenly much higher. And although there are people I don't want to meet, while I'm in my hermit-crab-without-a-shell state, maybe, as Alison has reminded me, there are still one or two old friends and acquaintances that I would like to catch up with.

I think, maybe, on the other side of the road, I've spotted Mrs Davies, and I'm grateful I've dodged that encounter. 'Oh, Jennifer, isn't it?' I can imagine her asking, even though she's known me since primary one when I sat next to her daughter, Penny. And then, no doubt, I would have to listen to what a raging success Penny has made of her life.

I keep walking briskly to the newsagents. As I open the door and step inside, a bell pings above my head, and I can't help thinking what a nice shop it is. Bigger than I expected with bright lighting, a clean black-and-white floor, the smell of coffee and pastries, and shelves neatly crammed with all kinds of products.

At the back is the counter and there's a man, dressed in a tartan shirt and a padded body warmer, in place behind it. He has a mug and a newspaper in front of him, and he's mid-doughnut, engrossed in a call on his mobile. He's a big guy with dark, wavy, overgrown hair.

When the call is over, only half glancing my way, he says: 'Good morning, how can we help you? KitKats are on special offer today only and there is no one in the world who doesn't love a KitKat. Right?'

I can't help thinking that he sounds familiar. Then as I say 'hello,' and step closer towards the counter, he looks up and a strong flash of recognition passes between us. I realise this is Rory Ferguson, from my class at school. Rory, he wasn't a close friend, but I do remember him as always the laugh-out-loud funny guy. I don't think I've spoken to him for... can it really be about eighteen years?

'Oh my god, it's Jennifer McAndrew,' he says immediately. 'Of all of the newsagents in all of the world, she walks into mine,' he adds with a grin. 'So, how's our London hotshot? The one who got the hell out of town.'

11

I laugh at this because I'm not sure what else to do. The thought of having to explain anything to anyone is making me feel slightly sick. I only came in for a newspaper and I already feel ambushed.

'Rory Ferguson,' I say, 'how are you?'

'She recognises me!' he splutters, 'and she remembers my name. Are you getting this, Doughal?' He looks over to the shelf beside his head and seems to be talking to an orange goldfish in a bowl.

'How are you doing?' I ask again.

'Absolutely awesome, thank you. How are you? And can I just say? You look amazing. Come here, come closer, let me look at you properly... in the light.'

It's a bit cheeky of him, but I draw up to the counter. I do remember what a nice, if totally irreverent, guy he was, and how he could always make the entire class and the teacher laugh.

Rory Ferguson – yes, he looks a bit heavier than he was, but his shoulders and chest are broad, so he carries it. He has below-the-collar hair and he looks kind of cool in his tartan shirt, at ease with himself. He's grown up into St Andrews' very own Jack Black I can't help thinking.

'Oh my god,' he says. 'I know exactly how old you are, November 12th is your birthday, right?'

I'm amazed he remembers this.

'So, you've obviously had a skiing accident, but nevertheless, you look *fantastic*,' he gushes. 'What is your secret? Botox? Fillers? A nip and tuck? Very expensive face cream, happiness, inner peace, Zen meditation, enormous wealth?'

I shrug and smile at the lovely compliment.

'You're too kind,' I tell him. 'I slipped on some wet tiles and cracked my knee, but never mind. You look really well too.'

'Har dee har,' he scoffs, and puts down the uneaten portion of doughnut. 'That's very nice of you to say, but we can all see that I'm a stress-eating lard bucket. You, however, have looked after yourself, Jennifer McAndrew, or been well looked after... so how is your millionaire property developer boyfriend-stroke-husband?

I laugh again: 'Oh very funny.'

'Miracle cancer-curing-doctor husband?'

I laugh but don't want to be drawn. I'm far too raw to be chit-chatting about my relationship status.

'OK... I sense a reluctance,' he says, 'so I'm stepping away from that question. And no children, no? I'm guessing from the radiant hair and make-up situation that broken nights and toddler jam fingers are not part of your lifestyle.'

'No,' I say simply because no matter how complicated my feelings are about children/no children/Jono's imminent children, I can keep my responses to the outside world simple.

'Well...' Rory continues, 'whatever may or may not be going on in your love life, it definitely can't be worse than mine. Remember Hazel Rudge from three years below us?'

'Emmm... no...' I admit apologetically.

'Well, I married her because I thought she was lovely. And I went to work on the oil rigs, offshore: two weeks on, two weeks off. We have three girls, by the way, ages five to fifteen.'

'Really... fifteen?' I can't help myself. This just doesn't quite compute... how old were Rory and Hazel...?

'So roll forward to the year twenty-lucky-eighteen when I find out she's been seeing someone else for *two and a half years*. Two weeks on... two weeks off.'

He gives a heavy sigh.

'Oh dear,' I say, as kindly as I can. Oil rigs, three daughters, one who is fifteen, the wife's two-year affair... this is a lot of information and drama to take on board so soon after meeting him again. Meanwhile, memories of teenage Rory are coming back. He was lively, fun, the class' social organiser, definitely a people person. A big, stocky guy even then, and not particularly good-looking, but cheeky and charming. I remember him offering to be my 'emergency backup' date at the sixth form dance if no one else asked, but Euan McKendrick did... and then I can't help wondering what handsome Euan is up to now, but I turn my attention back to Rory's story.

'So, one painful and extremely expensive divorce later, I live in St Andrews again, so does she. I have my daughters three or four nights a week, so does she. The one good thing to come out of it all is this shop. Owning this place instead of working on the rigs puts a smile on my face every single day. I love it.'

'It's a great shop,' I tell him.

'Thank you and you're looking at the tip of the iceberg; I sell loads of stuff online. So, Jennifer McAndrew, what about you? Still in London?'

In my head, I had planned a line or two that I was going to start saying to people to deal with this question and deflect too many others – they were along the lines of: 'decided to take a sabbatical' and 'wanting to spend some time with my dad' and 'pretty happily single'.

But instead, maybe because he's been so open, I hear myself blurting out: 'I've just had a really rough break-up. So, I've ditched my job and moved in with my dad because I needed to get away from it all for a bit.'

And slightly horrified with myself, I then add: 'But please keep that info to yourself.' Although my guess is that it is an entirely useless request. But I mean, let's be honest, Joan has probably already spread the word far and wide. In fact, I'm surprised Rory doesn't already know.

'Oh... that's horrible,' he says with sympathy. 'I'm very sorry. Shit has truly happened.'

And a look of real understanding passes between us. Here we are, totally grown-up, in our Very Late Thirties, and things are not turning out as we'd planned.

'So welcome to my mid-life crisis,' he says, throwing his hands wide, 'and welcome to my shop. Have a look around, *mi casa, su casa*. In fact, I'll show you round. Come on over to entrepreneur's corner. I've got the shop all zoned now.' He steps out from behind the counter and gives me a tour of the highlights.

'Over here: the household necessities, groceries, your traditional corner shop items. Then we have the chiller cabinets. Over there,' he waves an arm, 'we have booze, news and waterproof shoes. Yes, I know they're wellies, but that doesn't rhyme. You'll remember the *St Andrews Citizen*?' he puts the local newspaper into my hands. 'You've got to keep up with the latest, I've spotted all kinds of openings and opportunities through this paper. I'm sure you can too... Here we have golf supplies: scarves, gloves and golf balls right beside my beautiful tourist selection.' He points it out proudly.

I turn to the colourful display: St Andrews-themed mugs, *check*,

St Andrews-themed tea towels, *check*, Scottie dogs, *check*, golf-playing Scottie dogs, *check*, golf-playing Scottie dog tea towels, *check*, and then a whole raft of Kate 'n' Wills stuff because of course St Andrews was where the future King and Queen met and fell in love. Wills 'n' Kate mugs, money boxes, biscuit tins and framed photographs apparently signed by the happy couple.

'Thank god for *The Crown*,' Rory says, 'it has brought new life to the Kate 'n' Wills St Andrews romance.'

'Where did you get those?' I ask. 'Did Kate 'n' Wills actually sign them for you? Were they passing through the shop?' I tease. 'On their way to play a round of golf?'

Rory looks slightly sheepish.

'OK, OK, I signed them myself with a Sharpie. But who's going to complain? It's all about spreading the love, giving the customer what they want.'

'I don't know, Rory, that could be fraud. Or possibly treason!'

'Scribbling on a photo with a Sharpie? That's just gilding the lily, if you ask me. OK, so you've got to have this. This is a must when you're starting over, starting out in business again, starting out in life again. I recommend it to every single one of my customers. It will literally change your life.'

He hands me a copy of a book covered with bright purple and gold lettering and the puffed, Botox-ed face of a very pleased man in a suit. It promises:

Success Unleashed – Release Your Dreams.

I'm not convinced.

'You have to read it,' Rory insists, 'changed my life.'

'Really?' I can't help wondering. 'And have your dreams been released? I can't help feeling he means "realise your dreams".'

Rory decides to ignore this and carries on with an enthusiastic:

'Now, do you have stationery?'

The doorbell pings and he is busy for several minutes cheerfully serving a regular, so I take the time to admire his St Andrews Old Course Hotel snow globes.

As soon as his other customer has gone, Rory returns and helps me shop for all kinds of things I didn't know I needed. But this is the essence of shopping, after all.

He suggests shortbread and KitKats for my dad. I decide gin would be better, but then it turns out I can't buy gin because it's too early in the day and there are laws about that in Scotland. So, Rory makes me take the KitKats, four packs for the price of one, short-dated, I suspect. Then there are oven-warm croissants for mid-morning, packs of a brand of coffee he is crazy about ('Because you're definitely going to invite me round, aren't you?'), pasta because it's on a two-for-one, pens, paper, envelopes, stamps and Post-it notes ('Because everyone needs those all the time.')

'Right, so, will that be everything?' he asks when he can't persuade me to buy any more.

'Yes, that will definitely be everything. That's more than enough.'

He puts it all through the till, packs it into a carrier bag and announces the surprising total.

'Ouch,' I tell him, 'I just came in for a paper.'

He points to the framed notice up behind the counter:

Good thing no' cheap.
Cheap thing no good.

'Does that apply to the KitKats too?' I smile again. In fact, the muscles on the side of my face are aching slightly because I've done so little smiling and laughing lately that my face isn't used to it.

'It's fantastic to see you again, Jennifer McAndrew, I've missed you. Let's have coffee very soon.'

'Yes, give me your number,' I say.

So, we swap numbers, I say I'll come back with a date and I leave his shop feeling cheered.

* * *

Then, even though I have a heavy shopping bag, a stick and a still dodgy knee, I walk out to the long stretch of beach at West Sands. The view here is much lovelier than I remember, blue-grey waves on one side, the spires of St Andrews rising on the other.

The cold wind blows in sharply and watching the waves rush in and rush out again, the sadness I thought I was holding at bay washes over me again.

I have a chunk of deposit saved for a home I've never bought.

A heart bruised by a man who didn't love me enough.

I'm really good at a job I no longer want.

And I have no idea where I'm going to go from here.

I feel deeply, terribly sorry for myself. The phone in my pocket buzzes. I take it out reluctantly, sure it will be another Jono text that I should delete.

Instead, the name Rory flashes up. I open and read:

Still can't believe ur back, AWESOME. Never mind coffee, let's go do FUN!

And despite the weight of my heart, the weight of my shopping, the wind lashing my hair against my cheeks, my stupid decision to walk along this beach with my stick in suede boots that are now completely soggy, I manage a smile.

I'm not sure that I can do a lot of fun at the moment, but at least I can try.

12

On Saturday afternoon, I borrow Dad's wheezy old Nissan Sunny to make the trip out to Alison's farm. Once I've got to grips with driving in general – it's been a while – and driving this antique, in particular, I enjoy bowling along country roads where cold sunshine lights up the gorse bush flowers and the new daffodils shivering in the breeze. I may have spent years and years of my life in the city, but I realise the loveliness of the countryside still lifts my heart.

It's the earliest days of spring. Time to come out of hibernation and back to life. Time to risk greening, growing and blossoming all over again...

* * *

I pull up outside the comfortably shabby farmhouse Alison shares with her family on their small farm. I haven't been here for years. Although the back door is open, I ring the brass bell hanging there and soon Alison appears in her farmer's wife ensemble of tartan padded shirt and practical cords.

Alison and I have been through puberty, first boyfriends, first drinks, fashion crises, exam and friendship traumas together. We have spent literally thousands of hours together in our bedrooms discussing everything, from which pop star we would consider marrying (her, Gary Barlow; me, James Blunt), to what our lives were going to be like when we grew up. We may not have spent much of our adult lives together, but I hope we can rekindle our friendship and I realise how much I want to do that.

I also feel a little nervous that it might be too hard. Time has passed. We've both grown up and been changed by the way our lives are playing out. I worry that I fobbed her off once or twice in my busy London life. Did I reply to every email, message or invitation in the past? Probably not – I hope she can forgive and forget.

I've brought fancy wine and nice chocolates, at Rory's shop, of course, as a kind of peace offering.

'Welcome,' she says and scoops me up in a hug. 'It's a total state in here as always. And I'm in a total state... as always,' she adds, making me feel with a glance that my careful hair, make-up and clothes choices maybe weren't so necessary.

I follow her through a corridor littered with Wellington boots, socks, toys, tennis rackets, skipping ropes and large bags of dog food, calf food, fertilizer...

On a farm, the dividing line between home and work is blurred. The dividing line between indoors and out of doors is also blurred.

Alison's kitchen is a messy delight. There's a huge cat beside the battered old Raeburn cooker, the smell of toast, and two large, hairy dogs thud their tails against the lino floor as I come in.

'So, Jennifer M, it's so good to see you! Take a seat and start talking,' Alison instructs, directing me to a wooden chair at the kitchen table and clearing a space amidst the piles of paperwork, schoolwork, unfinished knitting, overflowing basket of gnarled veg half covered in earth and collection of used tea mugs from a round of earlier visitors.

'Tea?' she asks.

'Yes, please.'

'We have so much to catch up on and I want to know everything. Every single little detail. Don't leave anything out. Tell all. How are you? Why are you back? How is it going? How long are you staying? How often can you babysit for me? That's a joke, obviously, well... slightly.'

'I can babysit,' I tell her straight away.

'I'd have to pay you danger money,' she replies. 'They're a bit wild.'

Then she fires more questions at me as she fills a kettle with water and sets it on the hob.

I nearly sit on what I think is a furry cushion but turns out to be a rabbit.

'Can I put him on the floor? Or will the dogs eat him?' I ask, scooping the bunny up gingerly.

'The floor is fine, I think once rabbits are in the house the dogs accept them as members of the pack or something like that. Oh, you know what? Sod tea and coffee; let's have a proper drink. It's Saturday, isn't it?'

'I'm driving,' I warn.

'Right, so you'll stick to tea and and I'll have...' she looks at the bottle of wine I've brought along, 'thank you, my very fancy friend-from-London, and that is definitely going in the special occasions cupboard. Meanwhile, I have rosé from the *supermarché*.'

So she makes me a mighty mug of tea, then unscrews a bottle of supermarket wine from the fridge, pours herself a hefty glass and we begin to talk... and talk, and tell our stories and reconnect. And within an hour or so, the years we've spent apart have melted away.

I recognise her laugh and her way of listening intently with a little crease of concentration between her eyes... and I miss Alison, my old friend, her sense of fun, her sometimes-a-little-bracing honesty, and I tell myself off for being so careless with a precious friendship like this.

'It really is lovely to see you,' I say when there's a break in the conversation.

'Yes,' she says with a smile, 'I was just thinking that.'

She tells me all about her children and the money troubles on the farm, but there's a lifeline new potato contract, she's planning a farmers' market stall, and she has her part-time tour-guide job on top of her official one.

'That sounds like a lot,' I say, marvelling at this level of busyness.

'It is,' she agrees, 'but on the other hand, there is never a dull moment.'

And then I make the decision to let her hear at least some of what's going on with me. I tell her I've broken up with my boss after he decided to go back to his wife. And how that meant I had to leave my job. I keep the impending twin babies-to-be out of it, because I realise that is still too painful to talk about. Nope, it's not going to be possible for me to just come out and talk about it round the table, with a mug of tea in my hand. It's too raw.

'I'm so sorry to hear all this,' Alison tells me. 'You seemed to have it all sorted – your swanky legal assistant job, lovely clothes, a string of successful boyfriends...'

This makes me laugh: 'Is that how it looked?' I have to ask.

'From the outside, yes!' she admits. 'Especially the lovely clothes. The last time we met, you were wearing Joseph or Armani or something and I was wearing some hideous old maternity sack that the baby had just puked o'.'

'I'm sure it wasn't that bad...' I tell her.

'Oh, it was, believe me. I had a little cry all the way home.'

'Alison! You're so very lucky to have your lovely children and your adoring Wattie and this gorgeous home. String of successful boyfriends?' I snort. 'Well, there was certainly a string of them... Jono and I managed two years, that's my longest yet.'

'That's looking pretty exciting from where I'm standing,' Alison says, 'and you moved to London. You've had all that time there doing interesting things...' she holds up her hand, 'don't spoil it for me. You are my glamorous friend from the big city.'

I smile and don't say anything. No need to ruin my image with stories of unaffordable flats, terrible commutes, horror stories from the London dating scene, or anything else. For the time being, Alison can think of my life as on a par with Sarah Jessica Parker's.

She takes a sip of her rosé and says: 'I feel I should let you know that Take That are touring, and Gary Barlow has admitted he's come close to divorce. So, there is *always* hope. Wattie has said if I can snag Gary Barlow, he will happily stand aside!'

And although I'm only on tea, I find myself laughing like a teenager along with her. And it feels good. In my pent-up, serious little state, I realise I haven't had a real belly laugh for far too long.

So another hour, more tea and more wine goes by. At one point, I have to field some awkward questions about my sister.

'No... we haven't really managed to build any bridges,' I have to admit.

'What?!' Alison sounds genuinely surprised. 'But your mum's gone and you've got a niece and nephew... don't you want to get to know them? Can't you get on with Isla just for their sake?'

These are difficult questions and of course I've thought about them but maybe not as often as I should have. I haven't tried to make up with my sister and she hasn't tried to make up with me. We've both just left it. And now, I haven't seen my niece and nephew since they were tiny. They wouldn't even recognise me. I wonder if Isla has even told them they have an auntie.

'Is it just about Richard?' Alison asks me now.

Why is Alison using the word 'just'? Is it *just about Richard* as if it's not really a big deal that my younger sister should have snapped up one of my... well... 'string of successful boyfriends' is about right, and not a huge amount of time after he'd ended his relationship with me.

So, yes, Isla is married to one of my exes, which I think is quite a big deal, not to mention pretty awkward. And this has caused ongoing trouble and unhappiness between us, and that trouble and unhappiness played a part in my mum's death. So, building bridges... that's not something we've been able to do yet.

'Yes, Richard is part of it,' I tell Alison now, 'but there's more to it than that.'

'Do you think you'll try to mend fences now you're up here?' she asks.

'Maybe,' I say and hope that she can read from my face that I don't want to talk about it any more. It's not as if I haven't thought about Isla as I've walked past the door to her old bedroom night after night. It's just hard to know where to begin. At least when we ignore each other, we don't make anything worse, or cause any more pain.

'What's it like living back home again?' Alison asks, knowing this will be a more comfortable question to answer.

And then I'm discussing Dad and Joan with Alison.

'I mean, do you think they're... you know...?'

'At it?'

Alison is a farmer's wife; she's not for mincing about. I'm giggling again as I protest: 'Nooo, don't say that. Don't put that picture in my mind.'

'They're probably just good friends, but who knows?' she goes on. 'Who knows anything about anyone? And by the way, Jen, if you're going to start dating again and having a whole Exciting Sexy Life with Multiple New Men, don't expect to turn up here and be able to go on about it. Staying married is hard enough without the single friends bragging about last night with Mr Musical Fingers they found on Tinder.'

The muscles in my face are beginning to ache again. I have not been laughing enough recently.

'Actually,' Alison relents, 'you would be allowed to tell me a little bit... in small doses. I'm dying for a bit of excitement and even someone else's adventures would do.'

'Alison, there is not going to be any dating yet, I can promise you that,' I tell her truthfully.

'Too soon?' she asks.

'Definitely too soon,' I confirm. 'I'm burned... it could be years before I play with those matches again.'

And our conversation moves on, first of all to Alison's children and then to her elderly mother.

'She's not great,' Alison admits. 'I think she might have to move in with us and somehow, we'll have to find money for a carer when I'm out at work. And right now, my day job at the distillery is just completely *rubbish*.'

'Oh dear,' I sympathise.

'I would really like to find something else,' Alison says. 'Or, fantasy lifestyle, just be the lady of the house. God knows there's enough to do around here.' She casts a look around the chaotic kitchen and takes a gulp of wine to fortify herself.

'So what's happening at work?' I ask.

'I've annoyed them and they're not going to let me forget it,' she says.

It turns out that Alison still works for a small, local distillery, fine Scottish whiskies, hand-brewed traditional gin and that kind of thing, and she gives me the impression that the place is run by a pompous bunch of tweedy old farts.

'They're not making nearly enough money for the dynamic new managing director, so they've decided to concoct an extra-strong cider, in exciting new *fruit* flavours! So basically, they're going to be making alcoholic lemonade for kids. And I've let them know how downright irresponsible it is to target teenage drinkers. I tell you, at the school, in the town and the uni, we have a massive drinking problem. There are kids in hospital with alcohol poisoning every single weekend.

'So I told them I wasn't going to have anything to do with iDer, or whatever stupid name they've given it, and my boss said – "Well, Alison, no one's forcing you to work here..."'

When Alison looks at me again, there are tears in her eyes.

'Oh no,' I tell her.

'There I was hoping for a sodding promotion,' she goes on, 'because the farm income is absolutely drastic again this year and our old sheds are going to have to be re-roofed before they fall on top of us. But instead, I get called to a meeting with the chairman and he explains that for "operational reasons" they're going to promote my junior to the post above me. And would I like to work three days a week instead of five?' Her voice has risen and it would be hard to miss the tone of outrage. 'Turns out it's not just TV presenters who are getting bumped off because the boys at the top think they're past it.'

'What did you tell them?'

'I said I'd like to think about my response, then Mum went and got a chest infection so I've had to take two days off to look after her. I'm going to tell them that I really want to keep my five days. I need that job.'

For a few moments we are quiet and listen to the whoops and squeals of the two boys playing video games next door.

Then, ten-year-old Matty comes in, hair on end, dressed like an urchin, forages for crisps and a carrot, and goes out again.

Suddenly, to my surprise, I find that I'm blinking back tears.

'What's the matter?' Alison asks.

'Oh... I'm just sorry all this time has passed,' I say, wiping my eyes. And I'm not quite sure how to explain myself: 'I wish I'd spent more time with you and your family.'

'C'mon,' Alison says gently, 'let's have some shortbread. It'll help me to soak up the wine.'

We hear the back door opening and the clump of boots being taken off in the corridor.

'Did someone say shortbread?'

Moments later, Wattie, Alison's man-mountain of a husband, fills the kitchen doorway: 'Jennifer!' he exclaims, 'I heard you were coming over, how nice to see you again.'

When I stand up to greet him, I'm enveloped in a not entirely pleasant hug against an overalled chest that is dusty and smells of pig, straw, earth and other pungent pongs.

'Hey, Wattie, how are you doing?'

'Good, good, good,' he peels off the overall, letting it fall into a heap at his feet and pulls up a chair.

'Now... Alison tells me you've still not settled down, no family and single once again. Dear, oh dear.' He inhales a shortbread then despite my surprised expression and Alison's embarrassed warnings to 'shush, Wattie', he carries on. 'You need to take care of yourself, my girl...'

'Yes, thanks, Wattie, I'm trying to do that.'

'I've seen it so many times before with the sows...'

'The sows?!' Alison says, astonished. 'This is not the same! Wattie, please stop talking.'

'Well, no.' Wattie rubs his chin, deep in thought. He hasn't taken off his hat, which I suspect is not actually a hat but a knitted and very battered tea cosy.

'But the sows,' he goes on, 'when their piglets go, they can get moody, even ferocious. I've even seen them attack other mothers and eat their young. Not nice. So you must be careful, Jennifer, you don't want to let that happen to you.'

I nod solemnly. Maybe I should feel offended, but it's too funny. 'Wattie, I promise, I will not eat your children. OK?'

He looks at me and nods: 'And don't stay alone too long. I could try to find you someone if you like. That Justin MacAllister, at Nether Woodfield, he's looking for a good solid wife. Last one took off.'

Wine actually squirts from Alison's nose.

'For god's sake, Wattie!' she exclaims. 'Don't you even think about match-making! This isn't the farm, you know; this isn't cow meets bull. This is Jennifer, a sophisticated woman of the world. She's lived in London for years.'

'Yes, but a woman has needs, Alison, you don't want her turning all moody and strange.'

'Please, Wattie, just stop talking and eat more shortbread for god's sake.' She turns to me. 'Pay no attention. Let's talk about something else. Do you want to come on my tour tomorrow, if you're not doing anything else? We start at 10 a.m., takes two hours.'

'What kind of tour guide are you, exactly?' I ask. 'Famous landmarks of St Andrews?'

'No... you will wee yourself.'

My mind boggles.

'I'm a guide on the new Kate 'n' Wills Royal St Andrews tour... now that *The Crown* has covered their love affair here, bookings are non-stop.'

'The entire tour is about them? But... I definitely remember that you're not her biggest fan.'

'I don't *hate* her, I'm just... I mean, does she have to be so bloody perfect all the time? Didn't we love Princess Di so much because she was flawed and because she messed up? I want Kate to spill ketchup down one of her creamy coats, or have a hole in her tights or just a teeny crumb stuck to her face, or something, anything, to prove she's human, one of us.'

'Buttock-clenchingly perfect,' I agree. 'Just the smallest burp even, or an ever-so-slightly bad hair day. Does she have to go about looking like she's actually been photoshopped in real life and is posing for the cover of *Hello!* magazine at all times?'

'But she is posing for the cover of *Hello!* at all times. If she ever farted,' Alison muses, 'it would be a tiny squeak of a thing which wafted a beautiful smell like...'

'Acqua di Parma,' I decide.

'You what-ie?' Wattie asks, living up to his nickname.

And once again Alison and I collapse into the kind of hysterical giggles last seen when Take That was first in the charts and Gary Barlow was still single.

* * *

'Hello, Jennifer,' Dad greets me in the hallway on my return from Alison's.

'Hello, Dad, I think the clutch might be slipping in the Sunny.'

'Oh dear... that sounds expensive.'

Without hesitation, he hands me a gin and tonic.

Without hesitation, I start to drink it.

And so, another pretty tolerable evening at my dad's passes with its lulling ingredients of gin, wine, Elvis, the television, Joan and a mince-based meal.

But when I head upstairs to bed and pass the door to my sister's old bedroom, I'm not so lulled as to have forgotten Alison's questions about Isla, and how we should think about healing the rift now that I am back in St Andrews.

But I hardly think it's going to be easy. *Years* have passed since we last had a good conversation. We have grown apart and she's married to the man that... to be honest... I had wondered about marrying. And we all know that he broke up with me after his first visit to my family, or his first meeting with my younger sister. We all know he started going out with her five months later when she moved to Edinburgh to study interior design. I stuck it out for a bit... but then one day, I bumped into the two of them at the place I always went to with my friends and my sense of rejection and embarrassment was just too much to bear.

The next day, I packed up, left my room, left my degree course and got on a train to London. I stayed with a friend, applied for legal secretary work and quickly had the first of many jobs, an income, then a new place to live and a burning need to not think about Isla, Richard, Edinburgh, my unfinished law degree, how disappointed my parents were with me – or anything else that was too painful to deal with.

Now, there are just too many differences between us for me to be able to get on with her again. She chose to stay in St Andrews, while I moved to London. She has two children, while I don't have any and feel pretty sure I will keep it that way. Ever since uni, I've always worked, but ever since marrying Richard, she has never worked. She's on the perfect, stay-at-home Mummy track and so I don't think we would have much in common, even if we did want to hang out together. But there is also another major reason why we've had very little contact over the past four years – the fact is that I blame her for playing a part in our mum's death. And she blames me. There was a furious argument the day before the funeral when we both told each other what we really thought. And there hasn't been any attempt at forgiveness on either side since then.

I don't know if there can be now. Or if I even want there to be. Everyone always wants families to get on and 'play nice'. I know Dad would love us to get along the way we used to when we were primary school children. But sometimes siblings are too different, have different life experiences and, in our case, are too angry about what has happened to ever close the rift.

13

The following Saturday, Alison and I have a girlie date. I've agreed to come even though she didn't exactly pitch it brilliantly, phoning mid-week to say: 'Jen, I got a voucher at Christmas for spa treatments, dinner and drinks at the McIver Hotel, you know the one I mean, why don't I book us in on Saturday? I've got to use it before it runs out anyway. Sorry, that doesn't sound... you know what I mean. Come with me – a free massage, then dinner with wine. Can't go wrong with that.'

'Why don't you take Wattie?' I suggest. 'I could babysit.'

Alison sighs. 'Wattie likes shortbread, hamburgers, pizzas, and wearing his dungarees. Being dragged to the McIver in a suit and tie would not make him happy. A massage or any kind of spa treatment – out of the question!'

'Fair enough.'

'No, we'll go swim and steam, and have a massage, then we'll hammer that dinner and drinks for two voucher to death.'

So we do.

* * *

We swim a little bit. Then we talk and talk in the steam room, catching up further on everything that has happened over the years since we've seen each other. I remember all the things I like about her – she's warm and funny. I remember the few things I don't like about her too – sometimes she can be a little too blunt and matter-of-fact. We reminisce, of course, and all kinds of school and teenage memories come tumbling out.

'Have you bumped into Rory Ferguson yet?' she asks.

'Yes, I went into his shop the day I ran into you outside the café.'

'I think his wee shop is going a storm... I haven't seen him for months. Anyway, was he pleased to see you? And what's going on with him?' she wants to know.

'He seemed good... he's promised to take me for a coffee, or something, but we've not managed to make a date yet.' I tell her with something of a shrug.

'Why not?' she wonders.

I'm not quite sure what the right answer is here... Rory has suggested several dates, then he's cancelled because of daughter commitments, or I've cancelled because I've suddenly felt it would be too strange. What will we talk about I've wondered. Will he think I'm interested in him when I'm not?

'I'm worried we won't have much to say to each other,' I admit, 'and... I don't want to give him the wrong idea.'

Alison bursts out laughing.

'What?!' I ask.

'Well, number one, never worry about running out of things to say with Rory. He's a talker. If you had to take a group of awkward people out for lunch, you could take Rory along and it would all be fine. And number two, I think we can all see you are way out of Rory's league. I mean, he's nice, he's good fun, but he's chubby, on the short side and in a whole complex three-children-and-an-ex situation. You, Jennifer, are the glam girl from London who has had a string—'

'—*Of successful boyfriends*,' we say together and laugh about it.

'So yes, meet up with him. You'll enjoy yourself,' Alison adds, 'and you'll probably hear some incredible gossip. Rory hears it all.'

After our lengthy steam session, we are massaged, which releases a great deal of the tension knotted into my body, and then, after pre-dinner drinks, we make our way through a four-course meal, splitting a bottle of wine between us. Then we retire to the clubby bar to decide if we can manage any further alcoholic indulgence.

* * *

I buy us both a cocktail because I'm full of wine and it seems like a good idea. When we're halfway through these, Alison leans over and murmurs: 'White shirt, dark jacket, approaching the bar any moment now.'

There's a movement to my left and a tall, dark-haired, long-legged man orders a drink, gives a room number, and says: 'Good evening, ladies,' to us in a heavily foreign accent as he passes, then takes a seat at another table.

Alison doesn't take her eyes from him and I have a powerful flashback of nights out in St Andrews a long time ago. Vivacious with blonde curls, Alison did a lot of dating before she settled on the lucky Mr Wattie Watson.

'Oh my god, he is sitting over there so that he can keep his eye on you. He was in the dining room too and I saw him checking you out all the way through dinner.'

'I think you may have had too much to drink,' I tell her, but I can't quite resist pretending to look for a waiter, so that I can glimpse in his direction. The man, and he is definitely a handsome man, seems to be looking at us. But the lights are dim, so I'm not sure I can really tell.

'I bet he could put a few things right for you,' Alison says.

'What?!' I splutter.

'You know... some quality flirting time, a bit of feel-good friction.'

'Feel-good friction? What are you talking about?' I hiss at her. 'I think this is maybe what *you* are thinking, Alison. Is this a little bit of what you would like, maybe?'

'Except I'm married, Jen,' she says. 'And I'm not saying that doesn't have advantages, but being able to enjoy some quality time with a man like that, is not one of those advantages.'

The grass is always greener, I suppose.

'He's coming over,' she whispers, sounding thrilled.

'He is not...' I insist.

I take a glimpse in the man's direction. He does seem to be walking with intent in our direction. Maybe it's not our direction. Maybe we've missed something very obvious. Maybe he's just spotted his wife in the lobby and he's going to meet her and this walking in our direction has absolutely nothing to do with us at all.

But no, I'm tapped on the shoulder. I look up at a jutting jawline with a sprinkling of dark designer stubble and the man of mystery asks in a not-in-any-way unattractive, maybe even slightly husky, foreign voice: 'Would it be rude of me to ask if I could join you at your table?'

I am utterly astonished. What does he want? Seriously, he's a hot guy on a Saturday night and he wants to join *our* table? I can't help feeling this is some sort of scam or set up. Has Alison bribed him to do this?

'Umm... well, no... I think it would be fine,' I tell him.

'Yes, *of course*,' Alison says sounding like she might eat him up all in one go, 'come and sit down with us. That will be lovely.'

'That's good. I'm looking for company; I'm looking to talk to people,' he says, choosing the comfortable chair opposite mine and sitting down. 'I am working for hotel company. I have to stay in hotels all over the world and find out what guests want, what guests enjoy. I'm Sergei,' he holds out his hand. He honestly pronounces it as 'Sir Gay'.

And now I carefully avoid Alison's eye because if I catch it, we will both be in danger of squirting expensive cocktails from our noses.

'How interesting,' Alison says, once the threat of hysterics has passed. 'Where are your favourite hotels?'

So he begins to talk in his luscious accent, tripping over the odd word here and there. He's from Croatia, he's in St Andrews for a few days, staying in several different hotels, interviewing as many guests as he can.

'What do you think of this town?' he directs the question at me. 'Do you live here? But I think you have not always lived here? You look too glamorous.'

I've made a reasonable amount of effort for this dinner out. The hair and make-up is sorted, the one smart dress I brought up with me is on. I don't feel particularly gorgeously glamorous, but I let it pass and don't protest. I'm a grown-up, so I can enjoy the moment when Sir Gay of the huskily accented voice aims a compliment at me.

I tell him a bit about the mix at the heart of St Andrews: on the one hand, still a small, traditional Scottish town, but with the wealthy, glamorous edge brought by the influx of students, tourists, the Royal connection, and golfers.

'It's full of bright young people and wealthy foreigners, so there's a glamorous and rich element and I think that's all very interesting. But it's still small and tucked away. The bus journey from the train station, or that single lane road from the motorway that goes on for miles, these things still make it seem like a remote place on the edge of the sea. Quite romantic, really...'

This could be the booze talking.

'So tell me a little bit about yourself, why have you come back to St Andrews?' he asks and leans in over the table towards me. And I realise I'm looking into those dark eyes a little longer than I should. When I break off to glance at Alison, she is giving me a surreptitious thumbs-up.

'I used to live in London...' I begin.

'Ah, London!' he smiles. I smile back, enjoying his enthusiasm, his infectiously good mood and yes, his handsome face. 'I've been to London many times and I love it,' he says. 'Almost as exciting as New York.'

'Oh... New York,' it's my turn to enthuse. 'I *love* that city. I can actually feel quite homesick for New York sometimes.'

This makes him laugh: 'You live in St Andrews but you are homesick for New York... so why don't you go and live in New York?'

'You're right. Why don't I? Maybe I should...' I make a mental note to put New York at the top of my where-next list as Alison excuses herself and makes her way a little unsteadily to the ladies.

'What will your husband think?' Sergei asks.

'What?!'

'About moving to New York.'

'Oh – that's easy, he won't think anything because I don't have a husband.'

'No boyfriend?' Sergei is enough of a charmer to make himself sound surprised.

'Not any more.'

'Oh... did this happen not a very long time ago?' He grins then arches his eyebrows. 'This is quite interesting to me perhaps? If you are free once again?'

No mistaking what he means.

And I feel an unexpected lurch. I had been with Jono for two full years. I have forgotten all about flirting and the thrill of connecting and even feeling interest in a body I don't know. It feels like such a long time since I was single. And this suspended state... this tingling space between where we are right now and where we go next? It's much more of a buzz than I remember.

The anticipation in the air. The unknown. I wonder what is going to happen next.

'So... how old are you?' I ask.

I feel his knee bump against mine and he doesn't move it away.

'How old are you?' he asks straight back.

'Old enough,' is my reply.

'I like this,' he laughs. 'I am old enough too.'

I have to swallow. And re-cross my legs.

'I think it looks more comfortable on your side of the table,' he suggests, gesturing to the upholstered sofa.

I don't protest, I just move over as he comes to sit beside me. And then we are sitting side by side. His arm stretches out along the sofa behind my shoulders, and then my hand goes to his knee, and his hand rests on top of it.

I feel a little scrambled with the wine, the martini, and the tumble of thoughts. Sensible me is looking on and thinking: *'What are you doing? And where is Alison? What is going on?'*

Not-so-sensible me is cheering: 'Go, Jen! He's ridiculously handsome!'

Where *is* Alison? I scan for her bag, her cardigan, her jacket. She's taken it all. She's obviously left me here on my own because she thinks this is a good idea. Really? Does she honestly think I should be diving into the arms of a hunky foreign stranger?!

Sergei's hand moves from the sofa to my shoulder and remains there, warm and heavy. I stroke the inside of his palm and he half laughs.

I don't think he's much older than thirty.

We manage to keep up a conversation of sorts. The city he lives in... other cities we have been to... some of the best sights in St Andrews... films we've enjoyed. But really, all thoughts are elsewhere.

That hand on the shoulder has moved down to my waist, reaching just a little under my top. My hand on his knee has moved up a little, feeling the muscle under the trousers, feeling the impatient movement of a restless leg.

Impatience is coming over me, too, making me breathe deeply and willing me on. I'm watching his face, wondering what he would be like to kiss. His face is bony, skin pulled tightly over the cheekbones, dark stubble on his jaw.

'I don't know if your friend is going to come back... but maybe you would like another cocktail?' he asks. 'Or maybe something else?'

His voice is deep and dark, as unknown a quantity as he is.

'Are you going to drink something?' I ask, thinking he's probably right about Alison.

'I thought perhaps a café?'

'A coffee?'

'Yes, a coffee.'

I like the fact that he's not trying to ply me with drink. If I'm going to do anything with him, I'm going to be more sober than I am now, have my eyes open. I'm not going to pretend that I was under the influence and got carried away.

'Maybe I'll have coffee,' I say.

'Espresso? Single or double.'

'Macchiato, with a little milk.'

When he's at the bar ordering the coffees, I seriously consider running away. I mean, it's been well over a month since I left London and Jono. Generally, I try to concentrate on being over Jono and staying at a certain level of angry with him, but now and then come feelings of sadness and longing. Spotting his favourite brand of coffee in the supermarket aisle can make me feel teary.

But still too soon.

Too soon to imagine that anyone else would be able to help in any way.

But... then again, for two whole years, I've not looked at anyone else. And now I can... if I want to.

Sergei comes back, sets the small coffees in front of us and after a few sips I tell him: 'One of us should probably run away.'

But his hand is steady on my knee. The warmth of it runs between us, connecting us.

'Stay and talk to me,' he says. 'I am enjoying your company.'

So we talk a little more, but when the coffee is drunk, although he's powerfully attractive, I tell him: 'I think I should go.'

His black-brown eyes meet mine. His eyebrows are arched into a question. His hand over mine.

'What do you *want* to do?' he asks, darkly.

And I think about it. I really think about it.

I imagine kissing him. He will taste of coffee and hold me tight against his firm body. I imagine him persuasive and persistent... unhooking my bra strap, putting his face into my breasts. I look at his hand, holding mine, and imagine it on my thigh, moving under my skirt, reaching up to touch me.

Then, I'm not sure why, but I can't help myself from also imagining the comedy version: me hopping about his room, knocking things over as I try to get my leg out of my tights... him having overpowering garlic breath and dodgy-looking underwear – too tight and with a bad pattern or, even worse, wording... 'big boy' or 'OMG' – and just no, that's when I snap out of the daydream. That's my cold shower moment. Because I just know, no matter how much this could be just fun and escapism, pure fantasy and a one-night only event, I am not ready. I'll almost 100 per cent definitely end up crying on him, spilling out my sob story.

And as soon as that thought crosses my mind, I know I have to go. Sitting here, I'm just kidding myself.

'Good night, Sergei,' I say, sure of my decision. 'It's been amazing, really interesting, but I'm going to go now. Thank you for the coffee and the chat and the good time.'

'Don't go... no,' he counters, looking upset. 'I'll buy you another drink. Whatever you want.'

But I'm up on my feet, reaching for my bag and jacket. This is too much, too soon and I have to get back to my current job of working out where to go from here.

'Good to see you're getting back out again,' Dad tells me on Sunday morning when I appear in the kitchen to make myself breakfast much later than usual.

'I don't like to see you sitting at home brooding,' he adds.

Dad is big on the problems of 'brooding'. His answer to every kind of problem when we were younger was to get outside, go for a walk, take the bike out, phone a friend, get a hobby.

'I'm not brooding,' I say because this is the easiest way to get him off my case. Conversations about needing quiet time or time to think don't go down well with him.

'Keep busy, keep fit... take a leaf out of your old dad's book,' he tells me.

'Does this mean you're off to the golf today?'

'Absolutely, you can't spend a day as good as this inside! What about you? What will you do? And no staying in fussing about the house. The house is absolutely fine. I'm not saying you haven't done some nice things...'

This is reference maybe to the new pot plants, tea towels, hand soaps, mugs and other nice little touches I've brought in.

'But there's no need to do pernickety things around the house. Life is for living, so get out there and enjoy yourself,' he insists.

I pass him a mug with his favourite mahogany brown tea in it and decide I should maybe not tell him that I have a slight hangover and would really like to snuggle down on the sofa for a few hours.

'I'm going to go for a long beach walk...' I tell him instead.

'And what about organising some company for yourself?'

'Yes, well, I saw Alison yesterday, remember, and I've got another school friend lined up for a drink,' I tell him.

'Great stuff... right... better have some toast.'

Once Dad's breakfast is finished and his golf clubs are all packed up, he gets himself out of the door and into the Nissan. No sooner has the car pulled out of the driveway, than I am snuggled up on the sofa for at least a few hours of peace and quiet before I have to haul myself to the beach to keep him happy.

This is very teenage... I tell myself. But it turns out it's not possible to come back to your family home and not revert in some tiny way back into your teenage self.

Just as I'm considering which of the very limited TV options to dive into, my phone rings and I see it's Alison, obviously wanting to catch up on What Happened Last Night.

'Yes, he was very handsome but absolutely nothing happened,' I say, as soon as I've picked up. 'And by the way where did you get to? You literally vanished!'

'Nothing happened?!' Alison sounds horrified. 'But he was so gorgeous! Why did nothing happen?'

'Because this is real life,' I remind her. 'Not some daft movie... and I just didn't think it would have solved anything... plus, I began to worry about what his underpants might look like and then, you know, we have to consider that he could have been a travelling serial killer.'

'True...' Alison admits, 'this is the kind of thing people in ancient marriages do not need to worry about.'

'Did you have a nice night?' is my next question. I hope she did. I don't think she gets out of the house as much as she'd like to, so I hope Sergei didn't ruin the end of her evening.

'I had a fantastic time. Meeting Mr Gorgeous was the highlight. But it's back to reality this morning, I can tell you,' and I realise her voice sounds a little choked and unsteady.

'Oh no, what's happened? Is everyone OK?'

'Yes... and thank you for reminding me that things could be a lot worse. But I've just lost my job, the main one, with McWhirter & Sons. They've sacked me by email on a Sunday morning. That's just charming, isn't it?'

'They've sacked you?!' I repeat, surprised. 'But what on earth for?'

Alison sighs and sounds as if she's trying hard not to cry.

'I've got the bloody thing in front of me. They've "questioned my commitment to the company" and they're planning to make "organisational changes", that require a "streamlined marketing approach". So, I'm basically surplus to requirements,' she blurts out. 'They've told me not to bother coming back and they've said severance pay will follow. So, I don't even get to say my goodbyes. And Jen, jobs do not grow on trees in this part of the world and we really, *really* need the money my job brings in.'

I feel a rush of sympathy and take a moment to think about what's the next best step for Alison.

'How would you feel about speaking to a lawyer about this?' I ask her. 'You've worked there for a long time and the company might not be able to just cut you off like this.'

'Yes, exactly,' she says. 'Just what I was thinking. That's why I'm phoning you. I thought you might be able to find out who I could speak to and maybe you could come with me when I go to talk to them?'

'Of course I'll come with you. No problem,' I assure her. 'But in St Andrews, I wouldn't know who to recommend.'

We're both quiet for a moment, wondering how to solve this, when I suddenly have the answer: 'What about Rory?' I suggest. 'He seems to know everyone... I bet he can come up with some names for us.'

'That's a really good idea. Will you find out, Jen? And we'll go from there.'

'Yes, and look, try not to worry,' I tell her. 'You're a really good, really capable person. You'll get everything sorted out very soon. Keep telling yourself that.'

'OK... and thanks,' she says.

As soon as the call has ended, I send Rory a message and receive a prompt reply.

My divorce lawyer was Mick Munro. One-man band. Not flashy. But a clever man at a clever price. I'll forward his number. Now, about our get-together. How about next Thursday eve? And I PROMISE I won't cancel.

I reply with a quick :

Brilliant and you're on

In response, I get two little thumbs-up emojis, which makes me smile. Rory is himself something of a human thumbs-up emoji.

* * *

The next day, when Alison has finished her early morning tour-guide stint, we meet at the Northpoint Café and, after a bracing coffee, we go off together for her appointment at Mick Munro's.

We find the small side street and stand outside an antique three-storey building checking the names on the buzzers. Both the signs and the building's paintwork are flaked and fading and even from the outside, the place looks as if it could do with a serious clean.

I press the buzzer.

After a short wait, a man's voice replies: 'Hello, Munro & Partners.'

'Hello, we have an appointment with Mick Munro.'

'Who is this?'

'It's Alison Watson and Jennifer McAndrew.'

The door buzzes and I push it open. In front of us is a rickety wooden staircase, covered in stained brown carpet. By the time we're tackling the second set of stairs, the brown door at the top has opened and a small man with just a remaining ruff of dark hair at the back of his head, huge black-framed glasses and a domed fore-head is peering out at us.

'Hello, are you Mick Munro?' Alison asks. 'We have an appoint-ment. About an unfair dismissal?'

'Yes, yes of course. Come on in,' he beckons with a shy smile.

Now that we're at the doorway, I can see behind him, a grue-some mustard and tobacco brown office that was possibly last deco-rated back in the days when the Bee Gees, ties and trouser bottoms were all very big.

'Good to meet you,' he says and shakes both our hands. Then he ushers us into the uninspiring space. I take in ancient orange plastic chairs, a bashed-about wooden desk, a mummified pot plant and an old-fashioned and surely in the push-button, call-centre age, entirely useless, dial phone.

Most of the walls are taken up with floor-to-ceiling stacks of cardboard boxes, which are probably packed with ancient legal papers.

This place does not exactly scream success or even thriving local business. In fact, it looks as if it's teetering on the brink of extinction.

Mick, I see now, is accessorising his checked shirt and argyle tank top with cords and well-worn moccasin slippers. This is about one million miles from Jono's legal office, which was a temple of modernity, brisk efficiency, organisation and important legal cases. I clutch at my handbag nervously, exchange a glance with Alison and wonder if we should just back out and run away.

'I'm sorry about the reception area,' Mick says, maybe registering our horror. 'Mrs McKay, my assistant, retired a year ago now. I've not managed to replace her and it's got very cluttered without her. She wouldn't thank me if she came in and saw the place like this.'

As he sighs and gestures towards a grouping of plastic chairs, I spot a wedding ring on his hand. Someone has married Mick Munro. Someone else may have been involved in the purchase of the moccasin slippers. This is quite a surprise.

'Tea or coffee?'

'Tea, please,' Alison and I chime together.

Then Mick asks Alison to explain her dismissal, as he makes something of a mess with dribbling teabags and a carton of milk. I'm handed a chipped mug of stewed brown liquid and asked if I'd like some shortbread.

I decide it's friendly to say yes. But alas, the shortbread tin with the McIver Hotel on the lid is empty.

Mick apologises, then gets on with reading Alison's dismissal letter. And as he asks Alison intelligent questions about her job, the circumstances surrounding her dismissal, and discusses the options open to her now, the dingy office with its mess and boxes and dead plants fades into the background. I've spent enough time working with lawyers, Jono in particular, to understand immediately that Mick is very capable. He clearly knows the law inside out and he's good with his clients. Alison is already so much more relaxed than when we first came in. He's clearly just a bit of a hopeless organiser, without much practicality who hasn't paid any aspects of his business, other than the lawyering bit, any attention.

So, when he and Alison map out a plan of action involving a letter to McWhirter & Sons first of all, and then a potential unfair dismissal claim, and Alison asks with concern in her voice: 'So how much is all this going to cost?' I suddenly know exactly what I'm going to offer in order to help my friend and this struggling lawyer.

'You know, Mick... I've got a bit of an idea,' I begin. 'I used to work for a barrister in London as his sort of right-hand woman. I did it for three years, only left to move up here in January. So, can I suggest that I come and work for you for a week or so, for free, to help get you organised again? Get right back on top of your filing?'

I point to the boxes and explain that I'm sure I could get his office running smoothly again within a few days and maybe even help him find that replacement assistant. And, in return, I ask if he could consider taking Alison's case on for free, or at least on a no-win, no-fee basis?

They both stare at me.

'Jennifer, are you sure?' Alison is the first to speak.

'Yes, of course, I'm pretty much at a loose end and this is definitely my area of expertise.'

'Well...' Mick begins hesitantly. 'That's a very kind offer. I can't really say no to that, can I?' I think I can see something that looks a lot like relief cross his face. 'I could definitely do with some help around the filing. When do you think you would you like to start? I'm in court until the end of the week, but what about Friday?'

'Perfect. Let's say 9 a.m. on Friday morning then?' Because, to be honest, I'd quite like to don some rubber gloves and get started on this room straight away.

As I shake his hand, I feel an unusual burst of excitement. It turns out that I can't wait to be hanging about a lawyer's office making myself properly useful again.

15

My evening out with Rory begins when he picks me up from Dad's in an enormous, well-worn SUV that seems to have a pickup truck attached at the back.

'Well, this is a big car,' I tell him as I buckle up into the front seat once we've said our hellos.

'I have a lot of daughters and a lot of boxes to transport,' he explains, before adding, 'so... we finally got a time to suit.'

'Yes.' I smile at him and we look one another over.

He's casually dressed, just like he was in his shop – wearing a white T-shirt, tartan shirt and padded gilet combination. His hair may be longer and his face broader than I remember from the boy I knew at school, but there's still so much familiarity to it. I feel as if I still know Rory well and at this strange time when my life has been thrown up into the air and fallen back down again in scattered pieces, that's sort of comforting.

With my dad, Alison and now Rory back in my life, I feel as if I've gone back in time to before I left school, when life was simpler, people seemed kinder, and there was so much ahead, rather than a trail of mistakes behind me. Maybe this could mean that I'm back at a new starting point from where I can set out again in a new and better direction.

Mainly, I remember that Rory was always cheerful and funny, and I hope that's still the case. I hope life so far hasn't knocked the fun out of him.

'You're looking casually awesome,' he says with something of an eyebrow raise.

And it's true, I have made an effort – a new billowing blue and white blouse underneath a trusty navy jacket, favourite jeans, heeled boots, plus the hair done and the full war paint.

'Thank you.'

'This isn't a date, you know.' He accompanies this with a cheeky grin, '... unless you want it to be.'

'No! I know this isn't a date!' I laugh and it feels comfortable between us, not quite like old times, we can't go back to being seventeen-year-olds again, but maybe heading in that direction.

'OK, I thought we better just get that straight out into the open,' he says. 'I mean, people will wonder. People will want to know. They won't realise that we're old friends rekindling an old acquaintance.'

'That's a nice way of putting it... I quite want to sing "Auld Lang Syne" now.'

'Feel free... you're only three months' late.'

And then he starts to drive and tells me about what's been happening in his shop and with his daughters today as I consider the fact that I've not had a male friend since Rory. I've had boyfriends and many female friends, but Rory was my male friend at school. We never dated, we definitely did a bit of jokey flirting back then and that little charge of flirty tension between us made the friendship even more interesting. I'm glad that he's brought this up and cleared the air straight away. Now, we can just relax and enjoy ourselves, free of all that exhausting double-think. I'm only just crawling out of one train wreck of a relationship and he is not at all my type. Older, suave, sophisticated types, that seems to be what appeals to me.

* * *

Rory drives us to one of the town's lawn bowling clubs. This is something of a surprise, because I thought these bowling clubs were for old people, and as we go inside, it turns out I'm right.

After cheerily greeting the old boy at the reception desk, Rory turns to explain to me: 'I know this is not your typical venue for a night out, but I've come here once a month for – well, it's a long story – and you can trust me, bowling is much more fun than you think, the food is amazing and,' in a stage whisper, he adds, 'they are practically giving the drinks away.'

Inside the club, it's busy and there's something of a jolly OAP party atmosphere. Everyone seems to know Rory and he has to stop for little chats with many people.

'So, Rory, is this a new girlfriend, finally?' one oldster stops to ask.

'No, but thank you for the embarrassing question, Bill. I especially like the use of the word "finally". This is Jennifer McAndrew, she was my best friend at school.'

'Pleased to meet you, Jennifer. Bill Simmers. He's all right that one,' Bill says, pointing to Rory before giving me a wink.

'Yes... nice to meet you, Bill. And nice of you to call me your best friend at school,' I add, turning back to Rory, as Bill heads for the buffet.

'I know, especially as I wasn't your best friend, was I? No, that was Alison McBain.'

'But we were definitely friends,' I assure him.

'Yes, ah-ha, until you went off to London and Never Called Again,' he says.

'Oh...' I feel caught off guard. I'd hoped we wouldn't be talking about the past tonight, or not very much anyway.

'Yes... well, I know... I can see why you might have thought that...' I try to explain, 'but I just needed to...'

'Break away from us all when you dropped out of your law degree?' Rory asks, finishing my sentence. 'It's OK we all got that. But... I didn't expect you to never get in touch again.'

'No... I didn't expect that either,' I admit. 'I suppose I just got caught up with London life. I didn't mean to hurt your feelings.'

'Well, you did – just for the record. There are only so many unreplied messages a guy can leave without feeling like an unwanted stalker.'

'I'm sorry.'

'You didn't even reply to my wedding invitation. I mean... a wedding invitation, Jen. That always deserves a reply.'

'Your wedding invitation?! I honestly don't think I ever got that, Rory,' I say in my defence. 'I moved house a lot in the first few years. And changed email addresses and phone numbers... so I must have missed it,' and I realise as I say this that I tried quite hard to shake my past off. I did not want to be known as the girl 'who dropped out of her law degree because her sister married her boyfriend'. Still, I see now that I lost friends and hurt people by running away to my supposed fresh start. 'I'm sorry,' I tell him.

'Well, alright-y,' he seems to shrug it off. 'I'm glad we cleared that up.' His smile is back in place and he adds: 'OK, so we're here now. Time to enjoy ourselves. Time to sashay over to the buffet, load up our plates, then try out the indoor carpet bowls. And, believe me, the best thing about everyone else being over sixty-five,' he whispers, 'is that I feel young and limber and gorgeous.'

I have to laugh at this.

We eat what can only be described as a small mountain from the buffet, which is all home-cooked and just as excellent as he has promised. Rory closes his eyes when he eats and is a highly enthusiastic food critic: 'Oh my god... Mrs Harrison's *patatas bravas*, are to die for... she spent five years in Barcelona, you know, so this is *autentico* and you must try one of Nita's homemade veggie samosas – transcendental.'

After we've eaten, I knuckle down and give carpet bowls a go. I've never been bowling before, but Rory is an encouraging tutor and tells me throughout my disastrous attempts that I'm a natural, I should be doing this every week and I'll soon get the hang of it.

'You've got strong shoulders,' he says several times, 'and great hands. You could be quite the bowler.'

'Really, you think? I've not considered bowling as a sport before. Is it in the Olympics?' I joke.

'As with many things, your technique improves as you get older.'

'Woah,' I roll my eyes at him. 'That sounds a little bit cheesy.' I want to make it clear that we're not doing flirting, we're doing friends.

'Yeah? Rein it in? I'm just trying out my lines on you, so you can do exactly this – shoot down the bad ones. Believe me, I need all the dating help I can get. It's a tough crowd out there. Now eye on the ball and smoothly does it.'

When we retire to the as-billed unbelievably cheap bar, I drink wine, Rory drinks Diet Coke and we update each other on all that has happened since I ran away to London. We talk about the big city versus St Andrews. I tell him about the job I've left but skip the affair-with-the-boss part, and I say that I'm going to help Mick get organised, starting from tomorrow – which Rory approves of hugely.

'Yes!' Rory exclaims. 'That is going to work out perfectly for him.

Why didn't I think of putting you two together in a professional capacity before?'

Then Rory talks about his daughters, his previous oil-rig jobs and his shop. And inevitably our talk turns to the messy business of break-ups.

'It's the fight about the last gas and electricity bill. Once you've had that, then you know it's finally over,' he says, and takes a sip from his pint of Diet Coke.

'We didn't have any fights about final bills,' I tell him, not wanting to go into too much detail at all. 'He wasn't living with me... so none of that drama.'

I have the chilling thought of my former flat with someone else living in it and no trace of the time I've spent with Jono left anywhere. Apart from some photos on my phone and the gifts he gave me – all boxed up – there's nothing left of 'us'.

'You two sound as if you were pretty civilised,' Rory says. 'Hazel tried to claim back the cost of the stamps she used to send letters to my lawyer.'

'Wow, she played a tough game. You've got to admire that.'

'Yes, she did. She still does. And this is the woman I have to go on sharing my girls with.'

Our eyes meet for a moment. How could we have known at eighteen how our lives would be now? And if we'd had a glimpse of our futures, what would, or even could, we have done differently?

'We should probably try to look on the bright side. It could be worse, it could be much worse, we could still be with those difficult people,' Rory says with a shrug. 'So, let's not go on about the crappy times. Jono's loss is St Andrews' gain. Hazel's loss will be someone else's gain, eventually... here's hoping. Now, Jennifer McAndrew...'

'You'll have to stop calling me that,' I tell him with a smile,

'Why, is it not your real name?'

I prod him with my elbow.

'We've not really talked about school,' Rory adds. 'I've not given you the rundown on who is doing what. And I know it all, every little detail, you know, who became a millionaire and who became a heroin addict.'

'Really? Have we got both of those?'

'Well, Doughal Craig's farm sold to golf-course developers for £4.5 mill, but there are six of them in that family, so they got slightly less than a million each...'

'But still... very nice.'

'Yes... very nice indeed, *and* he's recently divorced, so you might want to... you know... get friendly with him on Instagram, stalk him on Twitter. Don't hang about. With that kind of pocket money lying about, he won't be single for long.'

'Rory!' I warn. 'If I need dating suggestions, I will ask.'

'At the other end of the spectrum, Joe Walker spent two decades on the whacky-baccy and died of lung cancer last year.'

'Oh... that's very sad.'

Joe Walker and Doughal Craig... I have only the vaguest memories of them.

And for a few moments we're quiet because it's a little overwhelming to think back to school and to being teenagers with our whole wonderful lives ahead of us. And now, here we are, over twenty years later, and I'm definitely not where I thought I would be by now.

'What about Euan McKendrick?' I venture.

'Oh, handsome Euan...? Your big date for the sixth-form dance... No longer single, I'm afraid.'

'Not what I meant!' I protest. 'I just wondered what he was up to.'

'Married with kids, gone a bit bald and broad, sells fertiliser or something.'

Fertiliser... I've been in London for so long, I've forgotten about rural life and the many strange rural jobs. Just about everyone I knew in London worked in something digital or virtual.

'So, Jennifer,' Rory breaks the small silence that has pooled between us, 'have you got yourself properly kitted out for Scotland yet?'

'Uh-oh, is this a sales pitch? Am I going to be £300 lighter by the end of this evening?'

'No, no, but I can point you in the direction of my favourite practical clothes shop.'

'Practical clothes?' I'm picturing myself in a sturdy sou'wester and massive green Wellingtons. 'Noooo, Rory, I don't think so. My favourite shop is Harvey Nichols and there's nothing very practical there.'

'Yes, I know, but we see it every year,' Rory goes on. 'All these beautiful people arriving off the bus and at the university in lovely shoes and light, breezy clothes without hoods. They're all make-up and curling tongs.'

'Or straightening irons in my case.'

'Yes...' realisation steals over his face. 'I knew there was something different about your hair. But I liked it curly. Anyway... within a few months with the wind and the dampness in the air, everyone realises that they have to change. And by the end of the year, all the beautiful people are wearing hiking boots, thermal long johns and anoraks with big hoods just like the rest of us.'

'That's not true,' I protest. 'I've seen the beautiful people out there all glamorously dressed on the high street every day.'

Well, to be honest, I've seen a sprinkling. Hiking boots and hooded anoraks is definitely the more popular look. But I am never, ever going to wear anoraks and hiking boots on the high street.

Rory shakes his head: 'No, I doubt it. They're either visitors, or the newbies. Even the Eastern European glamazon students end up in at least skiing jackets by the end of the first term. You can totally trust me on this.'

'No! Glamour and bad weather can be combined,' I insist.

He looks at me doubtfully. 'Well, I'll let you have a go, but when you need a big waterproof jacket, waterproof trousers and hiking boots, give me a call. I'll tell you where to get a great deal.'

Now it's my turn to look doubtful. There's no way I'm rushing to take fashion advice from a man in a tartan shirt and a gilet. 'No... look... even if I do have to buy a few weatherproof things,' I tell him. 'I'm sure they can be lovely.'

'Just don't waste your money on posh umbrellas,' he insists. 'For the winds we get, you need a hood with a drawstring. You've been away for ages, you might have forgotten.'

'Thanks, but I will never ever be pulling any drawstrings on any hoods.' I almost shudder at the thought. He'll be suggesting I wear a cagoule next...

'Bet you will,' he says.

'Bet I won't.'

'OK, Jennifer McAndrew, let's talk about something else. We've done work, exes, school, fashion... there must be something else?'

I lean back in my comfortably padded bowling-green bar chair. I'm on my third small glass of quite tolerable white wine and it feels cosy to be here, chatting like this.

'What about dating, Rory...' I venture, because although I'm months and months from even thinking about it, I'm still a little interested in how the grown-up dating scene works in St Andrews. 'Are you managing to get any dating done in your busy life?'

He rolls his eyes: 'This is a small town. I know just about everyone and there is not a huge pool of available talent.'

'Really? Isn't there a lot coming in every year...' and to make sure he doesn't think I mean he should be dating students, I quickly add: 'University staff, people who work at all the big events?'

'Believe me anything coming in from the outside gets snapped up pretty quickly. So, on the bright side, that is very good news for you.'

'Oh brother,' I fluster, thinking now of Sergei and his husky persuasions, 'I'm definitely not ready for dating.'

'No one our age is ever ready for dating,' Rory says. 'But it's like falling off a horse, right, you probably need to get straight back out there before you get too frightened to go back on.'

'Nooooo, I am allowed some time off after everything...'

I've not told Rory anything about the level of my break-up trauma... the fact that Jono was my boss, or the bit about him going back to his wife, let alone the unexpected twins. There are a lot of things you don't want to tell your old school friend in a bowling club on your first real night out in a couple of decades. But I still think I've managed to convey that I'm a bit cut up about it all.

'Fair enough,' he admits, draining the last of the Diet Coke from his glass, 'but when you are thinking about dipping your toe once again into the dating pond, then let me know and I will tell you everything I know about the St Andrews situation. Not that I know a lot,' he adds quickly. 'In fact... let's be honest, if you have any advice about dating – from the female perspective that is – I'll be very happy to hear it.'

And in that moment, I feel a little rush of sympathy for him. It can't be easy being divorced with three girls, running your own full-time business. No wonder he looks tired and a bit unfit and wears a straightforward uniform of tartan shirts and padded gilets.

'No problem,' I tell him. 'You're a good person. Someone will definitely spot that. Are you seeing anyone at the moment?' I ask.

'Well... there is someone who may, potentially, be interested,' he admits, suddenly looking a little bashful. 'I'm trying to tread that very thin line between making sure she knows I'm keen and not turning into her stalker.'

'Have you asked her out, on a date-type-situation?'

'Building up to it,' Rory says. 'Have to pick the moment. Have to pick the right kind of date-type-situation.'

'How about a long beach walk?' I suggest. 'Then there's no pressure to drink, no pressure to talk all the time. No obvious this-is-a-date vibe.'

'OK, I will add that to the list of helpful suggestions. Katie, who is five has also given me some good ideas, although they mainly involve ponies and sparkly shoes.'

'Awww...' this makes me smile, 'ponies and sparkly shoes are always good. I bet you're a good dad, Rory.'

This makes him smile broadly.

'I give it my very best shot,' he says. 'Right, talking of best shots, are we going to give the bowling another go? Get up there on the big green carpet?'

* * *

So, I drain my glass and follow Rory to the bowling space. Bill Simmers is there and Rory asks him to join our team. A surprising number of the older ladies seem to want to ask or tell Rory about something or other, and he makes time for everyone. Totally enjoys the attention, I think. I find I'm remembering more and more about what he was like at school. He was one of those precociously confident teenagers who was always on ultra-friendly terms with older pupils, younger pupils and the teachers.

'Do you know *everyone* in St Andrews?' I ask him.

'I've lived here all my life, plus I have a shop...' he reminds me, 'so I know a lot of people.'

And even though I fled from this town, first to Edinburgh University, and then all the way to London, and never wanted to come back, I can't help thinking how very nice, how grounded, to be the kind of person who always wanted to stay and be absolutely from a place, and know a huge range of people there.

At the end of the evening, Rory gives me a lift back to Dad's house. And when the pickup truck comes to a stop, I turn to him and grin.

'Thank you,' I tell him. 'I didn't expect to have such a great time at an old folks' bowling club, but I did! So thank you and I'm sorry I didn't reply to your wedding invitation and I'm sorry we've left it so long to catch up.'

'Yeah, me too. OK, good night and sleep well, my friend. It's great to have you back in town,' he says, 'and let's be allies out there in the dating wilds. We can advise, compare and contrast. And I can open my address book, remember, and come up with some suggestions.'

I laugh at this, but remind him: 'I'm not going out there any time soon.'

'Got to get back on the horse,' he insists, 'we could both do one date a month and report back. That wouldn't be so hard, would it?'

'I'll get back to you on that...' I say vaguely, part-horrified at the thought, but also just a little curious. A date a month? Meet some new people? Maybe even have some fun times... like Rory says, it wouldn't be so hard.

As I reach for the door handle, I wonder whether we should air kiss, just above the cheeks, like Londoners do, or would that be awkward? But instead, I see Rory is holding out his fist for a fist bump and I instantly like that idea much better than some awkward Londony air kiss.

'Goodnight,' I say, and fist bump him back.

'Let's do this again very soon,' Rory calls from the car window.

'Agreed!' I call back. And I mean it. I've had much more fun than I expected.

16

I arrive at Mick Munro's office at 8.50 a.m., dressed not in London office smarts, but in a crisp white shirt, flats and jeans because I suspect that today is probably going to get messy.

I'm carrying a large handbag full of fresh office supplies – pens, Post-it notes, a chunky stapler and many fresh paper files – plus a carrier bag stuffed with cloths, cleaning fluid, and the all-important roll of black bin bags.

I climb the stairs to Mick's office and when he lets me in, he seems a mixture of pleased to see me and quite anxious.

'So, well… I do appreciate this offer of help…' he begins, ruffling his hair and pacing about the reception area, 'but how will it work? What are you planning to do first?' he asks.

'I'm going to help get your office completely tidy and organised,' I tell him with what I hope sounds like brisk and efficient friendliness. I don't want him to get cold feet now when I'm itching to start. 'We'll clear out the actual rubbish…' I turn my head in the direction of the overflowing wastepaper bin behind the reception desk, then we'll set up some useful filing systems – older cases and paperwork stored in date order, recent and live cases filed and labelled but all at hand – and hopefully, you won't have to rummage through a pile of paperwork on your desk ever again.'

I cast a significant glance at his desk and then the reception desk. Both are stacked high with piles of paperwork that I suspect he rummages through daily.

Mick still looks concerned: 'That sounds fantastic, but my worry is—'

'That I'll throw away something you still need?'

'Exactly.'

'I won't, Mick. I absolutely promise. I've been working in this job for years and I know the difference between a legal document, an important document, an invoice, a receipt you need to keep and random, expired paperwork. If you like, I'll be extra-cautious and I can create a "throwing out pile" that you can go through before anything hits the recycling bin.'

This seems to reassure him and he offers to make us both a cup of tea.

'Yes, thank you,' I accept, although upgrading the mugs, teabags and coffee-making facilities is definitely on my to-do list.

'We're going to need a good storage space for all the older but important to keep files,' I tell him, and I approach the second door in Mick's reception area. I suspect this leads to a cupboard, but just as I turn the handle and open it up, wondering if there might be some useful space there, Mick looks round from his tea making and blurts out: 'Oh no, not in there!'

A solid wall of box after box and pile after pile of papers confronts me – years' worth of paperwork.

Oh! This situation is a bit worse than I expected, but my brain quickly comes up with a workable solution. This cupboard is really useful, so we need to free it up.

'Why don't I make some enquiries about renting storage?' I suggest. 'It doesn't have to cost much and all the things you have to keep but never need to refer to could go there. Then we can use this cupboard for more recent files.'

'I keep meaning to do that,' Mick says, 'but I'm always busy. I don't have time to do my filing; I've not had the time to find a new assistant... to be honest, I'd quite like to find a partner for the business too. But no time. There is healthy legal competition out there, of course, but the work keeps coming in,' he admits, looking somewhere between pleased and perplexed.

'You're obviously really good at what you do,' I say, giving him what I hope is a reassuring smile, 'but you need to build your support team. Otherwise, we'll find you collapsed in an overworked heap, buried under a mountain of paperwork!'

'Possibly,' Mick agrees with a hint of a smile.

And at that moment, I realise I'm glad to be here. After weeks and weeks of my very quiet life at Dad's, I realise that I am ready to be out in the world doing useful work again.

'Don't worry, I'll get this all sorted for you within a couple of days,' I assure him. 'We'll have rented storage for the much older files; we'll have office storage in this nice big cupboard here. Then we'll have files that are in use – plus invoices and receipts – out in a couple of filing cabinets over here and I'll put everything I think you can get rid of in a big pile for you to check through first. How does that sound?'

'That sounds incredibly good,' he says, almost astonished. 'Can you do all that?'

'Yes, of course!' I assure him. 'First the storage cupboard, then the reception area, and then the world!'

* * *

And so, for the rest of the day, I move and open boxes, sifting through them, reading, filing as I go and then hauling files around the reception area until I have one great big pile to toss and a neatly stacked pile to store: all date organised and client identified with brand-new labels. I book space in a storage facility, plus a man-with-a-van, who can be here at 3 p.m. this afternoon, because I cannot wait for the cupboard space to be clear.

For most of the morning, Mick generally hides in his office, only coming out now and again to pace around nervously.

When he does appear, I talk to him about Alison's case to keep his mind from the upheaval going on in his office.

'Do you think she has a case for unfair dismissal?' I ask, making us both fresh cups of tea.

Mick is the epitome of lawyerly discretion: 'I know you're her friend, but I would only want to say generally that unfair dismissal can be a hard one to prove. I obviously check contracts very carefully and have to establish if they have done something in breach of contract.'

'I noticed on their website that they have a big section on being an equal opps employer and how much they do around fair wages, maternity leave, returners to work, flexible working and so on – but Alison says it couldn't be further from the truth. Hardly anyone works part-time, maternity leave is strictly the minimum required and all the senior positions are occupied by men. Or "old dinosaurs" as she calls them.'

'Hmmm... well that's important to know. Can you screenshot that info from their website please?' Mick asks. 'Because you'd be amazed how often this kind of thing disappears from public view as soon as an unfair dismissal summons lands in a company's in-tray.'

'That's a good point,' I agree.

He asks once again how long I was with my previous employer and how long I've been working as a legal PA.

Once I've reminded him, I feel comfortable enough to say: 'I did two years of a law degree at Edinburgh Uni, but then... well... I left... maybe it wasn't for me.'

'But you've been working for lawyers all this time,' Mick points out.

'Hmmm...'

'There must be something about it that you like.'

'Maybe it's just what I know,' I say and turn back to my organising.

* * *

When the storage cupboard is finally emptied, I turn my attention to the reception area. I put rubber gloves on and deep tidy. I poke into dark corners cautiously, half expecting to find dead mice.

I open the windows wide to try and blow some of the dust out of the air and I book a window cleaner. I've already decided that Mick has to let me book a painter to change the mustard and tobacco-coloured walls to a much more uplifting and welcoming shade of pale-green.

With my cleaning cloths, I chase all the remaining dust and dirt out of the reception area and off the desk. I wipe down every surface. Then I set up new pens and pencils in a holder beside the phone. Labels, files, spare paper are all stacked into a drawer.

The day passes so quickly that I'm genuinely surprised when Mick appears in the reception to announce: 'It's after 6 p.m., Jennifer, definitely time to go home. You've done a terrific job. It's transformed,' he adds. 'I might even let you into my own office next time. It could do with a bit of a tidy-up...'

'I'd be delighted to help.'

He puts his hand on the back of his neck and goes on awkwardly: 'I mean... in just one day, you've done all this. It's amazing.'

It's true, Mick's office is close to the streamlined machine of efficiency I know it can be.

As I worked through the chores, I have tried not to think of Jono's office, but couldn't help myself. In the hive of efficiency I'd created for him in London, it usually took me just minutes to find files for him. And when he opened the files, the papers were neatly gathered together, the relevant pages stapled or bulldog clipped, so it was easy to look through them. 'I love the way your brain works,' he used to tell me. I tried to put that out of mind too.

Mick's reception area is now neat, calm and almost empty apart from the essentials on the desk and a small green succulent plant I've brought in. Next weekend, with Mick's full approval, two painters will be in the office over Saturday and Sunday to change the walls to a muted, pale mint-green. And the funny thing is, I've not had to talk Mick into any of this. I think he probably wanted to do all of it, but he couldn't gather up the energy. He seems genuinely pleased that I'm here, sorting it out for him.

I've thought a lot about the importance of energy, as I've motored through the chores. It always takes energy to move on from a difficult time, or into a new direction, or up to a higher gear. When your energy is low, or runs out, that's when everything gets stuck. And sometimes you can't rekindle it all by yourself, you have to borrow a little from someone else to get you started again. Helping Mick has helped me. Even though the day spent in his office has been long and busy, I have fairly bounced out at the end of it, fired up by my usefulness and achievement.

* * *

After my busy week, Saturday night at my dad's house is quiet. I make dinner to repay some of Joan's kindness and almost fall asleep in front of the Australian doctor-detective mini-series they are currently watching: '*Strewth, I knew that bloke was up to something.*'

I refuse all alcohol, which seems to upset Dad and Joan a little, but I clearly haven't got their ability to metabolise five units of gin per hour and I don't want to develop it either.

As a result, on Sunday morning I'm up way ahead of Dad and I'm sitting drinking tea in my pyjamas, looking out of the window when I realise that the bleak and wintry sadness is loosening its grip on me. Little bursts of cheerfulness are starting to break through. Instead of thinking obsessively about Jono and where it went wrong and the signs I should have spotted, other memories are popping up in quiet moments: Rory's raucous laughter at the bowling club, the astonished look on Mick's face as he walked into his completely organised reception, Alison's life-enhancing hugs and the sight of Joan's head resting on Dad's shoulder as they snooze in front of the TV. These good things are interrupting the stream of bad news that was playing 24/7 on Channel Jennifer. Jono's twins, our break-up, the loss – of my lover, my career, my would-be life – it's still there, but it doesn't feel as harsh, or as raw. The sharp edges of my sadness are beginning to blunt.

17

I'm startled from my peaceful Sunday afternoon reading time on the sofa by the sharp and insistent brrrring of the doorbell.

It's not so unusual for the doorbell to ring here. Post, deliveries, plus Dad and his friends being retired means they often call in on one another unannounced and make quite the occasion out of cups of tea and biscuits if it's before 5 p.m., or G&Ts and crisps if it's after. But right now, Dad and Joan are out with a full afternoon agenda of pub lunch, game of golf and 'a drive', which I hope the fragile old Nissan can handle.

I get up from the sofa, glance in the hall mirror at my entirely unglamorous outfit of Sunday sweats and hair in a scrunchie, but never mind, it won't be anyone for me, then turn the Yale lock, open the door, and stand face to face with my sister, Isla.

'Oh!' I say, out loud and with a tone of undisguised shock before I can think about a better reaction.

There she is, looking like a more grown-up version of herself, looking also like our mother and like the smart and respectable Mummy that she has turned herself into. Blonde hair in a bob, lipstick and classy earrings, leather boots and a navy knee-length woollen coat belted tightly shut against the chill. And right beside her is a girl, about seven or eight, long brown hair and a soft, shy face, who must be her daughter, Jessie.

It is such a powerful thing to see a face you knew so well, four years later. Her sweet, heart-shaped face has hollowed just a little further with age, throwing her cheekbones into sharper relief. There are faint lines around her eyes and across her forehead. She's still slim and graceful looking, but there is an undeniable motherliness to her now.

'Hello, Jennifer,' Isla says. Her tone is somewhere between neutral and brisk. 'I suppose we were going to run into one another, now that you've moved in with Dad.'

'I'm staying here, temporarily. I've not moved in,' I immediately jump to my own defence.

'How are you?' she asks. Again it's neutral and polite.

'I'm fine. How about you?' Two can play at this neutral and polite game.

'We're all good, thanks.'

There's a pause and we seem to size each other up. I don't feel I have any idea where I want this conversation to go next and maybe Isla doesn't know either. It's so painfully awkward. Two sisters, hardly knowing one another any more, not knowing what to say, so much hurt and bitterness spilled between us. No wonder it's much easier for us to ignore one another.

'So, is Dad in?' Isla asks next, and I'm glad of the question. It's practical and to the point, the answer is straightforward.

'No... he and Joan have gone out for the afternoon: lunch then golf then a drive,' I tell her.

'What?!' she exclaims looking properly annoyed. 'But I arranged this all with him on Friday. He said he would look after Jessie for two hours today. It's Peter's Judo exam and they only allow one parent spectator per child, and Richard's on a work trip.'

I have that tingle of weirdness that I can't help whenever the thought of Isla and Richard comes up.

'Is there any way of getting in touch with him?' Isla asks next, although I'm sure, like me, she knows that Dad has an ancient mobile phone, but never bothers taking it anywhere with him, or even charging it up. 'I suppose I could try the golf club...' she says next, but this is followed by a glance at her watch and further signs of irritation on her face.

'Good grief, we're on a very tight schedule... How has Dad managed to forget already?'

I see Jessie's serious face peeking out from behind her mother's arm and I remember what it was like to be standing beside my mother listening to a conversation that made you feel awkward and embarrassed, and as if no one was taking your feelings into consideration at all. And I feel a rush of sympathy for her.

I wonder if Jessie would consider staying with me... but a glance at Isla's face and I don't want to ask. She looks too annoyed, too closed off from me and it would be far more comfortable for us both if this conversation was over as quickly as possible.

But then Isla surprises me.

'Look, Jennifer... are you here for the next two hours? Would you mind looking after Jessie? She'll be no trouble. She's brought her colouring books and her iPad... if that would be OK with you, Jessie? Grampa will probably be back very soon... and this is your Auntie Jennifer.'

'Hello, Jessie.' I decide to concentrate on Jessie rather than Isla. 'If you'd like to come in, I'm sure we can have a nice time. I love colouring in – haven't done it for years. Do you think you could let me have a go?'

In return for this, I get eye contact and a shy smile.

There's a little more coaxing on both my part and Isla's part, but finally Jessie agrees to give it a go and Isla almost smiles at me before she kisses Jessie goodbye, then turns and hurries back to her shiny, navy-blue SUV. A very Isla kind of car, I can't help thinking.

'Come in, Jessie... where do you usually spread out your pens and colouring books when you're here with your grampa?'

'On the kitchen table,' Jessie tells me.

'Well, let's go and do that then. And what about something to eat? Are you hungry at all?'

'Maybe a little bit...' she admits.

'What would you like?' I ask, wondering if the kitchen will be able to provide something of interest to a seven-year-old. Although, thanks to Rory's sales skills on my first day in his shop, we still have plenty of KitKats.

'I like toast and I like ice cream,' Jessie says, her shyness beginning to wear off.

'You're in luck, we have both of those... maybe toast first?'

She smiles, nods and spills her bag of books, pens and pencils all across the kitchen table.

And a very pleasant hour follows. I make toast with butter and jam, Jessie eats it all up, and we look through her colouring books for pages to work on. I decide to go with coloured pencils, while she sticks to pen. It's both soothing and companionable to be sitting round the table choosing colours, filling in the little squares and chatting about the pictures, about drawing, about Jessie's art class at school.

And then out comes the question that I maybe could have expected.

'Why are you and Mummy not friends any more?' Jessie asks, her voice light and matter-of-fact.

'Is that what she said?' I counter, as I wonder how on earth to reply.

'Yes. I have an Auntie Lucy and an Auntie Nicola and I see them quite a lot, and my cousins. But when I ask about you, Auntie

Jennifer, Mummy says: "We're not really friends any more." And I know Grampa is quite sad about that... and I am sad too now that I know you're nice.'

'Thank you,' I can't help saying to the 'you're nice' part. 'You're very nice too and I'm sure your brother Peter is nice...' then I sort of dry up, not sure what to say next.

'Can't you say sorry and make up?' Jessie asks and turns her face towards me, letting me see glimpses of me, Isla, my mother, all of us when we were young.

'Did you ask Mummy that question too?' I realise I'm behaving like a politician, answering one question with another.

'Yes, and she said, "It's not that simple," but when I have an argument with my friends, Mummy says – "You just say sorry and forget about it, and that's that." So... maybe you could try doing that.'

'Hmmmmm... maybe...' I don't want to commit myself. But maybe when Isla comes to pick Jessie up later today, maybe I could try to be more friendly. At least we'll now have Jessie's visit to talk about.

'Mummy said she'd *writed* you letters to try and make up, but you never answered them.' Jessie adds. 'She sent you an invitation to my birthday when I was five, but you didn't come.'

I do remember several letters that arrived for me not long after Mum died, in which Isla put her point of view across very angrily. I read them, but I didn't reply. What was the point in carrying on an argument by post? I didn't want to do that. But letters to try and make up? An invitation to Jessie's fifth birthday party? Isla never sent these. She must have just said that to Jessie.

'Did you want me to come to your birthday parties?' I ask her now.

'Yes! All my other aunties came and Grampa came and they all brought presents,' Jessie says with a grin.

And suddenly I have quite the lump in my throat.

'I owe you quite a lot of presents, don't I?'

Jessie just shrugs at this, turns her head back to her colouring and says: 'You didn't get any cake, so don't worry about it.'

When Jessie has been with me for just over two hours, I happen to be glancing out of the window and spot Isla's car pulling up outside. In my head is the jumble of things I might possibly want to say to her now that I've spent time with Jessie, now that thoughts of reconciling, coming to parties, being an auntie have been planted.

I stand at the window, waiting for Isla to come out and cross the road. Maybe she'll also bring Peter with her. Maybe we could actually sit down, have a cup of tea and just try out being friendly to one another...

My thoughts are interrupted with a loud blare from the car horn. Jessie calls out: 'Is that Mummy?' and I can hear her start to pack her pens and books together.

Then she hurries towards the front door, where I hand over her lightweight pink anorak, before she skips down the steps towards the car. She opens the back door of the car and climbs in and all I get from Isla is a brief smile and a wave before she drives away.

18

'Mick, absolutely everything in the office is sorted.'

It's 11.45 a.m. on a Wednesday morning and after three and-a-bit working days, I have brought complete calm and control to Mick's reception area, storage systems, his filing, his case notes, his invoicing and his admin. I've also taught him the everything-in-duplicate, paperclips, bulldog clips and folders system I installed in Jono's office.

Mick's personal office is immaculate too. He finally freed up some time, allowed me in there yesterday to help him and after a marathon seven hours, plus fifteen bin bags of recycling, we were done. I even got him to throw away the clapped-out moccasins and sent him out to buy a particular pair of suede trainers I had spotted in a window, hoping this would meet his requirement for a totally comfortable, but totally presentable shoe.

He appears in the doorway that connects his office with the reception area.

'Oh my goodness... I suppose that means you're going to leave now, does it?'

I'm so happy to see that he looks properly anxious at the prospect.

'Well... that depends...' I say and I'm sort of thinking on my feet.

I like Mick. I've really enjoyed leaving the house every morning with purpose and it's been so satisfying putting his chaotic little practice back to rights. I've tried hard not to think beyond the next few days ever since I left London. But now, I imagine staying on in St Andrews for... well, some *months* even. And maybe I could come and work for Mick a day or two a week... keep him organised, keep him on track.

I mean, I have no idea what I want yet. Still tumbling around my head are wild ideas about escaping to New York, or those Argentinian Pampas and a whole mishmash of other thoughts.

'I've really enjoyed working with you...' I begin.

'Me too,' Mick says and adds a warmly appreciative smile.

'What about if I come in for a day or even two a week? And I do, well, everything you need me to.'

'That sounds like a fantastic idea,' comes his speedy response. 'I've needed someone like you to help me for... months. We just need to find a daily rate that suits,' he adds.

'Yes...'

We pause and look at one another.

'Do you want to go first?' I ask.

So, he suggests a figure that is a bit low for my London expectations. But I counter with one that could work for me now that I'm a resident of St Andrews.

And we agree on two days a week.

'Might as well start today,' I tell him. 'I thought as I've sorted out your actual physical office, I should probably sort you out online.'

Although Mick is possibly a few years younger than me, he rolls his eyes at this.

'Not social media,' he says. 'I don't do social media.'

'You know, neither do I at the moment.' I leave my explanation there. No need to tell him that gazing wistfully at the edited high-lights of other people's perfect lives turns out to be a hobby I hardly miss at all.

'But this is the twenty-first century. This is how people look for lawyers,' I insist. 'They put "lawyer, St Andrews" into Google and look at the results. If you're not on the first page, forget it and if they don't like your website, again, forget it.'

'I do have a website.'

'Mick, that website is quite old.' So old that you have a full head of hair – I don't add. 'Look, I'll make some calls. We'll get a smart new site at a good price. And then I'm sorting you out on LinkedIn. You don't need to tweet, you don't need to Facebook, or Instagram, or SnapChat, but you do need to make the most of your business contacts on LinkedIn. OK?'

'The Bold Partnership,' he says darkly, 'that's what we're up against.'

Yes, I have googled lawyers in St Andrews and top of the search results is indeed the Bold Partnership. Their website showcases a team of beautiful blondes in baby-pink blouses with hinting neck-lines and several ridiculously handsome all-jaw males in pinstripe suits smiling smugly. I have checked and the photos were not posed by models. Everyone at the Bold Partnership seems to have been chosen entirely for their looks. Even the senior partners have a touch of the George Clooney silver fox about them.

Their 'latest news' features cases they've won and successes they've had in the past week, along with a chatty blog posted just this morning. By contrast, the last post on www.munroandpartner-s.com occurred in 2016 when a 10 per cent discount was offered on will writing. And there is no longer a partner in Munro and partners.

Yes. It's high time for an update.

'A new website, a LinkedIn presence, maybe even a series of adverts in *The Citizen* and *The Courier* – what do you think about that? We want to spread the word, get plenty of new customers in now that everything's looking so ready for action.'

'Adverts?' Mick looks unsure.

'Time to be positive,' I tell him. 'Nothing flashy, we'll only do what you're very comfortable with. You just have to be yourself, Mick, a little tweedy, a little traditional but really good at your job. That's the message we'll convey and people will like it.'

As I say all this, I can see Mick starting to relax a little. Listening to myself, I also wonder if I've spent a little too much time watching *Dragon's Den*.

'Well, I suppose... as long as I can review things...' he tells me.

'Not one thing will go out there into the world unless you're 100 per cent happy with it.'

'Great.'

So, my busy day continues with contacting web designers for quotes, then trying out a range of different wordings for the adverts... and maybe even leaflets.

Finally, I'm happy with my efforts, but as it's now approaching 6 p.m., I decide I'll power down the laptop and review it again in the morning before I show it to Mick.

* * *

When I leave Mick's office at the end of the day, I decide to head to the beach for waves, bracing fresh air and a chance to exercise the knee, which is healing well and doesn't need a stick any more.When I get there, the wind is a little too bracing and I find I'm battling the kind of gusty blasts that make a brisk walk difficult, but I can't help admiring the savage loveliness. The beach is so long and so wide that even crowds of people wouldn't fill it, but there are no crowds here. It looks almost empty. The sky is a steely grey, so the water is too. It's approaching the end of March, but there's not a hint of spring warmth to the air today. I pull my woollen coat and scarf tightly around me and walk along the sand with the knee feeling quite smooth and improved, enjoying being outside with all this clean air and majestic scenery around me, despite the greyness and the cold.

I find myself watching the family groups, bundled in hats and coats, throwing balls and chasing dogs across the beach. And a strange feeling sets in. For years now, I've wanted a child-free, grown-up life, but I didn't expect to be alone. And now, I find myself wondering what it would be like to be part of a normal, everyday family, with children around me, a dog... a daughter like Jessie... needy little people who would fill almost all the time that I currently have to myself. I wonder what it would be like. A very different life, a very busy life. Would I ever want that?

One of the walkers seems to be waving. I look around but get the strong impression this man is waving at me. When he begins to wave with two arms and jump up and down, I realise it's Rory, so I quickly set a smile in place and walk towards him.

There are three smaller children with him and a fourth, almost as tall as him. As he gets closer, I can hear him telling them: 'Yes, that's Jen, remember I told you about her, she went to school with me. Yes, even though it's hard to believe because she looks about ten years younger. She moved to London, she's very sophisticated. Hey, Jen...'

We're just about close enough to talk normally now.

'How are you doing?' Rory asks. 'How's it going? Great evening for a wild walk.'

'Yes... all good,' I say.

'So, meet my girl gang. This is Samantha, then comes Maggie and absolutely no forgetting Katie.' He introduces his daughters in turn, from the oldest to the youngest. His teenager, Samantha, has mint-green hair with roots, a pale face and complex nose and ear piercings. Despite the scowly smile, she looks more shy than fierce.

Katie and Maggie are much younger; Katie, I know is five, her sister looks only about a year or so older. Maggie has a head of dark hair curlier than her dad's and an impish look. Katie sports a short blonde perky bob that flips out at the sides, at the back and, somehow, on top too. She has the most perfect chubby red cheeks and an unusually determined look for such a small person.

We all exchange hellos.

'And who is this?' I ask, looking at the shy little boy with dark hair and a pale face trailing behind the girls.

'Oh!' Rory looks at me in surprise, as if he's forgotten the little boy is there. 'That's Katie's friend...'

'Boyfriend!' Katie interrupts loudly.

'Yes, boy-dash-friend,' Rory adds. 'He's at school with Katie... and...'

'He's called Pooky,' Katie adds.

'That's not his real name,' Maggie explains.

Katie is the first to wade in with a question for me: 'Did you really go to school with Daddy?' She sounds suspicious.

'And what was Daddy like at school?' Maggie asks before I can answer. 'I bet he was really, really naughty. I bet he was at the headmaster's office the whole time.'

'And was he really the best person in his whole class at Maths?' is Katie's next question.

'And French?' Maggie adds.

'And writing stories?'

'Whoa, slow down girls,' Rory insists, 'give Jennifer a chance to answer. And obviously, Jen, I try to inspire my girls, hoping they'll be just half as brilliant at school as me.'

This is funny. Those cute-as-a-button but completely determined little girls are making me laugh. I'm trying to remember back to school, but I really can't recall Rory being particularly stand out good at anything. I think he did OK. Mainly he was the life and soul of the few classes we went to together, telling jokes and silly stories, brightening up the dreariness of another school day. But I'm not going to ruin the motivational plan he's obviously set in place for his daughters.

'Your dad was fantastic at school,' I tell the girls. 'He was especially good at Maths and English and French, and I don't remember him ever being in trouble.'

I give Rory a conspiratorial look because this is definitely not true, I do now remember something about homebrewed beer getting into the fruit juice one sports day, and he had something to do with it, but it's all such a long time ago now, I realise with a shudder. My classmate's *children* are now at school. I've not had to think about that until I came back here.

'And... I seem to remember something about him being in the school fashion show,' I add. 'Maybe I can even find some photos.'

'Oh no...' Rory begins as Katie, Maggie and even Samantha gasp and look utterly delighted at this prospect.

'Yes, please, please, please!' Maggie and Katie beg, while Rory insists: 'However much money you need to destroy that evidence, Jen, I can give it to you. Just name your price.'

The little girls and their friend break away to chase each other across the sand at speed and I can't resist telling Rory that his girls look so like him and even have his cheeks.

'Yes, yes, yes, chubby, adorable and only fit for squeezing – that's very nice when you're under ten, but I'm not flattered.'

'They are all lovely girls,' I add, loud enough for Samantha, who's fallen a little behind us, to hear.

'Yes and exhausting, *exhausting*! And the nagging for a dog... when will it ever end?'

'Just get a dog,' I tell him. 'We had a cat growing up and cats are rubbish.'

'Yeah, Dad, get us a dog,' Samantha adds.

'Yeah, Dad, stop being so boring,' I add.

'Do not join in, Jen. It's messy, cramped and busy enough at our place, I cannot add a dog. Look, horses!' he says, pointing some distance ahead in a bid to distract us from the dog talk.

And sure enough, three pretty, sturdy horses are cantering along the firm sand close to the water's edge.

'Wow,' I can't help myself, 'that looks amazing.'

'That's what you want to be doing, Jen, finishing your workday and then getting down to the beach for a gallop. You want the wind in your hair, feeling free and strong again. You used to ride, didn't you?'

'Well, yes... and I used to do handstands and cartwheels too.'

But that was all years ago and I haven't been back on a horse since. Not since I was a teenager, I realise. Looking at these big horses I wonder about my volunteering in Argentina idea. Could I ever be brave enough to cross the world and get back on horseback? Would it be good for me? Would it help me to put things in perspective? See my life in a different light? Would it make me happy?

'But it must be like riding a bike...' Rory begins.

'Nope, riding is definitely not like riding a bike,' I tell him.

'But you can't forget how to do something like that. I'm going to find out about getting you a beach ride.'

'No!' I protest. 'I'd be terrified. You don't care about falling off when you're a teenager, but now... I'd be holding on for dear life, even at a trot.'

'Trust me,' Rory says and before I can argue back, in a concerned voice he adds: 'Uh-oh, now that looks like a very black dark cloud. Time to quick-march home.'

We all begin to walk more quickly, but it doesn't help. With surprising speed, the sky darkens and it begins to lash with rain. Everyone hurries to do up their zips, except me. Everyone pulls snug hoods tightly up over their heads, except me. Everyone tucks their hands into deep and cosy pockets, except me. Everyone is wearing sensible hiking type shoes or welly boots, except me. Instead, my lovely soft wool wrap coat is soaking up water like a sponge and beginning to smell like a wet sheep. My sodden hair is clinging to my face, along with my now wet and sticky scarf, and my suede boots are once again letting in water like a sinking boat and are most likely ruined.

'Didn't I warn you about dressing for the weather?' Rory asks, dry and toasty under the kind of parka that looks as if it could double as an insulated tent. 'You're not in London now, you'll have to make some changes.'

'But I don't want to wear anoraks, or hiking boots,' I wail.

'I'm sure you can think of a nice way to do it. I mean you're not looking totally smart and together right this moment...' I can see the smile on Rory's face as he says this. Kindly, he adds: 'Waterproof mascara might be a start.'

'Oh no!' I start wiping under my eyes frantically as we hurry along the beach.

'So apart from a hot bath, what are your plans for the evening?' Rory asks as we all jog the final fifty metres or so to the car park, where I can see the Rorymobile.

'Making Dad his supper, a bit of light housework, a bit of Netflix... exciting times,' I reply, as we hurry towards the car, shepherding the little children in front of us.

'Now that is my usual evening, but not tonight. Tonight, the girls are going to Hazel's for the next three days and I am out...' his voice drops to a whisper, 'on a date.'

'Woo-hoo, go, Rory,' I tell him and I'm glad to hear it.

'Yes... but what do grown-up girls like?' he asks, almost anxious, checking Samantha is out of earshot. 'What's a good first date? Should we go to a bar? Go to dinner? No, I think dinner is too much pressure. Should we go to the bowling club? I mean, did you like the bowling club?'

'I liked the bowling club,' I tell him, 'but it's not very datey. A bar is good... or a long walk... there's no pressure with a walk... but the weather,' I look up at the sky; it's not promising.

'I think we can forget a walk,' Rory says.

'It will be fine, go somewhere nice and not too quiet. You'll be fine. What is she like? Do you know much about her?' I'm curious, wondering if she's local and already knows him a little, or if he's managed to find someone new on the St Andrews scene.

'I don't know much about her at all... she's a friend of a friend, lives in Dundee. In the photos I've seen, she looks like someone from a 1950s film about the future.'

The tone of slight dread that he delivers this in makes me burst out laughing.

'Beehive hair,' he explains, gesturing with his hands, 'massive beehive hair.'

'Well... that sounds very interesting.' I can kind of picture Rory with someone petite and busty with a unique dress style. I think it would suit him. She'd probably make him over as an American rocker from the fifties and together they would go on trips in huge, pale-blue convertibles.

'Is "very interesting" London-speak for "bizarre"?'

'No!'

'C'mon, into the car, everyone. You too, Jennifer McAndrew, we'll give you a lift.'

We have a mini debate with me insisting I'll be fine and that I'm wet already and I don't want to be any trouble, because I really don't. But Rory – ever kind, ever generous – insists I get in the car and let him drive me home.

Maggie and Katie join in with the chorus, so then I have to give in, although I'm feeling guilty and wondering how to repay Rory for all the unstinting friendship he's shown me. He's just jumped straight in, making it clear he wants to be firm friends and shown me up as all Londony and reserved.

So then I'm in the car and the heater is on at max power to warm us all and de-mist the windows. The CD player is also on full blast so Katie and Maggie and Pooky can sing along. Rory is already keen for us to arrange a time when we can get together to discuss how his date went.

'Come round to my place,' he offers as he slows up outside my dad's house, '*mi casa, su casa.*'

And as I wave the merry Rorymobile away down the road, I find I am already looking forward to seeing him and his girls again.

19

'I saw Isla today,' Dad tells me, trying to sound casual as he's handing me my first G&T of the evening. 'She said she'd like to see you properly... not like when she turned up on the doorstep the other day. Maybe you girls would like to meet for a coffee?'

I do expect my dad to mention my sister once in a while. It's only natural that he should, but every time he does, it feels unexpected and a bit like a punch to the solar plexus.

Nothing has changed between us just because I've moved from London to St Andrews. And if she really wanted to be friendly, then surely she should have come and said hello when she picked Jessie up? Instead of sitting outside in her car and tooting the horn like some power Mum in a very important hurry.

Or she could get in touch with me herself, instead of using Dad as a messenger.

'Do you know about any letters she sent me over the past couple of years?'

For a moment, Dad looks blankly at me.

Then he says: 'Well, I was the one who sent those on to you...

but she said you never replied, which I have to say... look,' he sighs and sits down on his favourite, saggy old armchair, 'I don't want to interfere with the two of you, in case I make everything worse, but when someone takes time to write, to choose their words carefully, and to try to put things right – as I believe she wanted to do – then don't you think they deserve some sort of reply?'

At first, I feel vaguely outraged, but then a thought that may explain it all comes into my mind.

'I moved into a new flat about eighteen months ago, in Pimlico. You did send the letters there, didn't you? I remember giving you my new address.'

At this, Dad goes over to the little writing table in the corner of the room. He rummages about and comes out with an old-fashioned address book. He opens at my page and reads out... my previous address.

'Dad, I didn't get those letters.'

'But don't people forward things on?' he asks, exasperated.

'This is London, Dad! People move house a lot and no, I don't know who lives in the place I rented before. Why didn't you tell me you were sending them?'

He sits back down in his armchair and takes a glug of his drink.

Then with a shrug, he says: 'I told you both to leave me out of it. You just need to get together, in person, and sort this out. Hear each other out, listen to one another.'

Then he clicks on the TV and the Aussie detectives are back, '*Strewth*', and our conversation is apparently over.

* * *

I head upstairs not really intending to end up in my sister's old bedroom, but I find myself outside the door, then turning the handle, stepping into the room and switching on the light. For a moment I stand there, looking at all the boxes... my boxes, that were stacked here only a few weeks ago and all the older boxes with other family treasures inside.

I lift open the flaps on the nearest cardboard box that isn't mine, sneeze violently, and spot an old mock croc handbag that I recognise at once as one of Mum's. She rises like a ghost, in one of her neat skirt, blouse and cardigan outfits. She was always smartly dressed for a housewife, but then she always seemed to have places to go to and people to visit. In my memories, she's always cooking, cleaning, ironing, smoothing, arranging, serving food or washing up in pink rubber gloves. Or she's out in the back garden, digging, weeding, planting little bulbs into pots, making it look neatly pretty. Or she's in a coat and a silk head-scarf against the wind, just 'popping out' or just returning to the house.

Isla, Dad and I never helped her much around the house and although she complained about it now and then, the truth is she didn't really like us to help. She was very particular and a perfectionist, who saw running the home like clockwork as her job.

I realise in a rush how fiercely I loved her when I was small. I thought she was so beautiful and so clever. I used to try on all her clothes, and her lipstick and brush my hair with her heavy hairbrush. And she was always there, such a reassuring presence – first thing in the morning till last thing at night, at the school gate without fail. There, to answer every question, soothe every woe, prepare every possible drink or snack. But I have to admit that around about age fourteen, this became so annoying. Mum seemed like the fussiest person in the world and I wanted her to be anywhere else but constantly around and constantly on my case.

As a teenager, I argued with her often and much more than Isla did. I accused her of being a housewife who'd wasted her life and set us a poor example. I was going to be a lawyer, doing an important job, and I longed to get away from her small-town standards.

When she died, our relationship had become better, but I still regret so many of those stupid teenage arguments and all the times that I could have said something nice, or expressed my thanks, instead of being a brat. The reconciling with your mother that I could see many friends going through later on, especially when they had children of their own, obviously did not happen for me. And so, I never had the chance to discover how much more I might have loved her again as she grew older. Maybe my full appreciation of how tricky mother-daughter and sister relationships can be makes me too wary to start a family of my own. With no relationship lasting too long... with my latest one being with Jono, who had said he didn't want more children... I've been able to dodge thinking too hard about it. Maybe I really don't want children. And maybe I've left it too late now anyway.

That final furious argument with my mum about going to the christening party... a chill passes down my back and tears slip down my face. I can't bear to think about it.

I close up the cardboard flaps again, hiding the handbag and choose another box. A puff of dust rises and once again I sneeze as I lift the flap on this one.

Here, several postcards and envelopes lie on top of the other contents. These are older letters addressed to me in my sister's handwriting, written very soon after our Mum died. I read them all back then and I didn't reply... and then, on a visit to Dad, I stuffed them into this box, not sure what else to do with them. For a few moments, I hold the envelopes in my hands and wonder if I want to read them over again. But I just don't think the explanations for what happened between us are going to be found here. And why did she always have to write?

Why did she write those more recent letters that never made it to Pimlico? If you can't say it face to face, if you don't want to discuss it, if you just want to put your point of view forward over and over again, then why bother?

I don't want to read about her justifying her actions all over again.

So, I stuff the envelopes back into the box, close the flaps, turn off the light and close the door on the room.

20

I'm in Rory's shop, but he is not behind the counter. I know that he's already at home, prepping his daughters for bed so that we can have a quiet debrief on how his date went.

'The beehive is even more impressive up close,' is all the information I've had so far.

'Hi, I'd like to buy a bottle of proper Champagne please,' I tell the student behind the counter, who has a straggly beard and is wearing a T-shirt with a Maths joke that I don't get.

'Can you just talk me through what you have?' I ask him, dithering slightly. Yes, Champagne is a little flash maybe, but I owe Rory a thank you for the bowling night and the lifts, plus I have to keep up my reputation as the sophisticated-girl-from-London.

I settle on the Moët. It's a classic and on at a pretty respectable price. As the student takes it down from the shelf, he tells me, 'Now, before I ring this up, orange Club biscuits and mint Aero bars are both on special offer today. And as for Easter eggs, we are practically giving them away.'

He's obviously been well trained by the boss.

* * *

Outside 24 Shore View, I park up in front of a two-storied, slightly shabby-looking cottage that seems to have been divided into two flats. I take the external metal staircase up to 24B and ring the doorbell.

It takes a little bit of time, but finally Rory opens the door looking startled to see me.

'Oh, Jennifer McAndrew, hello. It's you. Is that the time? Or are you early?'

'Oh... sorry...' I glance at my watch, I'm a little bit early I see now, but only by a few minutes.

And it almost feels a little awkward to be standing there on the threshold with him clearly in a state of some surprise, so I hold up my bottle, wrapped in tissue paper and say: 'I brought you some Champagne to say thank you for the lifts and our fun time at the bowling club...'

'Champagne! You total lush!' Rory exclaims. 'I hope you bought that in my shop – we have a good price on that.'

'Yes of course,' I grin at him and his expression softens.

'But I don't drink, remember?' he says and I think he looks slightly amused by me.

'What, not at all? I thought it was just because you were always driving.'

I feel taken aback at this. Silly that I didn't know. And now I'm wondering what I'm going to do with this pricey and a bit flash bottle. And I'm thinking about how the evening will go with no alcoholic bubbles to ease our chitchat along.

'I am always driving...' Rory agrees, 'but I suppose I didn't want to be that guy... you know, the big, divorced guy, who's always had a few too many. And is a bit sad.'

'Rory, I don't think you could ever be that guy,' I reassure him.

'What about one glass?' I ask. 'To keep me company?'

'Come in,' he says. 'And I apologise in advance, but it is still a madhouse. We're still at least one full hour from bedtime.'

'If you don't mind, then honestly, I don't mind.'

He pulls back the door and gestures me in with the words: 'You can come in and you are very welcome, so long as you don't judge me as the worst dad in the whole of Scotland.'

'Don't be silly.'

And so, I find myself in a small and jumbled, jangled home, where it feels completely natural to get caught up in the action and try to help with coaxing the little girls to finish their supper, tidy away their toys, brush their teeth and get into their pyjamas.

Rory's daughters, Katie and Maggie, are delighted to see me and completely monopolise me.

'Are you now daddy's girlfriend?' asks Katie, clearly a *Newsnight* journalist in training.

'Would you like to marry Daddy?' Maggie wants to know.

Before I can make any sensible replies, they are off on an unstoppable riff.

'I think you should marry Daddy,' Katie says. 'He's very nice and even though he has a lot of friends and knows a lot of people, I'm worried that he is lonely because he doesn't have a special person to cuddle in bed. I have Maggie, or Big-Ted-Behind-the-Head, Mummy has a boyfriend and he's called Ryan. He is quite nice but he's not as funny as Daddy.'

'Or as cuddly,' adds Maggie.

'He doesn't play silly games like Daddy. Or sing any songs. He does sometimes read us stories,' Katie concedes.

'But not with any silly voices.'

I can hardly get a word in edgeways they are both so chatty. But whenever I do, I try to assure them that I am Daddy's friend and I used to know him at school and yes, he's very funny, but marriage is probably not imminent.

'But why do you not want to marry Daddy?' Maggie asks tragically.

But before I have to think of a clever answer to this, Rory swoops in and insists: 'That's quite enough of that... good grief, poor Jennifer, stop asking so many silly questions or she will never come and visit ever again. And who said anything about me getting married?! Don't you think I'm busy enough without a wife to look after? I'd have to buy her shoes and boxes of chocolates and she'd probably want a chihuahua.'

This reduces the girls to giggles and inspires a long discussion about what kind of small dog they would most like as a pet.

* * *

But finally, the little girls are tucked up in their shared bedroom and Rory and I can head back to the small sitting room. It is quite the scene of chaos in this room, which is not going to be featured in *Elle Decoration* any time soon, but nevertheless, I plump up the cushions on the battered sofa, arrange the red tartan rug on top of its faded upholstery and collect abandoned crisps, partially melted chocolate buttons and Barbie dolls having very bad hair days, while Rory ferries dirty plates and sticky juice cups to the kitchen.

'And what about Samantha,' I ask, 'is she in her room?'

'Sam? She's out with her friends, she has a 10 p.m. curfew.'

'On a school night?' I ask and realise straight away that I probably shouldn't have.

'I know, I know it's late, but at least she does come in at 10. If I set it any earlier, then she whines and wails and doesn't.'

Because he looks a little stressed and agitated even discussing this, I ask:

'Is everything OK with her?' Although all I know about fifteen-year-old girls is that I once used to be one.

'Ah, what can I say? She's fifteen!' Rory collapses onto the sofa in surrender. 'Some of her friends are loons. She, of course, thinks I'm a complete loon. She's fifteen,' he repeats. 'No one said these years were going to be a breeze. And divorced parenting... it's not easy.'

I take a seat in the tired, but actually now that I look at it properly, quite charming room.

It has lumpy, cottagey whitewashed walls and a fuzzy brown carpet. There's a small window with a view of the harbour and the sea, growing inky blue in the early evening light. Bright paintings of fishing boats decorate the walls.

The other furniture is a bookcase, a TV and a heap of children's DVDs, new ones mixed in with classics I recognise even from my own childhood.

'I hope your children like *Scooby Doo*,' I say to Rory, who has now gone to the kitchen next door to organise glasses.

'My children have been brought up properly, and they love *Scooby Doo*, Scooby snacks and Shaggy and Velma,' Rory says coming back into the room.

'Of course they do,' I smile at him.

'Champagne glass?' he says, holding out a huge wine glass.

'Perfect. But you're not going to join me?'

'No, honestly, I don't miss the stuff at all. So, you have Champagne, my sophisticated London friend, I'll drink Coke and let's celebrate my first date in some time. The drought would appear to be ending.'

He pops open the cork, pours out my glass, cracks open his can, then sinks down into the sofa, close up beside me. It's not awkward. In fact, I like it; it's comfortable and comforting. It's almost like being back at school, squeezed together on the bench in the dining room. I can't quite believe how easy it is to be friends with Alison and Rory again.

'Here's to us,' I say, raising my glass, 'for getting the hell on with things.'

'Damn right,' he chinks glasses with me and lets out a long, 'aaaaaaaah,' after his first sip of Coke. 'Oh my god, having children is literally the most tiring thing in the entire world. Seriously, Mo Farah's weekly training routine is probably a doddle compared to this and I only have them for half of the week.'

I take another sip from my glass. Maybe I'm hungry, maybe I'm thirsty, maybe I'm drinking far too much gin at Dad's, because this Champagne tastes amazing and I decide on the spot that as soon as this glass is finished, I'm going to drink another.

'So, obviously I need to hear all about your date?' I prompt him.

'Yes... it was fine. It was nice,' he tells me. 'Her beehive is big, very stiff, very scary looking. It makes her about a foot taller than me.'

'Was she chatty? Easy to talk to?' I ask.

'Yes, she had quite a lot to say.'

'And was it interesting?'

'Yes... quite interesting.' I think Rory sounds a little hesitant here.

'Did she laugh at your jokes?'

'No... not really... but I was quite nervous, so maybe I wasn't doing the jokes justice. Justice for jokes,' he quips and I laugh.

'And the all-important question... were you attracted to her?'

'Yeeee-eees, sort of?' he replies and it sounds like a question.

'Hmmmm... care to elaborate on that?' I ask. 'I mean usually that's a straight yes or no answer. Either the buzzer goes off or it doesn't.'

'The buzzer... that's one way of putting it. To be honest, my judgement is off. I think I'd be almost pathetically grateful to anyone who showed even the slightest interest in me right now. It has been a while,' he confides.

'Ah... I see.'

'In fact... I am totally, completely available,' he adds, bumping his shoulder against mine, 'just so you know. I don't want you to be in any doubt about my status... just putting it out there, loud and clear.'

Oh, no... I don't want Rory to joke about this. I just want to be friends. I don't even want to admit there's any possibility of anything else. *Please, don't spoil what we've got developing here*, I want to shout.

'No! Don't even joke,' I protest, 'you're my long-lost friend. It's lovely to hang out with you again. Why would we risk messing anything up with... anything more complicated?'

'But isn't this what all the young people are doing now: friends with benefits?'

Something about the way he is now waggling his eyebrows at me makes me laugh. He is joking, isn't he? He is winding me up.

'You're thinking about it,' Rory says. 'Right now, you are picturing me *naked*.' He says this as huskily and sexily as he can.

And the next thing I know, I'm trying very hard not to imagine Rory naked. And then I can only imagine Rory naked. Rory would definitely be pale skinned, a little chubby, yes, but maybe with all that hauling about of boxes, on the muscular side of chubby, with strong arms... strong thighs. I glance down at the muscular legs next to mine on the sofa.

'Stop it,' I laugh and dig him in the ribs. 'You're my friend and I like it like this.'

He sighs and rolls his eyes, pretending to be angry.

'So, there is absolutely no moving you on from that then?'

'No! Look, we are not going to start dating, but I'm happy to help you... you know, on the path to true happiness. If I meet anyone I think could be good for you, I will let you know. And I hope you'll do likewise... when the time is right, which could take a while, I'm just saying.'

'OK, well I'm glad that's all out in the open and completely clear.'

The collapsed sofa has brought us very close together; our shoulders, hips and legs are touching. With Champagne buzzing through my veins, it feels very comforting and friendly.

I find myself slipping my hand into Rory's.

'You've really cheered me up,' I tell him. 'You and your girls. I was really sad when I arrived and... it doesn't feel so bad any more.'

'Thanks, Jennifer McAndrew,' Rory gives my hand a squeeze. 'You've cheered me up too. At least I'm not the only one riding blind through a shitstorm.'

'No,' I laugh, 'of course you're not.'

We let a few quiet, comfortable moments pass.

Then Rory has to ask: 'So, on a strictly theoretical basis, have you met anyone in St Andrews that you have considered shagging? Even just momentarily?'

I don't have to think too hard about that.

'Alison and I had a night out at the McIver Hotel,' I admit. 'And I met this very handsome guy called Sergei.'

Rory actually chokes on his Coke and coughs some of it up.

When he's recovered, I tell him about that flirtatious little interlude which came to nothing.

'You should have gone to his room and let him show you a good time,' Rory tells me. 'I would have. It's been such a drought for me recently that I might even have had sex with *Sir-Gay*. I mean he sounds hot. And the next time a hot man offers himself up on a plate to you, you should definitely say yes.'

'OK, I will try to remember that,' I say, smiling and not really meaning it.

'When your relationship has crashed and burned, you are allowed to go out and get some. That is the rule.'

'Right.'

My glass, which I seem to have already emptied, is refilled. Rory opens another Coke too.

'So if I'm Mr Best Friend who is good for cuddles,' Rory begins, 'all the way over here on the scale,' he holds one hand out to the left, 'and Sergei was Mr Shudders all the way over here,' he holds his other hand out to the right, 'then where on the scale is your ideal man?' Rory asks, still holding out his hands.

'Well...' I pause and consider the question as best I can after almost half a bottle of bubbly, 'you've got to have a lot of shudder, but also a good measure of cuddle. I don't know if there's an ideal. But maybe there's a sweet spot...'

Ooops, I inadvertently reduce us both to almost tearful giggles.

'I just mean...' I go on, when I can speak again, 'you need someone who can go on providing shudders and cuddles year after year. But maybe there's no winning formula. Maybe it's unique to every couple.'

'Hazel was one big, huge shudder to me,' Rory admits, 'but maybe I was Mr Cuddles for far too long. Maybe I need to work on my shudder. Maybe you could give me some advice there – what was Sergei's secret?'

'He was very tall and good-looking...'

'Uh-oh... Houston, we may have a problem...' he jokes.

My face is beginning to hurt from all the laughing.

'He seemed incredibly interested and did not take his eyes off me,' I add.

'Check and check,' Rory says, pinning his eyes on mine.

I slap his arm.

'Sergei also had a very sexy voice,' I add.

'Sort of like this,' Rory replies, low and breathy.

In a whisper, close to Rory's ear I add: 'And he also gave the impression that he was pretty practised in the sack.'

'Again, just like me. I could transform myself into the next Shudder King.'

Now it's my turn to choke on my drink, and Rory actually has to slap my back while I cough before we can carry on with our nonsense conversation.

'But I suppose the point is,' I say finally, when I can talk again, 'surely everyone shuddery does eventually become cuddly? I mean, probably even Mrs Daniel Craig looks at her hubby in his slippers and comfiest boxers and thinks "there's Mr Cuddles, what happened to the other guy?"'

'But could it ever work the other way?' Rory wonders, pouring another dose of fizz into my glass. 'Can someone ever move from Mr Cuddles into Mr Shudder?'

I look at his kind face and I know he's a friend, but maybe there's a little crush there on his part too. I don't want to encourage a crush, but I don't want to completely crush the crush either, so I say: 'Maybe... well, yes, probably happens quite a lot. Now, shall we watch something? Maybe a *Scooby Doo*? Must be decades since I last saw one.'

'No, not that. Hang on, let me get the remote.'

Rory sticks his hand under the sofa, feels about and something large and furry shoots out and tears across the room. I'm so surprised I actually scream. Rory shouts in surprise too, which makes me scream even louder. I'm sure it's a huge rat.

'*Jesus!*' Rory says, jumping to his feet. 'It's the bloody cat from downstairs. It sneaks in the kitchen window, hides under here and then scares the living daylights out of us.'

I turn to the door behind us where, sure enough, a fluffy tabby is scrabbling at the paintwork.

'I'll let it out,' Rory says.

Once he's opened both the sitting room door and the front door and encouraged the cat out with a brisk: 'Go on, off you go', then checked under the sofa for any kind of cat deposit, he settles back down.

'Mrs Morton downstairs keeps threatening to move closer to her daughter in England, wish she and her cat bloody well would,' he says.

I have my hand over my heart and it is going to take me a few moments to calm down from thinking I was about to encounter a great big rodent.

'I'm really sorry,' Rory says, realising what a shock I got. 'I can tell you're not exactly impressed with this place and your worst fears were nearly confirmed. Maybe it's a good thing that cat comes up regularly, or we would have a rodent situation.'

'Hey, no need to spiral,' I warn him. 'It can't be easy bringing up a small troupe of children on your own and running your own superstar-store. You're doing the best you can. And, people's homes are far too perfect these days anyway...'

'Yeah!' he agrees.

But at the same moment, I find myself thinking wistfully of my perfect little flat with every single little thing perfectly chosen and arranged. *Oh, get over it*, I tell myself crossly.

* * *

So, we spend a pleasant hour or so channel hopping, finding things to watch and laugh over together. Until gradually, my head droops and is then propped up against a plaid shoulder. It's a nice shoulder, warm and comfortable – a shoulder to lean on, a shoulder to cry on even. I really like my old friend, Rory Ferguson.

'I like your shirt,' I say.

'Cost me £6 wholesale. Had to buy a dozen though. And I

realise now that they are indestructible, so I have close to a life-time's supply – if you ever need a tartan shirt, you just let me know.'

'Very funny.'

'OK, I'm going to ask you one more awkward question...' Rory says, when the Champagne is almost finished and it's time for me to go so I don't fall asleep on his sofa. Plus, Samantha has texted to say she's on her way home and I really don't want a teenager's take on me on the sofa with her dad and a nearly empty bottle.

'What about Isla and Richard?' Rory asks. 'Are you going to go and visit them? Maybe you already have?'

I sit up feeling suddenly chilly and a bit more sober than I was a moment ago. I feel like Rory has kind of ruined it. He's brought up the topic I really don't want to talk about; don't even want to really think about. Especially after the blowing the horn from the kerb incident.

I shake my head.

'No... I've seen Isla in passing... kind of thing... but no plans for a reunion as yet,' I say coolly.

'I'm sorry,' Rory says, 'I didn't mean to...'

'It's OK,' I try to brush it off, 'everyone wants families to play nice, of course they do... but sometimes it just doesn't work like that.'

I realise I don't want any more chat about this, or any further probing into my state of mind tonight.

'Look, it's getting late,' I say, paving the way for my exit. 'And Samantha is on her way home. I should call a taxi. I'll pick dad's car up in the morning.'

What I really hate, most of all, is that it feels as if *everyone in this small town knows* that I used to go out with the man my sister married. People talking about me... that was one big reason why I had to flee the scene and take that one-way ticket to London back then.

Ha... and why I then had to take the one-way ticket back when it all unravelled with Jono.

As I sit in the back of the taxi home, yet again I find myself wondering: What do I want? Where do I want to be? What do I want my life to look like? And yet again... I can't decide. I just don't know.

Maybe I need to follow up on that volunteering in South America opportunity. Maybe a complete change of scene would bring the answers.

21

When I wake up the next morning, once I've drunk the water and cups of tea required to bring me back to life after the reckless Champagne swigging, I look at my phone and consider doing the thing I haven't done for some time, but find I want to do now.

How is Jono? I can't help wondering. Before coming here, I spent every single day with him, Monday to Friday, and usually some of the weekend too. I used to know everything about him, from the cases he was working on, to the colour of socks he was wearing, to what he would like for lunch. Now, I know nothing. Much as I'm trying to fill my time, have different people around me... of course, now and then, I find myself thinking about him. I don't want him back. It's too late, he's damaged not just what we had, but also my plans for our future. And he's made it clear he doesn't want me back anyway, so what's the use of even thinking like that.

But I miss him.

So, before I can even think about it too much, I tap:

Hi J, how are you doing? Jennifer x

And hit send.

I look at my message all small and lonely on the screen and decide I need to add:

I'm really well. Enjoying St Andrews life.

Hit send again.

Then to show I'm definitely moving on with my life, I also tap out:

I have news – planning to go to Argentina for the summer, to volunteer and have an adventure. Very exciting! Hope all is good with you and family.

I pause for a moment and read it over again before sending. Yes, it feels right to message him now, to hope all his well with him and the people he chose over me. And I definitely want to let him know that I'm fine and I have new plans. I'm definitely not sitting in my dad's kitchen, a little hungover, missing him and wondering what to do with the rest of my life... no.

Then I lose myself googling Argentina... looking at photos of the cities and the countryside, sending out requests to Airbnb hosts about possible accommodation in Buenos Aires in July, and when my phone bleeps after a little while, I'm half expecting to see an Airbnb reply.

But there, instead, is Jono's name and when I open his message, I see a photo that makes me gasp for breath.

There is his face, broad and happy grin in place, and on either side, against each of his cheeks is a tiny, red-faced baby.

Hello Jennifer, I have wonderful news. The babies have arrived. Meet Violet and Iris. They were 7 weeks early, but they are healthy and so beautiful. I've decided to take three months of paternity leave. Shock! To spend much more time with the girls and my boys, just as you advised. I'm so happy to hear you have new plans and life is moving on. All my very best, Jono.

I am moving on.

I do have new plans – sort of, even if they are still pretty vague and half-baked. But I still feel as if I've taken a blow to the back of the knees.

Did he have to send that photo? Jono as the perfect Daddy? With those two tiny, tiny faces.

And as for 'All my very best...'

I stare and stare at the photo and the message for a long, long time. Much longer than I should. All that time spent with him... all that time spent making plans for the future with someone who now has *two new babies*.

Someone who now wishes me *all the best*.

There are tears in my eyes, but I'm absolutely determined to see them off, so I raise my eyebrows and look up at the ceiling until the trick finally works.

I've shed far too many tears over Jono already. I will not shed one more, not a single one. And any time I spend thinking about him and his new life, is time away from thinking about me and my new life.

They look absolutely gorgeous. Congratulations to you all!

I really can't bring myself to mention his wife in this message. I mean, come on, I have to draw the line somewhere.

I wonder if she knows about me... I wonder if Jono has told all.

As I hit send, I can't help thinking that maybe this is the last time Jono and I will ever contact one another.

And with that thought, I burst into tears.

Damn.

As I mop up, my phone beeps and I tell myself, if it's Jono again, I won't even open it. But the name that comes up is Rory.

Saturday, 9 a.m. West Sands. I've got a surprise for you. Surprise! So b there or b square, as we used to say in skool. PS Dress for Scotland not Mayfair. Sensible shoes, lady!

I pick up the phone and call Rory because I think his cheerful voice is exactly what I need to hear right now.

'Hello, Jen!' he says brightly, 'how's the head? I've heard good quality Champers doesn't give a hangover, but that may be total bollocks.'

'Let's just say I needed that third cup of tea this morning.'

'But no existential angst? That seems to come hand-in-hand with the hangovers these days... according to friends. Obviously, I know nothing about this, nothing.'

And to my embarrassment, I burst into tears.

'What's the matter? Maybe it's just the existential angst kicking in... are you OK? No, obviously not. Is there anything I can do? What about a pub lunch? That usually helps everything. Or brunch with Bloody Marys? Fight fire with fire. I might be able to get away a bit early...'

'It's my ex...' I begin, 'he's had the babies. He got back together with his wife and they have had twins...' I'm blurting it out, but find that now I've started, I may as well keep going. 'And they are sooo tiny and so precious and he's the daddy...'

What on earth am I saying?

'And... why didn't he want to be with me, Rory? Was I not good enough? Was I not tiny enough? Or precious enough? And what did Sophie have that he had to go back to her for?'

'Oh boy...' Rory manages, when there is a chance to get a word in. 'Oh boy. I think a big lunch is on the cards. Why don't I see if Alison can come. Me and Alison, we'll bring you round, Jen. Don't you worry. And look, can I just make a wee suggestion here? These slick, successful, tailored-coat wearing tossers that you seem to be so intent on falling for – can I just point out that they are not working out for you. You need to rethink your entire type and concentrate on being with people who are worthy of you, worthy of your care and attention. OK... just saying... just an idea for you there.'

'Thank you, Rory,' I sniff and blow my nose noisily on a piece of kitchen roll, as that's all I can find. *Tailored-coat wearing tossers...* that's going to stick in my mind. I'm almost smiling at the thought of Rory shouting this at Jono.

Rory tells me he'll message the name of the place for lunch and see if Alison can join us.

'It's going to be OK,' he tells me. 'Honestly, you are well shot of the numbnut. Things can only get better from here on out.'

'Yeah...' I say, but right at this moment, it's hard to believe him.

22

'So, what do you think? Personally, I'm going for: uh-mazing.'

I put down the small half-pint glass and have to nod in agreement: 'It tastes so... fresh.'

'Unpasturised,' Rory informs me, 'they brew it right here on the premises. Five different types, including a non-alcoholic for me. Then on the menu, there's a beer or lager recommendation for each dish.'

'Really?' Alison picks the menu up and looks at it again, intrigued.

'Apparently, we need to think of darker, hoppier beers as red wine and light, crisp lagers like that one as...'

'White wine?' Alison adds.

'Yeah.'

I take another mouthful of the homemade pilsner. It is delicious. Creamy, fresh, not like any lager I've tasted before.

'Cheers, guys,' I say again, toasting first Alison, then Rory. 'Thank you so much for coming out and at such short notice. I feel much better. Much, much better for being here with you.'

And that's the truth. And I totally appreciate that they've had to scramble cover in the shop for Rory and someone to do the school run for Alison.

'Don't mention it,' Alison says. 'I was due a little trip into Mick's to drop off some documents and answer some more questions for the hearing... it's not long to go now.'

She makes a grimace at the thought.

'Try not to worry, if he thinks you have a case, you can be pretty confident,' I reassure her, 'he's really sound.'

'Fingers crossed,' Alison says, then turning to me, she adds, 'You will come to the hearing with me, won't you? I could really do with the moral support.'

'Of course,' I tell her, feeling flattered to be asked.

And because I don't think I've mentioned it to either of them, I add: 'Do you know that I'm officially working for Mick now – two days per week?'

This is met with hearty approval from them both.

'Good to hear it,' from Rory.

'That's fantastic,' Alison says with a smile. 'I bet his office already looks completely different from the day we walked in.'

'Oh yes,' I nod.

I look around the lovely old pub, recently made over by a friend of Rory's and sink back into my comfortable leather armchair.

'This is such a nice place. I need to bring Dad and Joan along. Would it be bad of me to say I don't remember St Andrews having such nice places when I was growing up?'

Alison and Rory exchange a look and both say: 'Yes!' together.

Alison adds: 'We've definitely gone up in the world over the past few years. Lots more wealthy golfers and tourists.'

'Yeah... I mean, this is nice,' I tell them again.

'Try not to sound so surprised,' Rory adds, 'London girl!'

There's an open fire in the corner, exposed brickwork on the walls and industrial style lighting. This is St Andrews hipster.

'We need a few more places like this, plus the town's own bowling alley and then there will be no reason to leave ever again,' Rory adds.

'Surely you like to get out now and then?'

'Well...' he loads up his fork with a mouthful of the mustardy steak he's picked, 'yes and no, I suppose. I'm a small-town boy and I can't imagine living anywhere else.'

'How about you?' I ask Alison.

She does think about it for a few moments before saying: 'Not really... I obviously need my work situation to be sorted out and don't get me wrong, every single cold and miserable February, I wish I lived in Mallorca, but when spring finally breaks out, I think it's beautiful here. And... I feel lucky to live so close to just about everyone I know.'

I let that sink in as we work our way through our delicious platefuls.

'Who's looking after the shop?' is my next question for Rory.

'For the next four hours, a very capable student called Li Wong. His dad runs nine grocery shops in Shenzhen, so he knows what he's about.'

'He sounds pretty good and what are you doing when we've finished here?'

'No plans until 4 p.m. when I have a meeting with a potential new greetings-card supplier and then it's on to pay a visit to my mum and dad.'

And maybe because the fire is cosy, the leather sofas are snug and the landlord plies us with his plum wine, we stay on for another hour, talking very comfortably. Even when Rory gets round to the 'so do you want to talk about Jono and his new twins or not really' question, it doesn't feel too unbearable, in fact, it feels as if it could be time to explain more of what has happened to my understanding friends.

'Jono and I were together for two years...' I begin carefully, 'and that's my longest relationship for quite some time.'

Alison nods gently.

'... and for much of those two years, we thought... or I thought... or maybe he let me think...' It occurs to me as I say it out loud. Could he possibly have been so calculating? 'That we had a real future together... He was separated from his wife, but I was never his official new partner. He said he wanted to wait until the children were older, the divorce was through...'

I'm aware it does sound a bit lame now. There was writing on that wall that I should have been reading.

Two whole years, I realise. All those conversations, and days spent together at work, snatching private talks together, the hours in bed, all the hopes and plans that I thought we had... all that *time*. And now there's nothing but heartache and disappointment to show for it.

Now, looking around this beautiful bar with my new-found friends beside me, I don't know if that's quite so true any more. Yes, I'm only into my third month away from the burned-out wreck of another relationship, but already, it feels as if the crash happened some time ago, in another place, to a different version of me.

I've got just a little bit of distance now, I realise, a little perspective on it all.

'I'm really sorry,' Rory says. He's leaning forward and his eyes are focused on mine. 'That sounds pretty hard going.'

'I'm absolutely furious with him on your behalf,' Alison adds.

'I thought he would choose me...' I begin, then pause wondering if I want to go on. This is so personal, so close to my heart. 'I thought he had chosen me. But then...' I can hear my voice waver.

Rory's face creases in sympathy and he puts a hand that's reassuringly warm and heavy over mine. 'I'm sorry,' he says.

And even though I've already given both Rory and Alison some inkling of all this, I feel like I have to go through it again, have to exorcise the pain some more.

'His wife got pregnant... with twins.'

'Well, there is some justice in the world then... I mean, twins – that is no parenting picnic,' is Rory's gentle attempt to cheer me up.

'Twin girls,' I add.

'Good luck, Jono,' Alison adds. She puts her arms around my shoulder and squeezes.

'And you know what's the worst thing... he didn't tell me. He didn't mention that he was back together with his wife and that she was pregnant. For quite a few months, he was with me and the wife. And I only found out when she phoned the office...' my voice has gone all teary and squeaky, 'to remind him about an antenatal appointment.'

'Oh my god, Jen, that is really horrible,' Alison says.

'So, then we had this big argument and that's when I fell and broke my kneecap.'

'Oh my god...' from Alison.

'I decided when I was in hospital ...' I go on, 'that I either had to accept being in second place in his life for good, or I had to break up with him. So, I went for the break-up.'

'That was really brave...' Rory says, giving my hand a squeeze, 'really brave of you. But it's for the best. Totally for the best.'

'Yeah... well... maybe... we'll have to see.'

My throat hurts and I sigh, realising that it has been helpful to share the full story with them both; I have been able to drag it out into the daylight and take a good look at it. And that is supposed to be the best thing to do with hard stuff – drag it out, look at it, understand it, stare it down and finally, hopefully, move on.

'It was pretty hard to see the photo he sent with the new babies this morning.'

And, on the verge of tears now, I add: 'I put my life on hold for him... I didn't think about what I wanted, I thought about what we would want in the future, when he was mine. And now, I'm alone and... don't know what I want.'

'Please try not to worry about any of it. You're such a smart girl, you'll work it all out, I just know it,' Alison tells me.

Rory tells me: 'And loads of people have to reinvent themselves because the track they were on didn't lead to where they thought it would. Look at me. I'm one of them. And some days, it's a bit rough, but sometimes it's even pretty exciting.'

Then he adds: 'You should know, by the way, that if I ever meet your ex-boyfriend, just for you, I'm going to punch him hard, several times, to try and bring him to his senses.'

This makes me laugh and I have to add: 'Yeah, one punch in the face and two to the gut, so he can feel just like I did when I found out.'

I sigh it all out and then smile at them each in turn: 'OK, that's totally enough about me. We have to talk about something else, now... how about your children... What's been happening with them this week?'

Now it's Alison and Rory's turn to sigh.

'Everyone coming home from school in one piece... that's about all I can ask for these days,' Alison says. 'Sometimes, I wish I had girls.'

'Ooooh... careful,' Rory interrupts. 'Girls are no picnic, especially in the social media era.'

'Would you like a boy?' I ask Rory. I think I meant to say 'would you have liked a boy?' but the plum wine is stronger than it tastes.

Rory leans back against the sofa, puts his hands behind his head and reveals: 'I absolutely love my girls. I'd have loved a boy too. But no more children for me, no. Three is quite enough, so I've had The Snip.'

Both Alison and I grimace at the thought.

'No, no, honestly, it was fine. Can't complain. The lady doctor was very professional.'

'Ooooh, painful *and* awkward,' Alison says.

'No, really it could have been much worse. But, for a lot of women, this is a big plus... man with his own contraception built in. I think I should probably put it on my dating profile.'

'Very funny,' I tell him.

'Now... I have news for you, Jennifer McAndrew, I may have found you a date.'

I hope my face conveys how horrified I am at even the thought of a date. How many times do I have to tell Rory that It Is Too Soon.

'No, no, no...' he insists, 'before you brush me off, let me just say the words: handsome, tall, runs his own building business... you've got to admit, that sounds worth a date, doesn't it? Even if you just want a contact for a kitchen renovation in the future.'

23

His name turns out to be Niall, the friend of a friend of Rory's who runs his own building business.

We exchange some awkward but chatty texts before I think to myself 'oh what the heck' and agree to meet for an after-work beer in a little pub just off the high street. We exchange some selfies too, so that we can recognise one another and Niall's selfie is fine, perfectly fine, but somehow as I look at this rugged Scottish bloke with dark, curly hair both on top of his head and escaping from the open buttons at the top of his shirt, I get a sinking feeling.

Nevertheless, we meet in the bar, we drink our way through two drinks, each paying a round and it is fine and friendly, but I feel... well... like I'm just going through the motions. He talks a bit, I talk a bit, we ask polite questions, we crack a few jokes. I worry quite a lot that he's thinking it's going really well, when I just want to finish this second half pint and be done with this.

'I mean... what do women go for?' he asks. 'That's what we really want to know.'

I'm tempted to answer: in no particular order, Niall, ambition, achievement, zest for living, top-notch personal grooming, proficient bedroom technique, kindness, empathy, determination, solid self-esteem, respect, wisdom, a well-cared for physique, excellent conversation skills... etc., etc.

But instead, I go with: 'Ummm... I guess humour is good.'

'Humour might be all I have,' he tells me with a grin, which is maybe meant to be self-deprecating, but I don't really want to stay and find out.

His next question catches me right off guard: 'So what are you doing on Saturday night?'

I can't think of an excuse fast enough, so get caught up in a whole unconvincing: 'Oh... Saturday... I think I promised my dad I would go with him to some... thing... oh god... I can't actually remember what it is... can I get back to you on that?'

We part soon afterwards and I text Rory with a simple:

Niall is nice, but nope, not one for me.

Don't worry!

He fires back.

I've got another lined up. Sholto is a seriously good-looking and fit tree surgeon. Don't say no, I've already arranged time and place.

Sholto?? Is that a real name?

Yes, trad Scottish. He is very hunky.

* * *

Much to Rory and my disappointment, the Sholto setup is a bust even more quickly than it was with Niall.

Sholto, not quite as a hunky as billed, in my opinion, seems shy, nervy and woefully underprepared for the rigours of blind dating.

Lulls in the conversation start to appear very early on, even during our first round of drinks. I start to wonder if there is going to be no round two and I should just put £5 down on the table and say I have to leave.

When Sholto asks, maybe in a desperate attempt to stop another conversational lull, if I've watched any good TV shows lately, my heart just sinks. I find myself looking around and thinking 'I used to be the girlfriend of a top London criminal defence barrister... now I'm here... with this guy... racking my brains for TV programmes I can talk about.'

The Saturday night question comes up again, but this time I'm prepared: 'It's so nice of you to ask me,' I say, 'but I'm going out for some cocktails with an old friend.'

Seems like a really nice guy,

I message Rory afterwards,

but can you stop arranging dates for me now?

Just, One, More...

Rory messages back.

* * *

Early evening the next day, I head for the beach after my day at Mick's before going back to Dad's. As I approach the shore, it's obvious that something is going on. There are crowds of people, mainly students, some of them wearing the traditional red St Andrews gowns, which are billowing in the wind from the sea. Some are carrying candles or flaming torches and they're all heading down towards the sands.

Of course, the *Gaudie*: the last day of April when students have a procession along the pier and throw a wreath into the water to commemorate a student who saved shipwrecked sailors from drowning.

Tonight will be a night of drunken parties and tomorrow, at first light, the hardiest students will jump into the sea to be washed of their academic sins – as tradition would have it. Or maybe, in the more modern hope, that they'll be rescued from their hangovers.

I stop and watch for a long time. Pulling my coat around me as it gets chillier and following the sun as it dips slowly, sending a line of gold along the water. There's a minute's silence, broken only by one drunken student's whoop before he's shushed into submission and I hear the little girl standing close to me ask her mother: 'Why has everyone stopped talking?'

Then with a soft splash, a wreath is thrown into the waves.

Hundreds of people are down here now; some taking it seriously, some larking around, glugging from beer and Champagne bottles. There are lovely young couples holding hands, whispering and kissing.

Just as the sunlight fades almost completely, the students begin to sing their university hymn in Latin.

The little girl tells her mother in a quiet, awed voice: 'I can't believe this is really happening. It's like in *Harry Potter*.'

I feel almost as bowled over as her. It's beautiful and moving and a little bit primeval, as if we're gathered here to make an annual sacrifice to the sea.

'Hey, Jennifer! I thought it was you.'

I turn at the sound of the familiar voice.

'Hey, Rory, how are you doing?'

'Good. Very good. I'd like you to meet Elaine,' he says and I catch the look on his face. Oooh! Elaine – Elaine of the first date that went well – this is Elaine.

'Hello, Elaine,' I smile at the woman now beside Rory and offer my hand.

I'm already loving Elaine. She is beautifully dressed in 1950s vintage. Her orangey hair is even rolled up at the front into one of those 1950s dos. She looks like a wonderful mix of Doris Day, doll and alien space lady.

'Your hair is amazing,' I tell her, but really everything is amazing; the thick eyeliner, the brows, red lips, the big black beauty spot, the fact I'm shaking a hand in a red leather glove.

'Thank you,' she says. 'Rory says you're an old school friend.'

'Yes... I've moved back to St Andrews and it's so nice to catch up with old friends again.'

Old friends – I make sure that's the plural so she doesn't think she needs to worry about me as any kind of rival for Rory's affections.

'Good to see you,' Rory says after the three of us have managed a few more minutes of small talk. 'I'll be in touch about Mr Third Time Lucky.'

I pull a face in response to this.

'Are the words Scandinavian, handsome, Economics lecturer of interest?'

'Oooooh...' I admit to a slight pique of interest, 'maybe...'

* * *

I'm hardly surprised that it's only a few hours later when he calls.

'What did you think of Elaine?' he asks straight away.

'She seemed lovely,' I tell him enthusiastically. 'Far too nice for you,' I add.

'Yes, that is what I'm thinking. What in the hell is she doing with me?'

'How did the evening go? In general...' I add quickly. 'No need for any detail. General is absolutely fine.'

'We kissed... and it was a bit weird,' he says. 'I mean the kissing itself wasn't weird, that was really quite nice. It was the fact that we were kissing. It's all been so long. I've forgotten how to do even snogging. I'm like a thirteen-year-old. I might need to practise on my hand. Like in primary school...'

'No, Rory, no details!' I cut him off. 'But... how did kissing come about?'

'We were saying goodnight and I just sort of leaned forward a little to see which way it would go. I moved slowly, I wanted to give her all the options. She could have veered for the cheek, but she went straight for the mouth. Took me by surprise, to be honest. So, we're at the full-on kissing goodbye stage. I don't know what will happen next. Well, actually I do know. I'm going to the cinema with her, but in a group. So, I'll have to wait and see.

'So about you...' he continues, 'and Scandi lecturer man. Is it a go? Will you at least meet the man? He's super nice.'

'I suppose I could,' I tell him, thinking a meeting... that could be OK. We could talk about Sweden, or Norway... or wherever he's from and there don't have to be any strings whatsoever. And at least it would be an alternative evening to G&Ts and mince-based meals with Dad and Joan – not that I'm complaining about her generous cooking.

'I suppose I could meet him... as long as you've not built me up too much,' I warn, imagining Rory giving one of his persuasive sales talks but with me as the topic.

'What do you mean built you up too much?' Rory asks. 'You are St Andrews' star catch right now – total strangers are discussing you in pubs, wondering how they can get you to pay attention to them and how on earth they can snag your phone number. As soon as you go on a dating app, you're going to be mobbed. All the single guys will SWOOP.'

'Very funny... just nothing too much... maybe a beer or two in that place we went to with Alison.'

'OK, leave it with me,' Rory says. 'Any nights in particular?'

'Friday night? Saturday night? These are usually good options.'

* * *

On Friday evening, it is my date night with the Scandinavian – Norwegian, I believe – university professor, Lars, that Rory has found for me. When I get home to Dad's, I set out a selection of snacks for him to have with his G&T and then I catch up with the day's racing news.

Dad's in a good mood, £45 up and Elvis is doing the 'Jailhouse Rock' from the stereo. When I tell him I'm not joining him for supper tonight because I'm going out for dinner, he looks at me in amazement.

'Really? Is it a date?' he asks.

'Yes.'

'Someone you've met before?'

'Nope.'

'Well best of luck to you, but if he's any trouble, you just run straight back here.'

The dad-like protectiveness of this makes me smile.

'I will. So how's Joan?' I ask, wanting to duck any further interrogation.

'Oh, she's fine; said she'd be later tonight because she's visiting her daughter or something.'

'Why don't you make her dinner for a change? I've got a shop-bought lasagne in the fridge, if you stick it in the oven, you can both eat that and she can take a night off.'

I expect him to protest, to say something like: 'Oh, no, she'll be fine, she'll want to do it,' but he surprises me with a simple: 'That's a good idea.'

'Maybe you should buy her flowers too once in a while.'

He turns away from the latest horse data on his screen and says: 'Oh, but I do,' and then gives me a wink. And I'm reluctantly dragged back to wondering what my dad and Joan's relationship involves.

'Good, glad to hear it,' I say. 'I won't be late. I'll be back before 10 p.m. probably and we can watch some TV together.'

'That will suit me fine, my dear,' Dad smiles at me. 'I like having you around, you know.' He squeezes my hand.

'Thank you, it's nice to be around.'

And this is true; it is nice to hang out with my old dad again. It is really, truly nice. Even though being here means I don't have a place of my own. And I'm not even close to deciding what I want to do yet. And despite the rekindled friendships and the part-time day job, I am still waking up every morning inside a room that looks like a hotel loo and asking myself *what next? Where to now?*

I head to my swirly pastel-blue bedroom and change from my work clothes into a satin skirt and a just ever so slightly dressy, silky top because for some reason, known only to Rory, I am not blind-dating in the low-key place but going out for proper, swanky dinner. I add a stroke or two of eyeliner, lipstick, a touch of perfume, mess about with my hair – my hair, which is growing longer by the minute and I am going to have to bite the bullet and find a new hairdresser in St Andrews. I see that it's already 6.30 p.m., so I dither

for a few moments about which shoes. Then hurry out of the house
and into my pre-arranged taxi in a pair of low-heeled slingbacks
which I'm hoping are striking the right 'I've made a little effort, but
not too much' note.

Oh my god... here I go. First actual, proper dinner date in...
almost three years.

24

It's a funny thing because the McIver is a wonderful, stately place, a *grande dame* of a hotel, but as soon as I walk in, me in my London silky skirt-and-heels finery, hair done and war paint, my heart just seems to sink, and I instantly regret the choice of this stuffy, formal venue.

I wish Rory had made sure the Norwegian and I were meeting in the hipster brewery with the roaring fire and the steak sandwiches. Or, I wish we'd just arranged cocktails at the swanky bar – like the evening with Alison and *Sir Gay* – or even fish 'n' chips on the beach, not dinner. Because... because... this feels formal, and stuffy, tense even and not a whole amount of fun.

I haven't worn high heels for so long that my toes feel cramped and squashed, my Achilles and even my hip joints are already aching. The silky skirt feels tight and scratchy and I'd forgotten until now that this top slips down, giving greater cleavage reveal than I intended.

But there at the bar, perched on a stool is the tall, slim man with curly blonde hair who I'm sure is Professor Lars Pedersen and as he already has a drink in front of him, and I don't feel I can arrive with the words: 'Hi, Lars, let's just skip this and go somewhere more relaxed,' because we're all booked in and dressed up and we've taxied over here.

So, instead, I go up to him and introduce myself. He orders me a drink and we make a start on all those introductory questions. What do you do? How long have you been in town?

And meanwhile, I am going through the first date thoughts: well, he's undoubtedly attractive... he's very slim, must do a lot of exercise, or worrying, or maybe he doesn't eat much... if he only likes skinny women, I'm not going to be right for him. Maybe he would try and put me on an exercise programme. He appears to be on his second cocktail. He's Norwegian... I don't know any other Norwegians well. Aren't Norwegians famous for being fond of a drink...? To be fair, they have to suffer a long, dark winter, like the Scots.

And after the first 20 minutes or so has gone by, I have to admit, we seem to be getting on OK, so we go on with the plan and are escorted to our table, tucked into our napkins like big babies, and we look through the menu and choose complex, tiny starters with gigantic prices.

Then we get stuck into the scarily priced wine and I think both of us are trying to relax and enjoy ourselves. I really do give it my best shot. And I also think that Lars is making quite a good show of liking it, but beneath the surface, I can't be sure. But then, he seems reserved and I wonder how well anyone would have to know him before they could really be sure what was going on beneath the surface?

When our fish main courses arrive, they look delicious, and I think I'm almost starting to loosen up. Certainly, a full bottle of wine has disappeared between the two of us and now Lars is ordering a second.

We eat fish, chat and he drinks glass after glass of wine with something approaching determined concentration.

'Steady on,' I tell him when the second wine bottle is drained and he's suggesting a third, 'I may have to rob a bank if we're going to drink a third bottle at these prices.'

'Oh... yes, you are probably right,' comes the reply.

'OK, Lars, time for more questions,' I say and then realise I sound like a game-show contestant... oh dear god, it's been too long since I've done this. 'So, what are the top three things you miss the most about Norway?' I ask.

'Oh, good question.' He gives it some thought for a few moments before answering: 'Number one, my parents, who are very nice by the way. Norwegian parents are much more involved and able to talk about things than British parents. I think.'

'Hmmm,' is all the answer I make as I try to imagine Lars enjoying a really good talk about things with anyone. He just doesn't seem the type... he seems incredibly reserved.

'Number two,' he goes on, 'the snow in the winter, which is deep and dry, not like the small, wet snow here, and finally...' he pauses, looks at me and for a moment, I'm convinced he's going to say something like 'the beautiful blonde women', but instead he says, 'salty liquorice.'

'What?!' I pull a face. 'Salty liquorice? Isn't liquorice bad enough without making it salty?'

'Have you tried it?'

'No.'

'Well... what is the expression? Don't knock it until you have tried it.'

'And you can't get it in Scotland?'

'No.'

'Or on the internet?'

'Well... if I'm desperate, yes, but it's very expensive. And I think it tastes better in Norway. You will have to make a visit to Norway and try it for yourself.'

'I suppose so.'

So, then there is dessert – a heavenly concoction of chocolate, tangy berries and cream – plus dessert wine. Only when the dessert wine bottle is drained and our heads are swimming, does Lars utter the words: 'Jennifer, I've told you all about my work and why I'm in Scotland and lots of light, conversational things... and you are very entertaining...'

He looks into my eyes and slips his hand over mine.

Wow, I think. He's pretty handsome when he does the deep and meaningful look.

'But there are some very important things I haven't mentioned.'

Uh-oh, is my first thought. What is coming now?

'Oh...' is the response I manage, and I also briefly slip my hand over his.

Going by the serious expression on his face, this does look like a big important thing, and I can feel my breath catch in my throat and hold. Why is he doing this here? Because only now has he had enough to drink?

'I have a son, Gregor, who is seven...'

'Right... well... no reason not to mention that earlier...' I say, but the freewheeling professor image is beginning to clutter up a little. If he has a son, there's obviously a mother for said son somewhere in his life.

'I have a wife...' he begins.

My 'Oh!' is much sharper this time and I extract my hand from under his.

'No, not like that,' Lars protests, 'not waiting for me at home while I say I'm at a business meeting.' He gives a harsh laugh and shakes his head. But that comment is too close to the bone for me.

'We've been separated for a year... she has depression and she's gone back to Oslo. Gregor lives with me in Scotland.'

As I pause, not sure what to say to this new information, he adds: 'We will get divorced, but just now, she's concentrating on getting better. And meanwhile... well, I find myself very lonely sometimes.'

Well, that is certainly all very complicated.

He seems like a very nice man, very serious... a professor, learned, thoughtful, father to a young boy. Part of me thinks it's interesting and there's definitely some level of attraction between us and maybe I could see myself getting involved...

But hang on, backing up there... haven't I just extricated myself from a man with a 'separated' wife and family situation? Do I really want to risk putting myself through anything like all that again?

I'm feeling a little bowled over by his revelations and by his handsome face. Those clear blue eyes seem to at once drill into me and yet give away so little. What does he want from me? Does he want anything at all?

'Well... I do like you,' I blurt out. The wine has made it easier to say this, along with the fact that he looks movie star handsome in the candlelight and my leg has been resting against his under the table for some time and he's done nothing to move away.

He puts his hand over mine again: 'I like you too. But it doesn't seem fair to start anything when I have all this going on.'

Our eyes are locked on one another's and I find myself leaning forward, as he does too. I think there is quite a strong possibility that I'm going to be kissing that very handsome face over our empty dessert plates and drained glasses of dessert wine.

But before our lips are within any kind of touching distance, there's a flare of light, a pungent smell and I realise I've dangled my poker-straightened hair over the table's central tealights for far too long. Lars snatches up his glass and throws a generous amount of water at my head. It lands with a cold slap on my face that makes me gasp. I bury my face in my napkin then sensing the embarrassing commotion start up around our table, I bolt to the loos to repair some of the damage.

* * *

I'm in the ladies, drying my face and my hair with tissues and repairing my make-up when I realise how many cocktails and glasses of wine I've consumed. I actually have to sit down on the little chair and steady myself.

He's still married with a small son. He might move back to Oslo at the drop of a hat. You don't need this, I tell myself. I haven't even kissed him properly. I need to take everything one step at a time.

But it's no use. My drunken imagination runs away with me. I'm already picturing drinking morning coffee with Lars from a white mug at a pale wooden table in a beautiful, pared down, Scandinavian-chic apartment, with a sea view. Wait, is Oslo on the sea? I don't even know. I have some serious googling ahead of me.

I look at myself in the mirror. I'm wine-flushed with frazzled hair on one side. Good grief I look about as mad as I feel. Right, we need to wrap this dinner up and get out of here. I need to sober up before I do anything else.

My phone in my dinky little London clutch bag buzzes. I take it out to see a message from Rory:

Hope you enjoying your date. Come have fish n chips with me tomorrow and we can swap notes.

I am almost sober enough to type back.

Will be there

' · ·

Amazeballs

This reply makes me laugh.

When I get back into the dining room, two surprising things have happened. The waiter comes over to tell me that 'Sir has decided it would be best to practise his singing on the terrace outside.'

What?!' How did I manage to miss Lars singing?

And when I get out to the terrace, hoping for an encore, I find my wine-fuelled Norwegian singer fast asleep in one of the chairs.

The waiter doesn't hesitate to present me with the enormous bill.

By the time our taxi arrives, it takes a huge amount of effort to get Lars up on his feet and into the back of the car and get his address out of him – fortunately not far from my dad's house. The taxi driver gives me words of sympathetic encouragement as I pay the fare, on top of the restaurant bill, and then try to manoeuvre Lars out of the cab and to his front door.

I have to frisk him for his keys as the babysitter appears to have locked us out and isn't responding to the doorbell.

'You are so naughty,' he laughs as I locate the keys in his trouser pocket.

'No really, just trying to get the keys,' I assure him.

The babysitter also needs to be paid, but this time, I get cash out of Lars' wallet and hand it over. Then I make him drink a glass of water before leading him up to his bed, at his insistence.

'Just help me up the stairs,' he slurs.

In the bedroom, I do just some of the things it might be quite nice to be doing to him if he was a lot more sober: I remove his jacket and shoes, undo some of the buttons on his shirt. I decide taking off his trousers is a bit weird under the circumstances, so I leave them on.

He makes a clumsy attempt to hug me and I take the chance to plant a kiss on his cheek, which is smooth and still clean smelling, despite all the booze. He must have had one or two post-dinner whiskies or brandies, while I was in the loo, to be in such bad shape. Maybe this is his first date in a long time. Maybe he needed the alcohol to see himself through it and has misjudged horribly.

Whatever the reason, it's a bit sad for this to be the end of the evening. I wanted someone to wine and dine and charm me. I didn't want to be looking after a guy too steaming to find his own way home. I spend a few moments worrying about what kind of people are left on the dating scene, as Lars collapses back onto the bed and pats the space beside for me to lie down beside him. Briefly I do, leaning back on his pillows, feeling his hair brush my face as he drifts into sleep.

'You're very nice,' he murmurs before falling asleep.

I wait for a while, listening to him breathe, making sure he's not going to be sick. Then I sit up and know that it's time for me to get out of here.

25

'So the Elaine situation? Is it still going well? Still kissing?'

Rory and I are perched on a harbour wall eating some quite sensational fish and chips because he, of course, knows not just where the best place to go is but also when the best time is because the oil has just been changed and the new delivery of fish has just arrived.

'I think it's going OK,' he says. 'There has been talking and driving, a little bit of wine drinking, on her part, and some more hello and goodbye kissing. She seems to be having a good look before she leaps.'

'Well... that's probably a good thing. At our age... I take it she is our age.'

'Four years younger. Four kids of her own. That's a lot of children between us. That is seven children – five of them under ten. For that reason alone, we should probably call a halt to this right now.'

'Wow.'

'We'd be running a crèche. In fact, are two adults allowed to be in charge of seven children? There are probably rules. We definitely wouldn't be able to take them swimming. Anyway... this fish is—'

'—To die for. Best ever...' I agree.

'So, Elaine and I went back to my place after our date yesterday...'

'I'm pretty sure I don't want to know about this.'

'No, but I have to tell you,' he says, leaning forward, 'things were getting pretty heated on the sofa, but where does she get that underwear? Is it genuine fifties vintage? I mean we are talking conical bras, *conical*?' he waves his hands. 'I'd need a structural engineering degree to undo them.'

'Rory!' I warn him, 'I don't need to know.'

'But I like telling you,' he admits, 'it makes it a bit less mad and random. I mean what am I actually doing with this woman? She dresses like she lives in a comic, but she certainly doesn't find much funny. Is it going anywhere? Should it be going anywhere? I don't know. And the seven children. I must not forget about the seven children situation... really, I should probably wake right up and smell the discounted, but branded, coffee.

'How about you?' he asks. 'I want to hear all about dinner with the Scandinavian.'

'Well...' I'm a little tempted to tell him that Lars with his bouncy blonde hair and grey-blue eyes had quite the affect on my heart rate, but instead, I keep it cool and say: 'I actually really liked my Scandi date, but there are a lot of problems...'

'Such as?'

'He drank so much, I had to take him home and put him to bed... and not in an at all sexy way.'

Rory's eyes widen: 'Uh-oh.'

'Throw in a small son... and the fact he is separated from his no-doubt lovely wife who is currently living in Oslo...'

'Double, triple uh-oh...' is Rory's take. 'And why the bloody hell did he tell me nothing about this when I set you guys up?'

'Did you ask?' I wonder.

Rory has the decency to at least look a little guilty.

'Yeah... that's what I thought,' I add, 'but I did really like him.'

'*Like* like?' Rory asks, before slotting a particularly fat chip into his mouth.

'I'll keep you posted.'

'Hmmm... that sounds quite like a yes,' he adds.

'I bought some cross-country running shoes,' is the next thing I tell him because... I don't know... the nights are so much lighter now and I find I don't want to just slump on the sofa, I want to be out... getting back into the good habits I used to have.

'Take my advice and put those shoes on and run about three miles away from that guy and his complicated emotional situation,' Rory suggests.

'Probably good advice... I might even crack and get myself a running anorak.'

'You're ditching all that fake London stuff and reverting to your true self.'

This comment jars with me: 'No, I'm not,' I say. 'Why can't my "true self" continue to be stylish? There are ways of being practical *and* stylish, you know.'

'Yes, but you were always down-to-earth, a natural, outdoorsy person. You just thought you wanted to be a big-city princess. But I don't think it was really you.'

I'm not sure if I want to be told what I'm really like by Rory. Aren't we supposed to be changing all the time? Evolving? Becoming the people we would like to be... if we're lucky?

When I think back to my school self, or my first-year-at-university self, I'm not sure what I was really like back then, other than idealistic and... just young. Yes, I probably was quite a small-town girl then, and I didn't wear clothes that were smart or expensive because I didn't have much money; I could hardly have afforded most of the things I might have wanted. But mainly when I look back, I think what a lot of time I wasted, hanging out with friends and reading ten thousand magazines, so busy imagining how my future self was going to live, I didn't work out how to achieve the dream.

'People do change,' I tell Rory. 'People probably want to do different things than they did when they were eighteen or twenty. People might like to wear high heels and label-ly clothes and live a more glamorous life than the one they grew up in.'

'Hmmm... I don't know,' he chews vigorously before adding, 'there are some people who are just more naturally princess-y than others. You have to be true to your real self.'

'So who is more naturally princess-y then?' I challenge him, tearing off a corner of the crispy fish, putting it into my mouth, convinced there has never been a more heavenly mouthful of fish, crunchy batter, grease, salt and vinegar.

'Well take your sister, Isla; she was always princess-y. She had that dainty look about her and that kind of very precise hair. She was so contained and neat and just... what's the word? Measured. You're not that kind of person at all. You're taller and stronger and have dark hair and a big laugh...'

I think Rory means for these words to be a compliment, but all kinds of upsets and anxieties are rearing up in me. I don't want him to talk about Isla; I certainly don't want him to compare me to Isla. I definitely do not want to listen to Isla's qualities versus mine.

'Whoa, Rory...' I warn him, 'comparing siblings, no matter what you mean by it, is a dangerous game.'

'Sorry,' he says, so he must register the annoyance on my face.

'Look, I know the whole of St Andrews wanted to paint me, Richard and Isla as a "love triangle" but it wasn't like that. Yes, Richard was my boyfriend first and he was quite important to me and he ended it, which was upsetting. Them getting together quite some time later was also upsetting. But...'

I pause because it's hard to explain.

'We could have got over all of this if we'd tried harder. But her getting married and being in St Andrews, me being single and in London, then her having children and...'

It is hard to explain where exactly everything went so wrong and got so snarled up that we're now in a situation where we blame each other for my mother's death and can barely exchange civil sentences with one another.

'There were so many differences and our parents would weigh in, take sides, just somehow make everything worse. It's hard to know how it's going to get better from here – but please know, and spread the word, that it's not because I'm still in love with my sister's husband.'

'Gotcha,' Rory says. 'The only way to deflect local gossip though is to do something else for everyone to talk about.'

I sigh with exasperation because I'm not sure that's even true.

'Honestly, I don't think it would matter if I won the Nobel freaking Prize or went into bloody space, someone in St Andrews would still say: "Isn't she the girl whose sister married her boyfriend?"'

This makes Rory laugh.

'What about this trip to South America then? Maybe that's what you need to do to shut everyone up,' he suggests.

'Yeah... what about that trip to South America?' I say and I can feel my heart jump at the thought. I've had the confirmation. They are willing to have me over provided I commit to a minimum of three months. I... just... need... to book a flight... and then I can go.

A flight to Argentina.

Three months.

I'm brave enough. I'm definitely brave enough.

26

I walk quickly all the way back to Dad's house. When I get in, only the hall light is on, the sitting room empty. I try to remember which of Dad's 'nights' it is tonight: bridge night, the floodlit driving range...

I head upstairs, wanting to go back into my sister's bedroom to see if there's any more evidence there of what we've really fallen out about and if there's any chance we can make it up in the future. Because isn't that what I would really like? Wouldn't it be much nicer to be able to come to St Andrews as Auntie Jennifer to Jessie and her brother? Imagine a big family get-together with Dad, Isla, Richard, their children and me... wouldn't that be a nice thing to do?

Maybe as Dad says, Isla and I just need to sit down together and somehow talk it all over, come to an understanding of how we got to where we are and how we can get over it. I have the thought that maybe I should at least read one or two of the letters that I didn't even open. I know they're not the recent lost ones that were sent to the wrong London address, but maybe even looking back to how she felt in those raw months after Mum's death would help me now, in a way that it didn't help back then.

I open her door, switch on the light and take in her room with its white walls and pale-blue curtains. This time I look at the room properly, not just the stacks of boxes. The small double bed is made up with a pale lemon duvet cover and pillows. There's a bedside table with an artificial rose in a vase; a tasteful framed picture on the wall. She always had taste and a restrained but flawless sense of style. Princess-y, just like Rory said – even if I didn't want to hear it. The kind of person who could carry off a velvet headband and a tailored coat that buttoned all the way up; the kind of person who ate hamburgers with a knife and fork and made tea in a china pot with real tea leaves and none of it seemed affected, it all seemed just exactly right when she did it. The person that, no matter how we feel about one another now, I once loved very dearly.

I open a drawer on the bedside table and see more envelopes, these ones opened, with my name on the front. Like many of her letters, I've taken a quick read and then put them back here, to make sure she knew I was rejecting them, because she was sure to come up here and check on her old room, now and then.

Now I pull this top one out of the drawer, out of its envelope, open it up, admire the flawlessly neat handwriting and begin to read.

Dearest Jennifer,

I hope you are very well and I hope you don't mind me writing to you again. I'm not sure where to begin, but the most important thing I want to say to you is sorry. I've asked for your forgiveness before and I've decided I'm going to go on asking because I go on hoping that there is some way you can find to forgive me. I shouldn't have said any of the things I did to Mum and I shouldn't have blamed you for what happened afterwards.

I didn't mean for any of this to happen. I hope you can at least believe that. And, of course, I wish every day that things had gone completely differently.

But, dear Jennifer, I miss you very much. My little girl, Jessie, is four now and Pete is one and they are lovely siblings together, just like we were. They have their little fights and disagreements, just like we did, and then they hug and make up and are close again. Just like we were.

They miss having you as an auntie too. They would enjoy your company so much and I know you could be a lovely auntie for them.

I hear from Dad that you're happy – enjoying London, work and apparently there is a new man in your life. I hope all is going very well, because that is what you deserve. So, if you can ever find it in your heart to forgive me, to forgive what happened between us, then I'm right here, waiting to be friends with you again.

I miss you very much and hope some day we can all be part of the same happy family.

So much love,

Isla

I sit down on the bed and read the letter over again. I'm not surprised to feel a tear slipping down my cheek because it's much nicer and sadder than I expected. Were the past letters like this? The ones I opened and read? Could I really have been so upset and angry before that I read these letters and misunderstood the words? Didn't hear the tone? Didn't feel the emotion?

Or maybe the letters were different before. Maybe Isla has changed her mind over the time since Mum's death.

So, what do I do now? I can't very well turn up on her doorstep and announce, I've just read a letter you sent years ago and you were right, we should make up and be friends. Look how she treated me last time. I think of the SUV on the kerb tooting to bring Jessie running out to avoid me.

But maybe that's all my fault.

Has Dad even told her that I didn't receive the more recent letters?

I'm too tired to think about any of it any more. I put the letter back in its envelope, close the drawer, turn out the light and go to my room.

That question – 'what do I do now?' comes back. What do I do about Isla, about finding new work, about dating, or not dating? So many questions, so many different directions I could go in.

And the temptation to just slip away from it all comes up... as it has done before. Board a flight to Argentina, I think. Look forward, not back. Enter a whole different world where no one knows about Richard and Isla, or our late mother, or Jono and his twins, and the fact that he was my boss... not to mention my other failed relationships. Yes, getting away from everything and starting over sounds very tempting.

27

'So what is this favour that you need from me?' I ask Rory, several days later, as I eat an apricot Danish, still warm, from a plush paper napkin in his shop.

'First of all, I want a full critique on the pastry. I'm trialling three new suppliers and your opinion, as a sophisticated woman of the world, is important to me.'

'The Danish is absolutely awesome,' I admit, 'crispy, but soft, flaky, buttery, the right side of tartly sweet.'

'You sound like Paul Hollywood.'

'You look like Paul Hollywood,' I fire back.

'Whoa,' he reels back. 'There's no grizzled white beard to see here. But if you're talking about the imposing, muscular girth, that's how we alpha males like to carry our power around the jungle.'

He bunches up his arms to demonstrate.

'Fine. Well, keep a note of your thoughts and come in next Saturday when we'll try different buns.' Rory says.

'So how are you?' I ask. 'Still making progress on the dating front?'

'Nooooo...' he shakes his head.

There's brief interlude while he serves a customer who comes in for a paper and then goes out with a paper, a Danish, of course, plus a twelve-pack of crisps, which are, needless to say, on at an amazing price and an enormous box of washing powder, which is on at a once-in-a-lifetime price, apparently.

'I may have to put a stop to the Elaine thing,' Rory admits.

'Why?' I ask.

'Irreconcilable differences,' he replies.

'Such as?'

'She just doesn't laugh at any of my jokes. I mean I'm trying to put up with it because of her...' his voice drops, 'amazing boobs. I mean, those really are some world class nunga nungas.'

'Stop it!'

'Sorry, you're right. You're right. I'm objectifying a very lovely lady. But, I've tried different jokes, and she is still not laughing. Not even cracking a smile. I think it could be a sign. I mean not even my favourite Buddhist joke about vacuuming without attachments...'

'What?!' I'm genuinely surprised. 'Give her a little more time, Rory,' I say. 'Then if it's still not great, there are plenty more fish in the sea'.

'Nope. Not really. Did it ever occur to you that because St Andrews is on the coast, we have half the radius of population to choose from. I mean, it must make a difference.'

'But people flock to St Andrews.'

'Yeah, well, I'm way past chatting up students, and not nearly old enough to chat up American tourists. So anyway, moving on to my favour, which you're going to do in return for a week's supply of Danishes.'

'Aha...'

'Samantha needs a new outfit for the school prom. A perfect outfit. An impossible outfit. It's a hideous problem, it's been going on for weeks. I can't help her. Her mother definitely can't help her;

they've already had two flaming rows in two different dress shops. And apparently, her friends aren't any use either. Sam's having a total nervous breakdown and the dance is next Thursday. So, I thought... maybe... you could... as a woman of the big city, a woman of sophistication and glamour—?' he smiles very sweetly at me.

'Rory, that's very nice of you to ask, but I've only met Samantha once.'

'Well, that might be a good thing,' he insists. 'You'd sort of be like the dress UN, a neutral force. A dress peacemaker. Anyway, I've asked her about shopping with you and she said she would be happy to give it a try.'

'Really? That's... sporting... and very nice of her. I'm flattered. So when does she want to do this?'

'Is there any chance you might have a bit of time on Saturday?'

'Yes and I'm sure it will be fun but, man, there really is no such thing as a free Danish in here, is there?'

* * *

On Saturday, I meet Samantha in a little café off the high street, buy her a Diet Coke and sit down with her because I feel I need to do a little research before we venture out there into the shopping jungle. We've only spoken once before and despite the punky green-tipped hair and the many earrings, I suspect she is quite shy and I'd like to try and put her at ease a little. I feel slightly daunted by the task I've taken on and hope I can get it right.

'So, first of all, are you sure you don't mind shopping with me?' I ask. 'Because this may just be a mad idea your dad has had and maybe you'd prefer to go it alone.'

'No, I don't mind,' she says. 'I've tried with Mum. I've tried with my friends and I've tried on my own. Nothing has worked.'

'So... what really didn't work and what kind of maybe worked?' I ask, wondering if I can play some sort of shopping-detective role.

Sam plays with her Coke straws with glitter-coated nails carefully painted alternate shades of dark-blue and dark-green. Her emerald-green hair is growing out. It's just below her shoulders now, with about three inches of her true brunette shade growing in. She is dressed entirely in shades of black and grey – I make a mental note of this. Something about the width of her face, her high cheekbones and small nose reminds me of Rory as a teenager, but I suspect she looks more like her mother.

Is she pretty? Of course she's pretty. She's fifteen and every fifteen-year-old is fresh-faced and in the full bloom of pretty.

'My mum made me try on pink, glittery ballgowns that were disgusting!' she protests. 'My friends liked all the black, slinky numbers with slits that were totally slutty and made me look huge... and...' she breaks off to sigh with exasperation. 'I just can't find one single thing that I even remotely like.'

I smile with complete understanding because truly, we've all been there.

'Do you want to go to this dance?' I ask, wondering if this is the cause of the problem.

'Yes... no... sort of.' Hair fiddle, look away, sigh. 'I don't know.'

We've all been there too. You want to go... but you'd like a different version of yourself to show up.

'When you imagine yourself at the dance, what do you look like?'

For a few moments, this question seems to stump her. But finally, very shyly, she looks down at her nails and mumbles: 'I look really punky and cool.'

'OK... any further clues?'

'I don't like stupid girlie shoes. I want to be able to dance, jump, even run.'

'What do you like?'

'Dr Marten boots. Black. Fishnet tights. And lots and lots of eyeliner.'

I am picturing a line-up of punky princess icons and I suddenly realise that maybe this task could be easier than it seems.

'OK, Samantha, take a look at these pictures. How do you like any of these ladies?' I bring out my phone and search images of Debbie Harry in Blondie, Madonna in full eighties garb, Cyndi Lauper and Courtney Love. I loved them all when I was younger, but I never had the nerve to dress like any of them.

'Oh wow!' she whispers, scrolling through the pics, with wide eyes and an astonished expression. 'Yes! This is how I want to look, but Mum and Dad would freak.'

'Well, it's your dance. It's your look. As long as you're happy, I don't think they're going to mind too much.'

'But won't they say it's slutty?'

I enlarge a picture of Debbie Harry dressed to thrill. 'I don't think she looks slutty. I think she looks creative and punky and strong. Pretty cool actually.'

Samantha takes my phone and looks at the picture carefully. 'So what do I have to do to look like her?'

'We'll need a dark-coloured ball dress, preferably cheap and short. And if it isn't short, we just hack off some layers.'

'Really?'

'Yes, of course. Rough and uneven round the edges is best. Then do you have Dr Marten boots?'

'Yeah.'

'How many holes?'

'Fourteen.'

'Well that's going to be perfect.'

Samantha starts to giggle.

'Then it's fishnet tights, maybe some long, black lace gloves. And let's look at the make-up and accessorising.'

We enlarge a few more pics and scour for tips.

'Black cross earrings,' Samantha says, 'black eyeliner, red lipstick.'

'If we can get a fake fur or leopard print jacket or stole that would be awesome,' I add. 'You're going to need a tonne of hairspray and backcombing.'

'Maybe go totally blonde,' Samantha suggests.

Inside I'm screeching: *Nooooooo*. But I sense that may just spur her on, so instead, I shrug and say: 'Meh, so harsh on the hair. What about some blonde highlights? Or get a can of that spray paint for hair. Go totally green?'

'Wow! You really think this is going to work?'

'Of course. Easy. What is your budget?'

'£120.'

'We won't need all that, especially as you already have the shoes. Right, finish your drink. It's time to go shopping.'

* * *

Even though St Andrews high street can be walked both up and down in about fifteen minutes, there are plenty of the kind of shops we need. Plus, there are side streets with charity shops and vintage shops and little designer boutiques.

Because we are on mission, with our desired look in our heads, it takes us only two hours to round everything up.

There's a charcoal-grey ballgown in a charity shop for £35 that fits well and it turns out Samantha's soft white arms and shoulders look dreamy in a ballgown. I assure her that once 15 inches has been hacked off the hem, it will look just the way she wants it to.

A beaded handbag comes with us from the same shop. In a high street chain shop we find fishnet tights with sparkly thread woven through them. There are also punky spiked bracelets and gothic earrings in the accessories section. We decide to blow £60 on a pale-green fake fur jacket from a little boutique because Samantha is in love with it and assures me she'll wear it every day for the rest of her life and will find spray paint so that her hair matches exactly.

* * *

Then we are done and a little exhausted, so we have to stop in a coffee shop, me to mainline a flat white, her to eat a millionaire's shortbread.

When we're all settled at our table, I ask what she's planning to do when she finishes school.

'It depends on my exam results.'

'What do you want to do?'

'I want to be a nurse.'

I'm genuinely impressed. I didn't expect this from the uncertain princess of punk.

'That's a very special career,' I tell her, 'not many people are cut out for that life. Only very giving people. What grades do you need?'

She tells me and says she hopes to manage them and get herself into training in Dundee.

'Is there a backup plan, just in case?'

'I'll do re-sits. I didn't work as hard as I could have this year,' she admits. 'If I have to do re-sits, I'll give it much more attention and make sure I get the grades.'

'That's very impressive. Your mum and dad must be very proud of you,' I say and realise how much I'm enjoying our chat. Samantha is so much nicer than I expected and more open and sensitive than I would have guessed.

I also remember how important it was at that age to have an older friend who wasn't your mum... and I surprise myself by thinking how cool it would be to be that person.

She acknowledges my compliment with a shy nod and then asks me: 'What was your end-of-school dance like? Do you remember much about it?'

I laugh at the question, then delve back in my memory to see what I can come up with.

'I remember wearing a strapless ballgown,' I tell her, 'and totally regretting it, because all night long, I thought it was going to fall down. It didn't fit nearly as well as your one does... I remember someone tipping a bottle of vodka into the fruit punch, but it didn't taste any different or even seem to make anyone drunk, because the punchbowl was so big and we were all so excited and high on the event anyway.'

Of course I remember who I went with, handsome Euan, and I remember snogging him for what felt like about three hours in the room with all the lockers, but I don't share that memory with Samantha. That was my first real experience of the wonders of snogging and those hours are still up there in the happiest hours of my life chart.

'What about my dad?' Samantha asks. 'Do you remember much about him at the dance?'

'Yes, of course!' There can be no forgetting Rory at the party.

'Your dad was the guy who got the DJ to play all the best songs and I remember your dad dancing right in the centre of the room, singing along, jumping and waving his hands in the air. He may, in fact, have slightly ripped the back of his trousers. Your dad is the man at a party,' I tell her, laughing at the memory.

'OMG,' she says. 'He was like that at seventeen too?'

'Yeah, we're all quite well formed at seventeen. We don't change too much from who we are at that age.'

'Dad told me he wanted to go to the dance with you, but you already had a partner.'

Now that Samantha's reminded me, yes, I realise that I do remember an awkward conversation on the school stairs about this. Back then, my impression was that Rory was just a good friend, who didn't mind at all that I had a new brand-new boyfriend. In fact, he seemed really pleased for me. And I thought he'd asked me to the dance just because he didn't want me to be stuck without a date.

'Did he mind?'

I realise I've asked this out loud.

'Yeah... he really minded. He said he had a huge crush on you at school. He would always be on the verge of asking you out, but then someone would always get there before him.'

'Oh...' I'm genuinely surprised and I feel a bit embarrassed too. 'I didn't know that. It must have been a temporary crush though. Because I've always thought of him as a good friend and we get on really well as friends still.'

'Sounds like you've had a lot of boyfriends,' Samantha says and shoots me a grin.

'I suppose I have...' A lot of damn disappointments too. I've had so many break-ups, I should probably be much more cynical and wary. But... then there are those times when I can still feel hopeful and maybe even a little desperate for it to be my turn. Why shouldn't it finally be my turn to be with the right person and for everything to finally turn out right for a change?

'Who was the best-dressed girl at your end-of-school dance?' Samantha asks.

And so our conversation moves on. But at the back of my mind, I hope I didn't hurt Rory's feelings back then when he was a schoolboy with a temporary crush.

28

The date has been on the calendar for a few weeks now and finally, it's the day of Alison's mediation session with McWhirter and Sons.

I've arranged to pick up my nervy friend and give her a lift so we can once again go over the points Mick's going to make on her behalf in the meeting. I'm hoping this will calm her down.

When I get to Alison's house, I find Wattie in the kitchen directing a very noisy breakfast and he tells me Alison wants me upstairs. I find her at the top of the stairs, waiting for me and still in her dressing gown.

'Hello... time to get set,' I say, a little surprised that she's not dressed yet. We don't have acres of time before the 9.30 a.m. appointment.

She waves her arms frantically: 'I can't, I can't!' she says.

'What do you mean you can't? Nervous? Don't be – we're here with you. Wardrobe crisis? Let me help.'

'Well, yes that, always. But, it's this brush!'

She points to her head and that's when I see the handle of a hairbrush emerging from the back of her neck.

'It's completely stuck in my hair!'

'Turn around, Ali, and let me take a look.'

Having assessed the whole hair-entangled-round-brush situation, I take hold of the handle and try to give the round bristle
brush a turn, but this just makes Alison yelp. It's wedged absolutely
firmly in the hair at the nape of her neck.

'What happened?' I ask.

'Oh, the *bloody* hairdresser,' she complains. 'He couldn't believe
I was still drying my hair on some old brush without bristles all the
way round so he made me buy this. Of course I had to try it for the
first time today, when I want to look half presentable and together
and *this* is what happens!'

I see the threat of tears in her eyes and put my hands on her
shoulders, as if I can literally hold her together.

'Look, you get dressed,' I tell her, 'and I'll google the brush
situation.'

'You'll google it and how will that help?'

'Someone, somewhere on the internet will know.'

'And I haven't made a final decision on what to wear.'

'Just some ordinary work clothes, Alison. Ones you're comfortable in.'

'That rules out pretty well everything then.'

She sounds on the verge of panic.

'Calm, Alison, calm. Come on, I'll help you with that too.'

I follow her into a charming bedroom with old-fashioned flow-
ered wallpaper, an antique four-poster bed, and a bay window with
a view of the fields in the bright morning sunshine. The bedroom is
unexpectedly neat, clean and tidy, compared with every other
corner of the farmhouse I've seen so far.

I look at the choice of skirts, tops and dresses Alison has spread
across the bed and quickly decide on a plain white blouse and a
pair of cobalt-blue trousers. There's a nice soft jacket in pale-grey
Alison can carry over her arm if she gets cold.

'And now shoes: comfortable flats or dressy heels, whatever you prefer, no pressure,' I tell her.

She turns to the wardrobe and looks as if she is obeying, while I take out my phone and google:

hairbrush stuck in hair

All the posts that come up seem to involve:

my six-year-old daughter

and:

when my four-year-old was playing in my room

There's nothing about being a mummy in a hurry, trying to look sorted and professional for an important workday.

Alison puts on the clothes and a pair of classy navy pumps.

'Nice,' I say.

'You don't think they're too good?'

'No, give them some wear, before you're actually too old to wear high heels.'

Then I fiddle about with the hairbrush again.

'It's not coming out, is it?' she asks.

'No...' I twist gently but make her yelp again, 'it's completely wedged.' And I'm flashing back to when we were teenagers and experimenting with henna dye and curling tongs and I can't help giggling.

'Do you remember the Sun In that turned our hair completely orange?'

Alison nods and manages a smile. 'I think we'll just have to get the nail scissors and chop the brush out,' she says.

"Fraid so,' I tell her.

I use the nail scissors as gingerly as I can. I snip bit by bit and keep wriggling the hairbrush in the hope that it will come free without too much damage. But despite my efforts, a substantial chunk of Alison's hair has to come off before the brush finally lets go.

'Oh, that's bad,' she exclaims, feeling the hole at the back of her neck with her hands.

'No, it's really not so bad,' I fib because it is kind of bad, but I really don't want to add to her anxieties.

'I'm going to use hairspray,' I say, spotting the can on her dressing table, 'bouff it up a bit and no one will notice! Then I'm going to get a few little tricks out of my bag.'

I find my make-up bag and it only takes a few minutes to add tinted moisturiser, smoky grey eye shadow, mascara, blush and a lovely berry lip stain. I find some nice earrings too and Alison applies a little burst of perfume as her finishing touch.

'Chin up, shoulders back, best foot forward,' I tell her. 'You're going to be fine. I trust Mick completely. He'll get this sorted.'

She stands up, almost as tall as me in her navy heels, and gives me a hug.

* * *

At the glossy mahogany table in the centre of the McWhirter's boardroom, Mick, Alison and I are on one side; Miss McKenna of the Bold Partnership and Mr McWhirter, of the third generation of McWhirters, are on the other. Between us, at the head of the table there's a, hopefully, neutral mediation lawyer. The point of this meeting is to try to reach an agreement and avoid a fully blown industrial tribunal case for Alison.

Although we're on McWhirter territory, I like the fact that it's

Mick who opens the proceedings. 'Good morning, everyone,' he begins confidently, 'are we sitting comfortably?'

In the time I've been at his office there have been subtle changes in Mick, which I like to think have been brought about by my good influence. He's dressed neatly, but still in a Mick-like way, in a blue tweedy jacket, a white shirt, chinos and a pair of comfortable shoes. He spreads out beautifully organised, colour-coded and bulldog clipped files and notes before him on the table. I've explained my ex-boss Jonathan's trick of putting out lots of immaculate paperwork to make it look like an awesomely substantial case has been built against the opposition – even if some of that paperwork is just the same files in duplicate or even triplicate if required.

'What I would like to do,' Mick explains, 'is outline the case that I could make for my client, Mrs Alison Watson, were we to go to industrial tribunal. I hope you'll listen and take the opportunity to reach an amicable settlement with Mrs Watson outside any official tribunal.'

'Thank you,' Miss McKenna of the opposition replies, 'we appreciate your efforts to mediate with us.'

Yes, I hear that snide little word 'efforts'. But Mick, a damn good lawyer, as I realised from day one in his office, returns with a solid: 'Thank you. As you know, it's much more in McWhirter & Sons interest than ours to keep the case out of the public eye.'

'Right, well, please go ahead,' says the mediation lawyer.

And so Mick picks up the papers and makes his points one by one, crisply and clearly. Every statement is backed up with the relevant piece of employment law that appears to have been breached. It's the lawyerly equivalent of letting them have it with both barrels.

I glance at Alison sitting on my right, smart and understated in the white blouse, her hair recovering from the stuck-brush trauma. She looks anxious and underneath the table, she's twisting a paper tissue in her hands. I reach out, put my hand over hers and squeeze to reassure her.

Mr McWhirter keeps an impassive face.

When Mick has finished outlining Alison's case, Miss McKenna asks: 'So what would Mrs Watson be hoping for in the way of recompense?'

'She would either like her full-time job back, with some payment to compensate for the distress caused. Or, if she's not going to return to the job, a full set of references and one year's salary,' Mick says.

'Thank you, Mr Munro.'

The mediation lawyer asks Mick if he's finished and he nods. Then Miss McKenna requests a break so that she and her client can discuss the terms of our 'request.'

* * *

Mick, Alison and I are ushered into a small adjoining room where I take a seat, but Alison stands and Mick paces about, not nervous, but deep in thought. I wonder if he's reviewing his presentation and working out if it could have been better.

'Do you think they're going to agree?' Alison whispers, too nervous to talk in a normal voice. 'I really hope they don't offer me my job back. I actually can't even stand being in the same room as McWhirter now, the pompous arse.'

I pour both of them a cup of tea.

'What did you think?' Mick asks me. 'Right tone? Good case? Convincing argument?'

I like the way that he's been asking me for all kinds of advice recently and he seems to trust my opinion. He seems to have a lot of respect for the job I did in London.

'Yes. I thought you put it across really well.'

'Agreed,' says Alison. 'Do you think they're going to go for it and offer me something today? Or do you think they'll make me go to tribunal?'

'As I've said all along: you've got a very good argument against them,' Mick says evenly.

We drink our tea without much other conversation. It hardly feels as if the teacups are empty before someone appears at the door to tell us: 'They're ready to see you now, if that's all right with you.'

'That was quick,' Alison says, looking startled.

'In the law, quick is often a good thing,' Mick replies.

Less than thirty minutes later, the three of us are walking out of the building with broad, triumphant smiles on our faces. In just a few days' time, Alison is going to be one entire year's salary richer and she is close to whooping with delight. They agreed – of course they agreed. To every point. To the lot. To full reimbursement for all the distress caused.

'I can't believe it,' Alison says, for the fifth or sixth time. 'And the tour guide company want to take me on for another two days. So I'll have three days of work a week, plus one year's salary! This is amazing. This is a bloody miracle. You were brilliant, Mick, and you definitely need to offer Jennifer a full-time job... if she'll take it.'

'Oh...' from Mick

'Ummm...' from me.

Alison's suggestion, blurted out in happiness and excitement, stops Mick and I in our tracks.

'Jennifer...' he begins, his face serious now, 'I'd love you to come and work for me full-time. I think with your help, we can bring in the business to make it worthwhile. Just tell me you that you might be interested and we can come up with a plan.'

'I'd love to work for you...'

'That's fantastic!'

He looks so pleased at this that I really, really wish I could agree. And working for Mick would be delightful. He's very good at his job; he just needs someone to run all the other things well, so he can concentrate on the lawyering.

That person should be me. I'm efficient and organised; I can boss him very nicely. I've got years and years of experience working for one of the best guys in London. Mick could look for twenty years in St Andrews and not find someone as perfectly qualified for this job as me. Plus, he's already told me that twice as many clients have come to use his services since I started working there. So, he could afford to pay me decently too.

'Ermmmm...' I stall.

'Of course, of course, take your time and think about it. I don't want to rush you,' Mick says, looking almost agitated now.

'There's nothing to think about,' Alison wades in. 'You're brilliant, Jennifer and the two of you make a great team.'

'Mick, I would love to do it. I really would...'

Neither of them is smiling. They can hear the regret in my voice.

'Then why not?' Alison asks.

'Because...'

This is only a recent decision. This is only just starting to come together and I wasn't going to be talking to everyone about it yet. But... I'm not going to stay in St Andrews. I've now committed to volunteer in Argentina over the summer. I've bought my flight. And after Argentina... I'm planning to go somewhere else...

'Well... I've decided to do some volunteering abroad. It's something I've wanted to do for years...' I begin, 'and this seemed like a really good time to go for it.'

'What?' Alison asks, looking surprised. 'Where??'

'I'm going to Argentina for the summer... or maybe longer... and I don't know what the next move is after that.'

Now both Alison and Mick are looking at me open-mouthed, as if I've said something completely bizarre... maybe I have.

I realise I've not exactly kept everyone up to speed with all this.

'You're going to go to Argentina... this summer?' Alison asks. She looks shocked and almost quite upset.

Mick looks crestfallen, but he doesn't say anything.

'Yes... for three months. I hope... there's an element of see how it goes.'

'So when are you going?' is Alison's next question.

'In about a month's time... I was building up to let you know, Mick.'

Both Mick and Alison look completely astonished.

'So... when were you going to mention this to me?' Alison asks and Mick would be perfectly entitled to ask the same.

'Soon. I was going to mention it soon.' And this is true. Maybe I've hardly wanted to talk to anyone about it in case I somehow jinx everything.

'I'm sorry...' I add. 'I was just feeling so stuck and unsure... I wanted to go off and do something useful,' I blurt.

Alison surprises me with a hug. She holds me tight and puts her cheek against mine.

'I thought we'd just got you back,' she says, 'and now you're off again... But that's wonderful for you.'

'I'll be sorry to leave,' I say and feel an unexpected threat of tears.

Then holding me at arm's length, Alison asks: 'But I just want to check, Jennifer – I mean, are you sure? I mean Argentina? That's pretty far away. And working with Mick would be—'

'—Pretty good,' I finish her thought, looking at him. 'I'm really sorry, Mick, but I want to have an adventure, go somewhere new... spread my wings.'

'Get away from us all,' Alison adds.

'Well... as the saying goes,' Mick begins. 'Our loss is Argentina's gain.'

29

'It's been an absolute pleasure working with you,' I tell Mick, several weeks later, as I prepare to leave his office for the last time.

'Thank you, Jennifer,' he says, looking around the room with something close to confusion. 'I genuinely don't know what I'm going to do without you. If you change your mind, you know you can come straight back – well... if I've not found someone to replace you, obviously.'

'Just at least keep the place tidy and organised, promise?'

'I'll do my best.'

And even though I know it's control freakery and I should just say goodbye and go, I've made an arrangement he needs to know about: 'Mick, I've organised for a weekly cleaner to come in. If you don't want that, her name and number are here, beside the phone. But if you think it's a good idea – and I do – she'll be here on Friday at 5 p.m. for two hours.'

'Great idea,' Mick says.

I take the set of keys on the yellow tag out of my handbag and drop them onto my desk. Now, I feel properly sad.

'I hope things work out for you,' Mick says and then adds, 'Well, except for my sake, I sort of hope they don't.'

'Now, that is what you call a mixed message,' I smile at him, 'but I appreciate the sentiment. All the very best, Mick. I hope business booms.'

We look at each other... and hesitate. I'd quite like to give him a hug and a kiss, but I think that might be too shocking for him. So instead, I hold out my hand and when we shake, I clasp my other hand over his, putting as much warmth and feeling into this as I can.

'I've had a great time here,' I tell him truthfully, 'I hope I can find another job as good as this one.'

'Wishing you all the best,' he replies.

And then I'm out on the high street, where it's suddenly surprisingly warm with June sunshine and I have shopping to do because I told Dad and Joan I would make them a nice supper. It's high time to break the news about Argentina to them too.

* * *

'*Argentina*?!' is my dad's first, astonished reaction, 'you want to move to Argentina?'

There's a pause, which is filled with Elvis telling us he '*ain't nothing but a hound dog*'.

My beautiful, creamed potatoes, the roast chicken and the green beans in a tomato sauce are cooling on our plates.

My dad is looking at me with raised eyebrows. He looks completely unconvinced. Of course he does. Even I'm not entirely convinced. Volunteering to ride around the Pampas of Argentina sounds completely far-fetched and crazy.

I try to explain to them both what I'll be doing for the next three months.

'I don't know much about Argentina...' Joan begins, 'but why would you want to move somewhere so far away from Scotland? When people move from Scotland, they move to Spain or Portugal where the weather is lovely and you can still get plenty of recognisable food.'

The fact that she hasn't mentioned someone's son or daughter having gone to Argentina before me is almost ominous.

'Didn't Terry and Bridget's daughter...'

Ah, here it comes.

'Wait, I think it was Argentina. Or was it Antigua? One or the other. Began with an A.'

I stifle a giggle.

'Jennifer...' my dad begins, topping up first of all his own wine glass and then mine, 'you're a grown-up, you're entitled to do whatever you decide to do. But you will make sure you come back, won't you? Argentina is a very long way to travel for an old boy like me.'

He reaches out and squeezes my hand. There's no denying the look of kindness and concern in his eyes.

'Of course, Dad,' I say, then take a steadying slug of wine, 'that's nice of you. I'm going to go for about three months or so and see how things work out. If I enjoy it, I might stay for longer.'

'I think it sounds very adventurous,' Joan says magnanimously, then she holds up her glass and offers me a toast: 'I hope you'll have a wonderfully happy time, dear. You deserve it.'

'Thanks,' I say and take a sip.

'Oh now this is a great song. Listen to this one,' Dad urges us refilling glasses all round.

We finish the bottle of wine and then the chocolate mousse dessert to several Frankie hits: 'Fly Me To The Moon' and 'My Way', but we wash up with Elvis: *'One for the cupboard, two for the sink...'*

'TV?' Dad asks, settling down onto the sofa, while Joan insists on making the round of teas. 'You might as well cosy up with us while you're still here.'

'Of course.'

He pats my knee affectionately: 'It's been very nice having you around,' he says. 'We've both got used to it.'

I think this is his way of saying he'll miss me.

'I know, I've enjoyed being around,' I say.

'In fact, I have something for you, Jennifer.'

While I protest and tell him that he doesn't need to give me anything, putting up with me for so long has been quite enough, Dad gets up from the sofa and disappears off to the hallway. I can hear him for quite some time rooting about in the drawers of the sideboard there, where he keeps his paperwork.

When he comes back into the room, he comes over to the sofa and hands me a little passbook for the TSB Bank with my name typed on the cover.

'What's this?' I ask, smiling, a little bemused, wondering if he's found some savings account I set up when I was a schoolgirl.

'Have a look inside,' he says, 'I got it updated just a few months ago.'

I turn the pages and see details of a bank account, which has been paid into first of every month after month, £20 after £20, beginning way back in the 1990s, then with sums of £350 here and there, year after year. On the final page, is the recently updated, plus interest, total of £17,435.40.

'It's the money I've been saving for your wedding.'

'Oh... my god, Dad...'

I'm actually lost for words. I'm quite overwhelmed by this tireless saving he's done for me. Even in his retirement, when I know he's been on a tight budget. This is a big sum of money.

I hug him tightly for as long as he'll let me. My *wedding*? He's been saving all these years for my *wedding*. For a hope, just like mine, that I'll find someone just right for me. Arching my eyebrows and looking up at the ceiling is doing me no good at all. I'm definitely going to cry.

'I think you should have it now,' he says, 'and do whatever you like with it. It's yours.'

'No, no, Dad, this is way too much... I really couldn't...' I protest.

'Jennifer,' he folds my hand around the passbook, 'I've been saving this just for you for all these years. It's all yours and it will make me very happy if you have it now. Do whatever you want to do with it.'

'Thank you,' I tell him, tears spilling now, and even though I'm not supposed to say this kind of thing, because we're Scottish, I add: 'I love you, Dad.'

* * *

That night, it's hard to fall asleep. I lie in the bed in the blue bedroom and find myself staring at the orange glow coming from the edges of the curtain as I find myself wondering all over again about what I want. Yes, I have a whole new adventure planned and booked, and now I have an amazing and unexpected chunk of money. So, why can't I feel more excited? More convinced?

I can't help wondering if I will ever have a wedding. And would I want a wedding? Do I want to be married? And what about children? Have I ever really taken the time to think about that?

I had convinced myself I didn't want them, when Jono made me feel like it couldn't possibly be an option. But now... oh god, I'm in danger of spiralling into another one of my 'who am I, what do I want?' sessions.

Shut up, Jennifer, I tell myself firmly. You're going to fly halfway across the world. You're going to go somewhere completely new, completely different. You're going to meet entirely new people. It's going to be bloody exciting.

And maybe if I throw all the pieces of my life up into the air, they'll land back down again in a much better arrangement.

30

It is clear and cool, but sunny when I get down to the beach for 8.45 a.m. on Saturday morning. Rory has promised me a big surprise and I know I'm going to surprise him too – I've sworn Alison to secrecy because I want to break the news about Argentina to Rory myself.

I've been to this beach so many times before, but it's still breath-taking especially on a calm blue-lit day like today. The sand looks smooth and empty, golden in the early light, with the sea rushing back and forwards against it. But I'm bowled over by the huge sky above, demanding I look up, look ahead and throw off my inconse-quential little worries.

There's hardly anyone here. Stick figures in the distance throw balls for racing dogs.

In the nearby car park, a big horse trailer is unloading two ponies and two sturdy-looking horses, one chestnut, one white.

That's when I see Rory's bright red pickup truck bouncing over the terrain into the car park as well. His younger daughters, Katie and Maggie, are in the back, waving and smiling when they see me.

And sitting beside them is the dark-haired, serious-faced little friend, Pooky.

'Hello, Jennifer,' Rory calls over to me, 'you beat us to it. But you haven't worked it out yet, have you?'

'No!'

Katie and Maggie tumble out of the back doors. They're uniquely dressed as usual: padded gilets like their Dad's, jodhpurs, riding boots, plus sparkly tiaras and ballerina skirts. Maggie is holding a wand.

'Hello, girls!'

'Hello, Jennifer!'

I'm touched by how pleased they seem to be to see me. Rory is raising three delightful little people persons in his own mould.

'C'mon, Pooks,' Maggie adds, encouraging their much more typically dressed friend from the back seat.

They race over to treat me to enormous hugs and something of a side smear of jam from one little face. All are now in a frenzy of excitement, spinning about and hopping from foot to foot.

'Can we tell her, Daddy, can we?' Maggie asks.

'Please, Daddy, we can't keep it a secret any longer, we're going to burst,' Katie says, jumping as she speaks.

Wait a minute...

I look at the outfits again. Jodhpurs. Jodhpurs??

I turn my attention once again to the horse trailer. The ponies and the two horses are tied to the side of the trailer as saddles are fitted to their backs. There's only one woman with the four animals.

'No... you're not expecting me to...?' I ask.

Rory is nodding and grinning.

The girls are wheeling around.

Each girl takes one of my hands, then they pump my arms up and down and shout: 'We're going riding, we're going riding, we're going riding!'

'Riding on the beach, riding on the beach,' Katie chants.

'And it doesn't matter if you fall off, cos you land in the sand,' Maggie replies.

'Hahaha, that rhymes – land in the sand,' Katie adds.

'Ride with the tide and land in the sand,' Maggie suggests and this sets off another volley of chants.

'Are you riding?' I ask Rory, a little astonished at the prospect.

Rory whips out his phone: 'No, I am chief cameraman, Jennifer, because I can't ride. But you can ride. One of those horses is for you.'

'But I can't ride...' I protest, 'it's been years.'

'No, you're fine. I spoke to Charlie over there who has a riding school. She owns the horses and she said if you were OK at seventeen, she's got a boring old trotter for you and you'll be absolutely fine.'

'What?!'

I feel rooted to the spot with fear.

'C'mon, let's go over and say hello.'

'No, I'm not going to do this. I'm definitely not getting onto a horse.'

'Land in the sand, land in the sand,' Katie, Pooky and Maggie chant.

Land in the sand? I'll probably break fifteen bones in one go.

But Charlie is lovely, Maggie and Katie are inspirationally fearless, Pooky looks a little rattled, but says he will give it a little go, Rory totally believes in me and the horse has calm, wise eyes that soothe my fears immediately.

And so this is how I find myself on top of Sparkle walking at a steady pace as Charlie leads the two little ponies out across the sand, while the two little girls bounce on top almost delirious with excitement and Pooky runs alongside, waving Maggie's wand and waiting for his turn.

'Sparkle is a good old boy,' Charlie has assured me. 'He won't do anything exciting. He's police-trained.'

It's so high, is my first thought. I've forgotten how high up you are on horseback. My hips are groaning at their unaccustomed straddle position. But the reins feel comfortable in my hands and somewhere, at the back of my head, or maybe in my muscle-memory, I sort of remember how to do this. We walk steadily along and I get used to the rhythm of Sparkle's pace.

Charlie and the ponies are already managing a little trot ahead of me and I can hear the children's giggles of excitement.

Sparkle and I head towards the water's edge where the sand is firmer. I already feel relatively confident of the walking bit, so now I think maybe a little trot wouldn't hurt. I can probably manage that. So I tuck my heels a little more firmly into his side and say, 'C'mon, boy, trot on, trot on.'

And as if by magic, Sparkle picks up the pace and I'm bouncing about, completely mistiming my rise up and down in the saddle. There's nothing but glorious empty beach ahead of us, with the ponies behind us and hardly any dogs or people in front.

Trotting is tricky, I remember as I bounce about uncomfortably; cantering is faster, but smoother. I lean forward a little, tighten my grip on the reins, tuck my fingers around the front of the saddle and with a burst of courage, dig in my heels and say, 'Go on, boy, go on.'

The gears change and I feel the surge of speed immediately. Yes! Yes! Oh my god!

Thud-thud, thud-thud, thud-thud, thud-thud. This is my heart thumping with excitement and the heavy hooves landing in the sand. Mighty legs are pounding beneath me. Water is splashing up into my face. The wind is whistling at my cheeks and tears are flying from my wind-whipped eyes.

This is just incredible... unbelievable and totally exhilarating!

I feel seventeen again. And seventeen is a very good place. My whole life is ahead of me. Anything can happen. I feel light and happy and strong, as strong as the horse's legs moving underneath me.

This is the *Chariots of Fire* beach, so of course the theme tune begins to play in my head.

'Go on,' I urge him and then, to my mind at least, we are fairly flying across the sand.

A grin begins to spread across my face as I wonder why have I left this so long?

Why has it been over twenty years since I've been on a horse's back? Yeah, I fell off a few times, but I just needed a good old boy like Sparkle to rebuild my trust.

'And whoah... easy now...' I lean back, gently tighten the reins, take the pressure from my heels and we are bouncing about in a trot again. Easy.

And then we're walking again, as he takes great lungfuls of breath to recover from his run. I turn him round and realise how far away from the others we are now.

'Ready to go again?' I ask him, patting the side of his neck. 'Or do you need to breathe some more?'

I'd forgotten how lovely it is to have an animal – a real, big, living being – to work with and to talk to. Riding is a meeting of two minds, but one is human and one is animal, which makes it quite magical.

When Sparkle's breathing is level again, we trot and work up to another long canter back to the car park. Hooves, sand, water all flying out behind us. Tears streaming from my eyes, snot from my nose, jacket flying, my hair matting into a great pillow behind me.

Who cares?!

'Who cares?' I say out loud as we pass frisbees and barking dogs and the early walkers out for a stroll.

'Who cares!!'

Until finally, we slow down and trot, my up and down in the saddle a little more practised now, towards the girls, the ponies and the trailer in the car park.

'Yeeeehaaaaw!' Rory yells, still filming with his phone.

'That was amazing! He's absolutely brilliant!' I shout back at Rory, Charlie, the little girls, and their friend, still on top of their ponies.

'You were brilliant!' Rory replies. 'You totally nailed it.'

'You must have been a very good rider when you were younger,' Charlie says as I climb down from Sparkle and lead him towards his hay net at the side of the trailer, 'you looked like a natural out there.'

I can't stop grinning. My face will literally not revert to the non-grin setting.

'You should definitely get back into it,' Charlie adds, 'just call me. I have a riding school on the edge of town and we bring the horses to the beach three times a week. We do riding lessons and competitions – you'll love it.'

For a moment or two, I picture cantering, even galloping, up and down the sands three times a week. I wonder if they ever come at sunset. It would beat jogging hands down, that's for sure.

Quietly, so Rory won't overhear, I say: 'I wish I'd known before, but I'm leaving St Andrews and... well, first stop Argentina for the summer... and after that...' I smile and shrug, 'Who knows?'

'Oh,' she says, pulling a disappointed face, 'well... that sounds nice.'

'Yes...'

I help Maggie and Katie down from their ponies. Pooky insists he can manage by himself. The children are allowed to feed the animals and brush their manes. I go and stroke Sparkle's soft nose too. Let his rough whiskers brush against my hands and feel the soft fur of his ears.

'Aren't you handsome?' I ask him.

'Oh yes, I definitely am,' Rory says, coming up behind me.

I turn and laugh at him.

'You. Were. Amazing. You are amazing,' he adds and his smile is warm and still boyish, almost exactly as I remember it from school.

'Thank you so much. I would never have done this without you. I'd totally forgotten how awesome it is.'

'I'm sending you the footage right now,' he says, tapping at his phone.

'Thank you. And thank you so much for organising this. It was amazing. I owe you... I owe you something equally brilliant,' I say, my hand on his forearm to let him know how touched I am and how much I'd like to do something as thoughtful for him.

He's grinning at me: 'I knew you would love this. You've forgotten how much you loved riding... maybe you've forgotten some other things about yourself.'

'Maybe,' I agree. 'Look... Rory...' I suddenly feel myself shrink a little at the words I'm about to say. My eyes have connected with Rory's. He has warm brown irises and an expression that always looks friendly and kind, even when he's not smiling. I suddenly think of that expression 'smiling with the eyes'; I've not understood it until right now. We've quickly become such good friends and I've enjoyed every moment I've spent both with Rory and with his girls. I suddenly realise that he will mind, maybe quite a lot that I'm about to leave town... and I will mind leaving him too.

'What's up?' he asks. 'This suddenly looks serious... you're not about to run off with the Scandi man, are you?'

He's joking, but I am about to run off.

'I've decided to get a volunteering job...' I begin.

'Well... that's... you're not giving up working for Mick though, are you?' Rory asks.

I nod.

'I'm going away... I've booked a flight... it's a three-month commitment...' My eyes are still fixed on his and I'm finding it hard to continue.

'It's OK, whatever you've planned is OK,' Rory is smiling. 'So?'

'I'm going to Argentina,' I blurt.

'Whoa... Argentina?! For three months?'

I realise I'm trying hard to read his expression. Is he surprised? He looks surprised. Does he look hurt? Worried? Disapproving? No... I think just surprised.

'Yes,' I say.

'And then?' he asks.

'Not sure yet.'

'Well... Argentina sounds fantastic,' he says and a big smile splits his face, 'might be just what you need. Horses, the open Pampas, hunky cowboy gauchos... yes, I can see you in Argentina... and what an adventure to tell your grandkids.'

This makes me laugh. And his enthusiasm is infectious.

He starts asking questions about where I'm going, when I'm leaving. And of course, reminds me: 'You need to drop by the shop. We have passport covers, luggage tags, mini hairdryers... all kinds of necessities for the international traveller... all on at an excellent, once-in-a-lifetime deal... this is so exciting!' he adds. 'Wow! How brave! Put it here,' he says, opening his arms for a hug.

We bear hug and I'm held for a long moment feeling strong arms grip round me tightly. He smells nice, I notice, of coffee and citrusy soap, washing powder and cinnamon.

'And if you ever, ever need a lift to or from Leuchars Station, you only have to ask,' he says against my hair.

'I'll miss you,' I tell him.

'That is nice to hear,' he says.

'Daddy, why are you hugging Jennifer?'

'Yes, Daddy, is Jennifer sad?'

'Is she cold?'

Maggie, Katie and Pooky are beside us, still a little crazed with the excitement of the morning.

'She's going away soon. It's an early goodbye hug,' Rory explains, letting go of me.

'Oh no! Why are you going away?' Maggie asks.

'But we want to go riding with you, every day,' Katie says, putting a cosy hand into mine.'

Before I can reply, a new chorus starts up.

'Daddy, can we get a pony?' Maggie begins.

'Daddy, can we get two ponies?' Katie adds.

'Yes! Two ponies!' They both start bouncing up and down again. Katie is laughing and Maggie hugging herself at the thought of TWO ponies.

'What about that puppy?' Rory asks.

'No, we've had a chat, me and Katie and Pooky,' Maggie says, 'and we've decided we'd like three ponies instead.'

'Well, we'd like one puppy too,' Katie says, 'and one kitten. And if you get the puppy and the kitten at the same time, then they're friends and they don't chase each other... well, hardly at all.' She looks up at him so hopefully that if it was up to me, I would be buying that puppy and kitten today, yesterday.

'And where exactly will we have room for a puppy, a kitten and *three* ponies?' Rory asks, eyes wide with amusement.

'The ponies will be in the stable, silly Daddy,' Katie smacks his leg.

'And if Samantha goes away to college, then there will be space in her room and we'll make a little nest for the puppy and the kitten,' Maggie says.

'But they could fit in our room, under our beds,' Katie adds.

'Yes!' Maggie looks hysterically excited at the thought, 'but not under the beds, on top of our beds!'

The horse trailer drives away first, then the red pickup truck with Rory at the wheel and the children buckled securely into their seats in the back. Once it's gone, it's very quiet and I feel alone. This isn't goodbye, of course. I'll see them again before I leave, maybe several times. I'm not off for another couple of weeks. But I still have to acknowledge a feeling of real and unexpected sadness at the thought of leaving them.

* * *

That night, I wake up in the small hours, heart thumping. I feel the bed beneath me, sense I'm lying on my back and I realise gradually that this was just a dream. Just a dream. An anxious dream. Not surprising really. I'm on the verge of a big change. I'm about to pack and up and leave all over again.

My heart is still racing and my mouth feels dry. As soon as I'm properly awake, I'll have to go and get a drink of water.

Some dream. It comes back to me in little bursts: I saw a blue SUV that turned out to be my sister's in the high street and I went quickly down a side street to get away from it. Then I bumped straight into Mick, but had to run on, with no explanation, to get away from that blue car. And then I was trying to get into a house door – I didn't even recognise the door – but I didn't have the key. I was searching all my pockets, knowing that I had the key, but I could not find it. I was looking in my handbag, unzipping every section, unearthing all the contents – still no key. Checking my pockets again, frantically knowing I had to get the key and get inside this door, before the blue car drove down this street.

Then the car was approaching and I was banging on the door in a panic. And there were the keys, in a big, jumbled bunch, dangling from the lock.

That's when I woke up.

I sit up now and turn on the sidelight, illuminating the bankbook with my father's careful savings for my wedding.

Tears slide down my face.

Just a dream, just a dream, I tell myself.

I'm leaving town.

Goodbye, St Andrews. I'm escaping from you again. Getting away from all the distress and disappointments of the past. No chance of bumping into Isla's blue car in Argentina and having to worry about whether I should try and reconcile with her or not.

But then there's the little whisper: what about Dad, he's getting older and you'll be far away. What about your friends? What about Rory and Alison and Mick – will they all be OK? Of course, of course they'll be OK, but I will miss them.

It doesn't feel nearly as easy to leave town this time. The last time I packed my bags and left 'for good', I was twenty-two and I had no intention of coming back. This time, I've booked an open, fully flexible, return to Buenos Aires because nothing is at all so simple any more.

31

And then there are some goodbye drinks, and packing, and much more serious googling of where I'm going and what is going to happen there.

Until it is finally the night before I go. My big travel suitcase is packed. My cabin bag too. My passport and tickets are in my handbag. I'm leaving very early by train for London, flying out in the late afternoon from Heathrow.

I say goodbye to Dad before I go to bed because I don't want to wake him up in the wee hours of the morning. Then I toss and turn in the bed for a short and restless night. Every now and then I wake and wonder if it's time to go to Argentina yet and I can't quite decide if going to Argentina is real or part of the landscape of my dreams. *Argentina*? Really? Did I really decide this? I am hurtling towards it and it still feels unreal.

When my alarm goes off at 3:45 a.m., I'm instantly awake as well as tense and nervy. I get out of bed and get dressed quickly. Almost as soon as I'm ready, with my bags in the hallway, the taxi is outside the door. So, I get everything outside and lock up. I dither for a moment about whether I should post my key through the lock or take it with me... and decide to take it.

So then I'm in the back seat of the taxi, feeling a little sick with nerves. In my mind, I'm waving goodbye to my childhood home. I'm so grateful to Dad for giving me a home when I needed one... but I do think I'm ready to move on. Here in the cool morning air, I'm much more sure of that than I was tossing and turning in the bed last night.

I wave goodbye to the high street, then the town and then we're on the twisty countryside road to Leuchars Station.

The early morning sun is rising over trees and hedgerows, which are all in the bright-green flush of summer. There are lush leaves and blossom, yellow, pink, white and green, on every side.

I arrived here six months ago when it was still winter. That journey is still etched on my mind, my heavy heart and all the hopelessness and hurt.

I smile and try to relax. I wonder why I'm not feeling a lot happier about my prospective adventure. Just nervous, I think. This is such a big step. I'm worried about everything that could go wrong.

At the station, I buy a cup of coffee and board the first train to Edinburgh.

It's a beautiful journey, through soft, green landscapes coming to life under the early morning sun, past sparkling blue coastline. I'm not sure Scotland has ever looked more lovely to me. I find there's a line of poetry running over and over in my head.

> 'the little white rose of Scotland that smells sharp and
> sweet – and breaks the heart.'

I think back to when I first moved from Scotland to London, and I wonder if I felt so deeply moved to be saying goodbye then.

That's not how I remember it. I'm sure it was an afternoon train and I have a vague memory of downing a bottle of rosé wine and throwing up in the toilet around about Peterborough.

But I was in my twenties; I was pent up, rebellious and desperate to get away. Now... it's different and I find myself partly excited, and partly sad and quite uncertain.

My thoughts are all tumbled and jumbled. I seem to be setting off on a major journey without having quite committed.

I'll be fine, I'll be fine – I tell myself. *I'm just nervous.*

On we travel, hugging the coastline, then crossing the majestic Forth Rail Bridge as the train approaches Edinburgh.

When we get off at Edinburgh station, I remember my bewildered self, just six months ago, alone with my suitcases, in shock, heading north to I knew not what. The time hasn't gone quickly, it's gone slowly. Every day has been filled with not only the new, but with getting to know the old again. St Andrews no longer feels like a place I've left behind, where only my dad lives. It feels like a warm and friendly home to me, full of people I know, full of things I can do, full of life... my new life.

I am sorry to be leaving.

There. I've admitted it to myself. Maybe I've only just realised it. I'm sorry to be uprooting, when I feel as if I've only just managed to get established once again. It's suddenly painfully obvious why I am so nervous and in such a flap.

I don't think this is going to work.

I think leaving right now... or maybe running away... might be a big mistake.

* * *

Right there in the middle of Waverley Station, I stand still, my bags beside me. It's a Saturday morning, so I'm not looking at the usual commuter crowd. Instead, there are mainly couples, of all ages, and groups of friends and families. One busy Mum and Dad are shepherding a noisy rabble towards a platform, along with bags, a small dog and a helium balloon number 5. Children's birthday parties... cake, balloons, being an auntie, being an important part of a family, hanging out with my dad regularly, looking after him even... I didn't think I wanted any of that. When I went to London, I was turning my back on small town and extended family life... I didn't want it, didn't like it. I ran away from it all.

But now...?

Right now, I'm watching a woman I don't know tie a helium balloon safely to the handle of a trolley case while a small boy, not much taller than the case, looks on seriously. He's five. My nephew, Peter, must be five. I haven't seen him since he was a baby. I wouldn't be able to pick him out in a crowd.

I still haven't properly spoken to Isla about the important things. I haven't even opened all of the letters that she wrote to me. I've not gone through my boxes from London. Or any of my mum's things. And there's another thing, I realise, as I watch the little boy take his mother's hand, that I do finally need to allow myself to think about... maybe even talk about, when the time is right. Maybe I would, some day, like a family all of my own.

Maybe I don't need to be in Argentina to think about this much more carefully.

I look up at the screen announcing the next departures. In fifteen minutes, the train to London King's Cross leaves from platform 3. But in six minutes' time, there's a train back to Leuchars from platform 12.

And so, I'm on the train again, heading north, back to St Andrews. Once again, I have had a cry in the toilet, as I've said goodbye to my South American adventure, plus whatever far-flung ideas I was going to follow it up with. But my tears have dried now. My inner rain has cleared. My face has been dabbed, my make-up has been repaired and I sincerely hope that it's all going to be OK.

If I'm honest, I feel partly numb and partly lightened, burden lifted and that sort of thing.

Yes, I am travelling *back*. I think of the people I'm travelling back towards. I realise that coming back is going to make me happy and, even better, it's going to make them happy too.

Dare I even think of myself as travelling *home*?

I have an hour left on the train. I look at my phone and realise I have a lot of calls to make and messages to send. For a moment, I'm not sure who to call first. Then I decide, to calm my scrambled mind, that I'll go alphabetically: Alison, the Airbnb flat in Argentina, Dad and onwards.

* * *

The train is held up and when I finally arrive in Leuchars, trailing my two suitcases behind me, I've missed the bus and I watch the last two taxis leaving the rank.

I park the suitcases and bring out my phone to search for taxi companies. I suddenly feel very tired.

'If you ever need a lift from the station, you're supposed to phone me...' says a familiar voice behind me.

I turn and see Rory, unusually smart for him, in a pale-blue suit and white shirt open at the neck. He's all clean, groomed and freshly shaven, looks like he might be on his way to a casual wedding or something important.

'Hey... hello, how did you know?!' Is my first question. 'I mean, I know you are the eyes and ears of St A's... but this...'

'Alison,' he replies, 'she was in buying sixty-four packets of crisps, assorted flavours, when you called her.'

'I've changed my mind,' I say.

'Well, I can see that...'

'A bit short notice,' I admit.

'Yeah... chances of getting a refund on that flight are...'

'They might be next to zero, for the outward... but I ticked some sort of fully flexible box... so maybe I can rearrange the flight back. I'll contact them and check.'

'A flight back from Buenos Aires is not so helpful if you aren't there.'

'True...' I admit, 'maybe I can sell it on ebay?'

I realise I feel all strange and light-headed and not sure if I'm going to burst into tears or laughter. I can't decide.

We're all alone on the platform now, the other arriving passengers have scattered and there isn't another train due.

'It's not that I was scared... or didn't want to go,' I try to explain myself, 'I did actually want to go quite a lot. It sounded pretty awesome, but it just felt as if there was still too much to sort out here. Too many things I haven't done... people I haven't...'

When I peter out, Rory just holds out his arms.

'The amazing Jennifer McAndrew is back,' he says. 'Put it here.'

I could really do with a hug right now, so I don't hesitate. I throw my arms round his waist and bury my face in his shoulder. His arms are tight and cosy around me.

'Welcome back,' he says, 'we want you back.'

'Thank you.' And it's obviously been a long and very emotional morning because I start to sob and all I want is my bed and it's only 11:45 a.m..

But instead, Rory convinces me that what I need is a pub lunch with several bracing drinks before, during and after.

'But... you look so smart...' I protest. 'Are you not on your way somewhere?'

'Oh, my lady-slayer suit?' he jokes, rubbing the lapel between his thumb and forefinger. 'I had a business networking thing... St Andrews movers and shakers,' he gives almost quite a shy smile. 'I can tell you about it over lunch.'

'You scrub up well,' I tell him with a smile and I mean it. Out of the lumberjack shirt and gilet, he looks quite different. Trimmer, less dad-ish and more serious.

Because I don't quite want to face my dad's doorstep just yet, I'm pretty easily convinced that I need a lunch, so we load my bags into his Rory-mobile and drive back towards town, while he negotiates cover for his shop for another 'hour or maybe two.'

* * *

'I don't usually encourage reckless drinking,' he says as I sip at the brandy and soda he's ordered for me, 'but there are some exceptional days,' he adds.

'Do you need another one after that? Shall I get Stuart at the bar there to line them up along the table?'

'No! No, one is absolutely fine,' I tell him, 'or there's a danger I might vom and that would be a tragic waste of an amazing steak pie.'

'No problem. And I'd like to say for the record – that was impressive steak pie demolition, considering the level of upset you've been under.'

'It's all the drink,' I tell him, 'it's made me very hungry.'

He's kept up a steady stream of comforting and friendly chat throughout the car journey and the meal. But now, sitting next to me, in the quiet corner of this quaint old place, he asks gently: 'Are you OK, Jennifer? And have you done the right thing? Or should I, in fact, be rushing you down to Heathrow to still try and make the plane.'

'Yes, I am OK. And yes, this is the right thing. No, I should not be on that plane,' I tell him, issuing a sigh that is somewhere between grief and relief. 'I think it's for the best. But I am a bit... sad, confused... muddled...' I admit.

I bump my head against Rory's shoulder and manage a, 'I need to shut up. I'm actually bored of listening to myself about all this.' I even close my eyes momentarily because it's so warm and I've had a lunchtime pint and a brandy and I am so tired.

Rory gives me a smile. 'You seem to be doing OK,' he says. 'This doesn't even look like it's going into your top ten worst days of your life ever.'

'No... it isn't. No... probably, on balance, it will turn out to be a good day,' I say, trying to sound cheerful, trying to get the thoughts straight in my mind: 'I thought I was all ready for the big adventure, the big "'leaving my past and my small town behind" but actually, I wasn't. Try to run away from things and they just follow you around when you're a grown-up. It's so much more easily done when you're younger.'

And then because we're comfortable and talking about the big stuff, I feel I owe it to Rory to explain: 'Obviously, the worst day was the day my mum died, but what you don't know, Rory, is that...' I'm surprised at how hard it is to say this aloud, to someone who doesn't understand how that day went. 'Isla and I both blamed each other for Mum's accident. And that is at the root of why we don't talk now.'

I feel a warm hand take a hold of my shoulder. Once again, I feel as if Rory has got enough warmth, energy and optimism to be able to lend me some. His arm hold feels as if it is holding me together.

'I think the important thing is to keep looking at all the difficult stuff,' Rory says gently, 'keep it right at the front of your mind. Look at it from different angles and work out where to go from here. You can and you will,' he adds.

He doesn't say anything else, and he doesn't need to.

You can and you will.

'C'mon,' he says finally, 'you need to go home.'

* * *

Back at Dad's house, I keep the explanations brief and drink down a glass of water, then I tuck myself into the funny old cane-framed bed in the pastel-blue bedroom and sleep for three hours straight. When I wake up, I see my suitcases lined up along the bedroom wall and I remember exactly what has happened.

For a few moments, my head reels. For weeks, the plan to move to Argentina has been right at the forefront of my mind and now it's all over. But, I still think this is the right decision.

I think there's a lot I need to get sorted out right here in the hometown first before I can go looking for anything, let alone anyone else.

I get out of bed, pull on jeans and a sweatshirt, and know there's one obvious place where I can go to look for the evidence.

I open the door on my sister's bedroom. The walls are still white, the curtains blue. The small double bed is still made up with a pale-lemon duvet cover and pillows. The artificial rose still stands in a vase on the bedside table and there's still the framed picture on the wall.

But messing up the tidy tastefulness of this room are all the cardboard boxes: my boxes from London and the boxes of Mum's things, and boxes of Isla's old things too.

No matter how painful it's going to be, no matter how many memories, how many ghosts of the past are going to be disturbed, I have to get stuck in here.

I have to sort this room out, sift through the evidence, unearth the real story and throw some of the past away – keeping only what is important and true.

I tackle the boxes from the London flat first. This now feels almost too easy, rifling through books, pictures, photos, letters, all the flotsam and jetsam of my life, and quickly deciding what is important and what has to go. I make four piles and sort accordingly: rubbish, recycling, charity shop donations and keep. The keep pile is the smallest one. It includes a necklace with an enamelled butterfly on a chain, which I like very much. It is one of the few gifts I have from Jono. He gave it to me for my birthday, when I was sure he hadn't remembered the date. I'll wear it now and then, when the memory of my hurt over his twins has faded further and I can think about our happy days again.

Then it's time to open the lids on my St Andrews past. The oldest and dustiest boxes in the room, the ones that haven't been opened since I left my hometown aged twenty-two, when I pushed everything that I thought I wanted to keep, but didn't want to take with me, into these boxes. I've never looked into them once since because I've always assumed that there was nothing but bitter memories here.

I pull the dried-out packing tape away easily. At the top of the first box, pushed in under the flap through a gap in the taping, are some of the letters Isla has sent to me over the years. Only a few are opened, but they are all un-replied. I put them to the side for now. I am going to read at least some of them later, because I'm almost ready to see things from her point of view.

I delve further into the box, bringing out the contents. There are clothes and shoes I haven't seen for over a decade; I put them straight into the charity pile.

There are envelopes of photos too and I glance through them as quickly as I can. Most are terrible: the subjects overexposed by bright sunlight or flash, the faces too far away to read their expressions. A few hold my attention though and these I put carefully onto my 'keep' pile. There's one of Isla and me, as teenagers, laughing as we decorate a very lopsided cake in the kitchen. I've not thought for years about how much we used to make one another laugh.

More photos... these dating back to school: Alison and me, Alison with a shockingly bad perm, me with homemade streaks of blonde turned orange. Class photos, and oh my god, photos from the sixth-form dance – me in a dubious purple dress on the arm of a boy whose name I momentarily can't remember... oh yes, Euan. I smile when I spot Rory in a kilt – so young! And more handsome than I remember with his square shoulders and muscular legs. He's not smiling though, he's looking at the camera with an expression I can't quite make out – thoughtful, wistful even. I put this photo on my keep pile, along with a close up of Richard and me grinning, his arm around my shoulder. Now this is a lovely photo. We look happy and we look so young – newly twenty-one or so. Our faces are smooth and quite unformed. In many ways, I prefer my face now. It's a more sculpted version of the baby moonface I had at that age. There's more cheekbone and more character to it now. Richard is startlingly good-looking: blond, tanned, fine featured. The details – his ironed white polo shirt, his short hair standing to attention, the pristine strap on his watch – all remind me what a perfectionist he was. This photo I keep too, because it's a souvenir of the two of us young and carefree. It shouldn't all be spoiled.

Ribbons, T-shirts, sunhats, Champagne corks, letters, postcards, tickets for concerts, menus... I scoop it all out of these boxes from the past and consign most of it to the black bags. Only a few things – ones that make me smile and bring back really good times – are to be kept.

Just as the boxes of my past are almost emptied, Dad appears in the doorway to the room.

'What are you up to now, my dear?' he asks.

'I'm finally sorting through my boxes,' I tell him. 'Old ones and the ones from London.'

'Oh my goodness,' he says, coming in and sitting down on the edge of the bed.

'I've done six,' I tell him, pointing to the flattened cardboard piling up in one corner of the room. 'Most of the stuff is going to Oxfam or the bin.'

'Goodness,' he repeats again, taking in the surprisingly high piles.

'Dad... what do you think about going through Mum's boxes with me? Would you be up for that?'

I expect him to say no. I expect him to shuffle off to the TV making an excuse to put it off for another day. But instead, he surprises me with the words: 'No time like the present, hey?'

So very carefully, we lift the flaps on boxes that have not been opened since the weeks after my mother's funeral, four years ago. I place the things on the bed and both Dad and I are bowled over with the memories that come rising so completely from the past.

That little green cardigan. The neat lizard-skin bag. Framed photos. Memorable jewellery. Hats. Even a small bottle of perfume that neither of us dares to open. Scared we'll uncork memories too powerful.

We gave away many of her things after she died. These boxes contain the mementos we couldn't bear to part with. Dad couldn't bear to live side-by-side with the memories either and must have thought that keeping everything in these boxes would somehow be easier.

* * *

Nothing about my mother's death is easy. But as I lift out item after item, Dad and I both growing teary eyed in the process, I try to rethink the sequence of events.

Until now, I always thought that it went like this: Isla married Richard – I found everything about this awkward and ran a mile. Isla had a baby girl, Jessie, and a few months later, Isla invited me to the christening. I came along and gave the best auntie vibes I could, considering I actually overheard cousins talking about how 'Jennifer probably wanted to marry him, but Isla was the one who got him.' I fled back to London again as quickly as I could. Over the next two years, I came up to St Andrews now and then. I would always go and visit Richard, Isla and their baby, even though I only ever seemed to get questions about: when was I planning to settle down? Had I met anyone special? Didn't I want a baby? and so on.

Then, five years ago, Isla had a baby boy. A few months after his birth, I was invited to his January christening. I was already planning to come up to see everyone at Christmas, I'd just endured a messy break-up with someone very important to me and definitely did not want another big family party with all those questions, so I said no thank you. I thought I did it gracefully, saying I was really sorry, work commitments, I'm not going to be able to attend. But Isla and I had a big row on the phone about it – maybe things were not as solid between us as they could have been anyway – with her calling me completely self-centred, and me... I wince at the thought, saying: 'You never go to church anyway, what the hell is this all about?' And then there were all the other hurtful things siblings can throw at each other when their tempers are up. I remember her saying I would never find anyone to settle down with because I was just too 'difficult'.

Isla made our mother phone me about it and so then Mum and I had a horrible row. I pointed out that I'd be travelling up from London again, just two weeks after Christmas, when no one ever came down to see me, by the way.

'Oh god, London's a dreadful place,' was my mum's take on this.

And after that argument, well, Isla insisted Mum drive over to her house afterwards for another big discussion, although they were both angry and upset.

In the wet and dismal darkness of a narrow country road on an early December night, Mum's little car drove straight into the back of a massive metal plough, attached to a tractor which had just come to a stop because the driver had missed his turnoff. She had to be cut out of the wreckage by the fire brigade and rushed by ambulance to the A&E department in Dundee, but she'd suffered catastrophic head injuries, internal bleeding, broken bones, a broken pelvis. She didn't regain consciousness and died eight hours after the accident, with my dad and my sister beside her intensive care bed, while I joined in with the absolute horror of it all on speakerphone.

Until now, I have laid the blame for this awful sequence of events and tragedy on Isla. If Isla hadn't married Richard...

If Isla hadn't made such a fuss about a christening...

If Isla hadn't cried down the phone at Mum and insisted she come over.

I have always pinned the blame on Isla.

And at Mum's funeral, Isla made it clear that she blamed me: 'If you hadn't upset Mum with your great big, selfish refusal,' she had screamed at me that day. 'She was probably crying in the car and that's why she didn't stop in time.'

'Who was the one who made her drive over?' I'd screamed back.

As if the funeral wasn't bad enough. We made it even worse for ourselves.

But now, I am following Rory's advice to really look at it and try to see it differently.

I say to Dad, in a voice that's husky with grief: 'There were several reasons for that accident, weren't there? I mean... several different factors.' I sound almost a little lawyerly it occurs to me.

'Oh yes, of course,' my dad replies, sounding husky himself. 'She'd have come out of a really up-to-date car with barely a scratch. That car was eight years old. Didn't have particularly good safety features, and was so small, there was hardly any crumple zone. And a modern tractor wouldn't have had its taillights down low, all clogged up with mud and such poor headlights that the guy missed his turn. And the fire engine took a while to come... the poor tractor driver talking to her through the smashed window all the time... horrendous to think about. The paramedics couldn't do much until the fire brigade turned up.

'So, yes, there were lots of factors... lots of reasons why it didn't work out for your poor mother that night... very sadly.'

He presses his eyelids with his fingers for a moment, then picks up a framed photo of the two of them, sitting at a garden table, decades younger, smiling at the camera. This same garden, I think, glancing out of the window. But it's so long ago now, it might as well be a photo taken on the moon.

'That's a nice one,' he says, 'let's get it a new frame and put it up in the sitting room.'

I nod, but I'm only really focusing on the fact that my dad holds the car, the tractor and the delayed fire engine all responsible for Mum's death. He doesn't mention me and my furious phone call, or Isla and her emotions, or the christening, as reasons for the crash. So maybe I shouldn't put so much blame these things either. Maybe I should focus too on an old tractor, driving too slowly without proper lighting, and an elderly small car without many safety features, and of course, terrible luck and weather and timing. I should let the other elements fade into the background.

'Should we keep all of her things?' I ask Dad, when all the contents of the boxes have been spread over the bed.

'I'm going to pick out a few bits and pieces,' he replies. 'Then you and your sister should do the same. Anything left after that should go to a good home.'

'Good plan,' I tell him.

'Ha...' he says, raising his bushy eyebrows and looking at me expectantly.

'What?'

'Well... that's the first time for a very long time, that I've mentioned your sister and you've not made the face.'

I don't say 'what face?' because I know.

Instead, I say, 'Ha,' too.

33

Over the next few weeks and then months, I'm busy setting up my new St Andrews life. Mick Munro is delighted – well, in a low-key, tweedy, Scottish kind of way – to see me back and offers me the four-day a week job I want at a pretty decent rate. And with a bit of time, the impeccable filing system, the understated advertising campaign, brand-new website and excellent word of mouth bring in many new clients.

And because it's just me and Mick, I find myself taking on more and more of a responsible role. I take client histories for him, research legal documents, draft wills and transactions. I find my work increasingly interesting.

Once a month, I babysit for Alison and Wattie, so they can go out and enjoy each other's company, while I try my hand at crowd control in the farmhouse. Also once a month, I take Alison out by myself, ply her with gossip and cocktails, and help rebuild both her interest in fashion and tolerance to alcohol.

Twice a week, I pay Charlie to bring my beautiful Sparkle horse to the beach along with the ponies, so that Maggie, Katie, Pooky and I can race around the sand, the shoreline and even the dunes until we are aglow with exhilaration.

I'm so grateful for Maggie and Katie and their little friend, they are small laughing dervishes, energy and hilarity in motion, who take me straight into their hearts.

Pooky is much more reserved, but I know all about Maggie and Katie's lives now. Their favourite teachers and BFFs, the type of puppy and kitten they would choose (choices one down to seventeen) if their mummy or daddy ever relented on this front.

'Daddy has said maybe when I turn eleven and Katie is ten, because we will be more "responsile".'

'Jennifer, what does 'responsile' mean?'

'It's when you're ready to look after pets properly,' I tell them as we get into the car after another beautiful riding session. 'But I know how well you look after the ponies when we see them. I'll tell Daddy that you're getting more *responsible* by the minute. So, fingers crossed, it won't be long before he gets you a pet... or maybe even two.'

Rory's teenaged daughter, Samantha, becomes my art-house film buddy. We regularly go and check out the latest moody foreign film to make it this far north of London.

I take up some new hobbies: kick boxing which I find hysterical; I can hardly kick straight because I'm trying so hard not to laugh and Japanese cookery, which turns out to be the most fiddly but beautiful thing I've ever done.

I also discover that I like visiting the small businesses in and around the town and buying myself and my little circle handmade pottery mugs, Shetland wool jumpers and all the other carefully made items that can be found. There's far more to appreciate about being here than I ever realised before.

I'm still living with Dad, so I clean and cook for him as much as

Joan will let me – 'keeps me fit,' she insists, 'a rolling stone gathers no moss.' Whenever I mention getting a place of my own, Dad insists I should stay just a little longer. But I'm registered with the estate agent and looking for the right kind of thing.

I buy myself a little red car, so that I can get right out of town at the weekends and explore the hills and coastlines and picnic venues from my childhood without worrying about the exhaust falling off the old Sunny. Soon it's full-blown summer and I'm in love with the light, which begins at four in the morning and doesn't finally fade until late, late into the night.

Once or sometimes twice a week, Rory and I go out for non-alcoholic beers and bowling and sometimes, he even wears his suit, if I twist his arm. Sometimes, when he's child- and shop-free, he comes on one of my trips out to the countryside too. And we do a long, bracing walk while I bemoan my tragic lack of dates, but only in jokey way, because really, I know that I've never felt calmer or happier.

'I've got a wedding to go to in two weeks' time,' he complains to me in the bowling club on one of our meet ups, 'and going to a wedding all on your own is no fun. What about—'

'Are you wearing a kilt?' I interrupt to ask him.

'No, I'm thinking the smooth, dinner-suit look.'

'Very nice... have you seen my photo of you in a kilt? Did you know that I had one?'

'No!'

So, from my bag I take out the snapshot from our sixth-form dance I've been waiting for the perfect moment to show him.

'Oh my Lord...' he says, taking a hold of it. 'Look at that gorgeous young dude. No wonder you've been carrying this around with you. Phwoar... how could anyone resist him? Yet so many did and so many times!' he laughs at the thought.

'What is that expression on your face?' I ask. 'You look all kind of... wistful really...'

'Oh yes, what a dreamboat,' Rory says and he looks up at me and makes the very same expression. I'm still not sure what to make of it, and I laugh at him, but I feel quite disconcerted.

'Don't worry about it. I think I'd had several puffs on my very first joint. Mind you, it was rolled by Douggie Mather so it was probably mainly made of hay. Let's talk about you... you know I had an idea for you.'

'OK...'

'You might need a real beer though.'

I shake my head: 'My kick boxing instructor wouldn't approve. He's all about living clean and kicking mean.'

Rory gives a laugh. 'I need to see you kick boxing.'

'So you can laugh? Like I do, by the way.'

'No! I think you kick boxing would be... quite an amazing sight.'

'Are you being flirty with me?'

Rory smiles quite flirtily and waggles his eyebrows: 'Would you like me to be flirty with you, Jennifer McAndrew?'

For a moment we hold a look.

'You're thinking about it,' he teases, 'you're seeing me in a whole new light. Why on earth did I not put on the lady-slayer suit?'

'No! I'm not,' I protest. And I'm not quite sure why I feel so stirred up. Rory is my best friend in St Andrews, closer than Alison really because he has more time to see me, but he's single, I'm single... but no, I don't want him to even hint. No spoiling anything between us.

'Sorry, sorry,' he bumps his elbow against mine, 'I'm talking rubbish because I'm exhausted. I stayed up till 1.30 last night eating chocolate and watching a Torvill and Dean documentary on YouTube.'

'What? *Why*?!' This is so unexpected I'm not sure how to react.

'I have no idea... fell down a YouTube rabbit hole. But have you seen the Torvill and Dean *Paso Doble*? I mean have you seen it?'

'I'm not sure. I don't think so.'

'Everyone thinks *Bolero* is the sexiest one but in that, he's the matador and she's the cape. And they are hot. On fire. He does look a little bit like a waiter though, not a matador. But a white Lycra onesie with flared trousers is a difficult look to pull off. But look up the dance where he is in orange harem pants and a gold waistcoat. I mean that is a brave, brave outfit choice.'

'You did not watch a whole Torvill and Dean documentary.'

'Did too. It was quite emotional. Had a little cry into my family pack of Minstrels. I mean could they be more British? We all wanted them to be shagging just the way they were dancing...'

'Shhh...' I warn him, as this is the bowling club.

'But no. It was a purely professional relationship. Although, I think he had a thing for her. Next time you're watching them...'

'I won't be watching them...' I insist, 'why on earth were you watching them?'

'I don't know. The night was young. There was an awful lot of YouTube to get through. What is your YouTube rabbit hole of choice?'

'Erm...' It's not as if I have to think about this for long. 'Interior décor,' I admit, 'the before and after videos... and especially those people who clean really dirty places, hoarder homes, kitchens that haven't been cleaned for a decade. Why is that so satisfying?' I ask as Rory laughs at me. 'And I might as well admit, I have quite the cookbook reading habit, even though I never seem to cook much that's very exciting.'

'But maybe you're prepping for it – your future home... your future meals.'

'Yeah...'

Is it just me? Or do we seem to be catching one another's eye a little too much this evening. Is there a joke I've not got? Why is Rory almost grinning at me.

'What?!' I ask.

'So... I met Mick the other day...' he begins.

'Oh... and...'

'He's so happy you're working with him. And he said...'

I feel as if Rory is pausing for dramatic effect.

'Yes?'

'He said you should finish your law degree because you'd make a great lawyer.'

'Oh!'

'Ever thought about it?' Rory wonders.

And before I can even reply he's mentioning online study, the Open University and have I thought about all the other places that might now offer online degrees?

'A law degree?!' I pretend to sound astonished. 'A law degree?' I repeat... but really, lately, well... I have begun to think about it. But maybe I needed someone to say it out loud. To make me believe that maybe I could.

'Yeah,' he says, 'all that time spent working for barristers and legal firms, I bet you could be quite the lawyer now, not just the brilliant assistant.'

I give a little laugh at this, drink more beer, promise him I will think about it and change the subject, but the next day, and the day after that... and beyond, the idea starts to take hold.

Another idea is taking hold too. Blue cars in the high street don't make me flinch the way they used to and I don't have bad dreams about them either. In fact, I find myself almost looking out for big blue cars. I'm curious. I'm already involved with Rory and Alison's families... going along on play dates, doing a little babysitting, baking the odd birthday cake and coming to the party too when required. But there is another family, another set of children that I really should get to know much better.

I realise the time has finally, *finally* come. Dad could test the water... and then he could make the arrangements with a simple phone call.

34

It's 2 p.m. on a beautiful Saturday afternoon in late August when I drive my little red car out to the address five miles or so south of the town. There's no denying I'm nervous. My mouth is dry, my heart is thudding and even when my phone insists '*you have reached your destination*,' I have to drive past, gather my thoughts for a few minutes, glance at myself several times in the mirror to make sure I look OK – more than OK – and then I finally drive back.

I indicate and pull off the road, parking in a gravelled driveway in front of a very pretty grey stone house. There's a blue front door and a trellis of pink roses climbing up the wall and nodding to the cool breeze. The lawn in front is neatly mown, blue pots at the door burst with flowers and everything looks cared for.

I walk slowly towards the door, aware that my heart is racing and when I reach out to ring the doorbell, I see how much my hand is shaking. The doorbell rings so loudly I'm startled. My throat's so dry, I can't swallow. Quick steps are heading towards me and I know I just have to stay here. It's too late to turn back. Too late to run away. I think of Dad and even my mum, try to lower my shoulders and breathe.

The door opens and in front of me stands the all grown-up, mid-thirties version of the girl I once knew almost as well as myself – Isla.

For a moment, we just stand and stare. It's striking how much she looks like our mother now. But her beautiful, beautiful smile is just as I remember.

'I'm sorry, Isla,' I say.

'No, I'm sorry,' is her reply.

And with that, we open our arms and fall forward, catching each other in the most heartfelt embrace.

Tears spring from my eyes, there's nothing I can do to stop them.

Her tears fall freely onto my shoulders as mine fall into her hair.

For several long moments, we can't let go and again whisper, 'I'm sorry. I'm so very sorry,' against each other's ears.

All that regret, and anger and heartache.

What a waste.

What a waste of time. Long years of pain that we didn't need to have.

Sorry doesn't seem enough.

I'm laughing and I'm smiling but I'm crying hard too. Look at this lovely person, my sister. My family. Part of me. Us.

'Come inside,' she says and takes me by the hand. So, in a blur of tears, I follow her through an elegant hallway into an immaculate white-and-wood country kitchen where she gives me tissues, cries and blows her own nose hard, then hugs me some more and makes me tea.

Alongside the mug of tea comes a plate of her homemade cake. She's picked one of our mother's recipes and I'm almost afraid to take a bite because the memories will be so fierce.

Once we've both stopped crying and started to talk and laugh again, Isla begins to tell me all about the parts of her life I have missed, and she asks questions and listens to me too.

We have so much time to catch up on.

We talk about her children and Dad and my new job; we talk about London and St Andrews; we worry about our elderly Dad together. She doesn't make me feel at all sorry for my rootless, undecided, single status; instead, she makes me feel quite exciting, different, adventurous and hopeful. The two hours we spend together fly past and with every passing minute, the years apart break down until we are sisters again, who want to grow much more closely together in the future.

'I've missed you so much,' we say to each other, over and over.

And when I'm brave enough, I look her in the eyes and say: 'I am so sorry, truly sorry that it's taken me so long to...' I have to pause, and scramble for the words, 'get over it.' I settle on. Those are the words I can manage.

'I wish so many things didn't happen the way they did,' Isla says in reply. She has warm brown eyes that look deeply into mine.

I put my hand over hers.

'Time to just forget about all that,' I say hoping she can read how much I mean this. 'It's the past. It's happened. We can choose not to rake over it all, but to move on.'

'Are you sure?' she asks.

'Yes,' I say, as I notice how light and relieved I feel. 'Absolutely positive.'

* * *

We are sitting on comfortable chairs in the sunny garden when tyres on the gravel announce the arrival of the blue car and the rest of Isla's family.

Once again, my heart begins to thud and my hands tremble as I realise I'm going to have to face Richard for the first time in years. And I'm going to meet my niece and nephew, properly, as two little people and begin my new, involved relationship with them as an auntie.

We stand up and wait as doors bang open and shut then, two children, much larger and much livelier than I expect, come hurtling into the garden. A boy and girl –Peter and Jessie – but...

As he approaches, the little boy stops in his tracks. He's looking at me in as much of a state of total surprise as I am.

'Pooky!?' I exclaim.

'Jennifer?!' he says back and after a moment. 'Are you my auntie?"

'Yes,' I'm kneeling now, so I can level with him. 'I'm going to be a much better auntie now,' I manage, all choked up.

He just runs into my arms for a hug, as I try to blink the tears from my eyes.

'This is Jennifer,' he tells his sister. 'She's nice and she's our auntie.'

'Hello, again,' Jessie says shyly, 'And I know,' she tells her brother.

'Hello,' I reply, thinking there's so much time I've missed. But no matter, I'm going to make up for all that.

'How do you know Pete?' Isla asks, almost as surprised as I was.

'I'm friends with Rory... and his daughters, Maggie and Katie.'

'Oh... of course! Pooky loves visiting them.'

'We have to go and swing, because that car is an oven!' Jessie announces, then she and her brother race to the swings at the bottom of the garden.

And then into the garden steps a middle-aged dad. He's tall and long-legged with something of the sportsman to his build. He's shaven headed, wearing a sturdy pair of dark-rimmed glasses. I look at him and honestly wonder who he is.

'Oh my goodness, Jennifer!' he says.

At the sound of his voice and at the sight of his smile, my brain makes the final adjustments and lets me know that this is Richard. Maybe it was letting the information in slowly, giving me time to react.

'Hello, Richard,' I say, hoping I don't look too startled.

I walk towards him and yes, we had a brief thing, and yes, I was sad when it ended and all confused when he and Isla got together. But I'm here now. I'm strong and capable and I've got over all of that. I can let that baggage go. And I can move on with the life I want to live.

We hug and nothing about this hug stirs up any kind of flashback. The younger Richard I was with has long gone. He's grown up, grown older and changed into Isla's husband, the children's dad... my... brother-in-law. This Richard looks like a really nice guy.

'You are looking so well,' he says.

'You too. I'm sorry it's been... so long.'

'Me too. I'm sorry. Really sorry.' I hear the seriousness.

Our eyes hold one another's for a moment or two. He pulls me in for another hug, holding me tight. This hug releases some last kaleidoscope of memories. And then it's over, forgotten and swept away. All in the past now.

Time to look forward.

I can see Isla is watching us and I give her a broad smile that I hope conveys that everything is really all right now.

I feel as if I have a brand-new family. And these two lovely children, so closely related to me. I'm Auntie Jen now.

This is much more wonderful than I could have imagined. I am totally bowled over and may have to hide for a few minutes in the guest bathroom and shed a few more tears.

* * *

When it's time to leave, I get into the red car and as this new family of mine stands at the door to wave me off, I'm struck by the look Richard gives Isla. That look is so tender and fond and wistful and loving. He looks at her still, after all these years, with such love.

I pull out of the driveway and onto the road. As I move up the gears and accelerate, I realise how full of love my heart is... I feel absolutely forgiving and understanding and touched and generous... this is love, I think. And I am full to the brim of it, ready to share it out.

And that's when the astonishing thought occurs.

In that photo from our sixth-form dance Rory wasn't looking at the camera, he was looking at *me*. And the other night in the bar, he did it again. He looked at *me*.

Quite like that.

My mind goes blank for a few minutes. I take in the road, the grass, the trees clad in darkest summer-green.

I'm not sure I can really think about it. I'm not sure I can think straight at all.

But the thought takes hold. And it won't go away, until I'm actually asking myself... Rory Ferguson did have a thing for me back then, according to Samantha... and was he trying to let me know with this look? Is there any possible chance that Rory Ferguson could still have a bit of a thing for me?

And has he been trying to let me know?

I think about our drinks together... and that sense of a shared joke, a shared secret almost. And his lady-slayer suit... I laugh at the thought. He looks good in that suit. Really good.

And I realise, all of a sudden, how much I love being with Rory. He makes me laugh, cheers me up, listens to me, cares... and looks actually pretty hot in the lady-slayer...

So...

So, could Rory have a thing for me?

And if so... what do I think about that?

This new possibility whirls around my head until I feel as if I'm spinning.

I... I seem to find this idea pretty interesting.

I mean... you could be very flattered by that. A girl could be completely bowled over by someone who has been in love with her years and years before and has fallen in love with her all over again.

Rory?!

Rory?

Rory!!

Rory is the nicest, kindest, funniest person I know. He has looked after me ever since I first came back to St Andrews. He has cared for me. He always has me, and my very best interests, at heart. I am only just appreciating how kind he has been to me.

But it's more than that. When I'm with Rory, I'm myself. I'm not trying to be anyone else. It's always for real.

When I've talked and joked to Rory about things, they matter more to me, or they make sense... or in some important instances, they hurt less. His opinion matters the most.

He knows me. I don't have to pretend to be anyone else or anything else.

And he's fine with me. Just me. And we laugh together... we really laugh. He makes me laugh and, almost as good, he makes me feel fun and funny too.

Oh my god.

I scream out loud in the car. And I'm not even sure why.

Excitement!

Uncertainty?

Happiness.

Really?!

Rory?!

Do I love Rory?

Have I decided this? Is it Rory?

Oh dear god, I have no idea... but I do know I need to see him. I definitely have to ask him. Yes. I urgently need to see him. Be wrapped in one of his bear hugs and try to work out how I feel about him.

Then I remember he has a wedding party to go to at 7 p.m. tonight. He's making a speech. And what about Elaine? Where is he with Elaine? They did break up, didn't they? Or is there any chance at all that she is his date tonight?

The atmosphere at wedding parties can get infectious. What if he gets together with Elaine or someone else, I think, almost a little hysterically – just when I've decided that *he* is *the one* for me?

Have I really decided this? Oh my god...

It's already 6.15 p.m.. No time at all until he's due at that wedding party. It may be too late to get to him tonight, but I really have to get to him tonight. All I can picture is him announcing his engagement to Elaine to me and... just no, no! I turn the volume up on the car radio and speed through the sunny lanes straight back to St Andrews, through the tourist traffic, cursing at every delay, every red light and finally make it to the cottage on the seafront.

* * *

It's 6.40 p.m. by the time I park outside. I'm sure I'm too late, so I actually run up the metal staircase, and knock loudly on his first-floor door. All I can think is: I need to see Rory, right now straight away, before he goes out with his date. I need to see him now. Of course, I've not prepared anything to say at all, which turns out to be a mistake because when he opens the door, I'm speechless.

But this has a lot to do with how he looks. The black trousers and white shirt is fine, the heavily done grey eye shadow and bright pink blusher is more unusual. There's a strong smell of nail polish and I spot his pink and glittery fingertips.

'Hi, Jennifer, how are you doing?' he sounds totally flustered.

'I'm fine... hi, how are you?' To my ears, I sound all strange and nervous, totally high-pitched. I realise there's some kind of stampede of heartbeats going on under my ribcage.

'I'm in a bit of a hurry,' he says, 'got to finish getting dressed, got to make my way over there... got to go through my speech again. I fell asleep in front of *Frozen*, that film is like Temazepam, I just need to hear the opening credits and I can feel my eyelids droop.'

'Did you sort a plus one?' I ask and this is a critical question.

'Yes! Dramatic new developments,' he says.

I give something of a gasp and think my heart might actually stop.

'Well... right...' I take a step backwards. I feel as if I'm reeling backwards.

'So, I'm in a bit of a hurry,' he adds, 'to put it mildly, but what's up?'

And I just stand there on the doorway and look at him, feeling like a total dufus, to be honest. Can I maybe convey this without words, the way they do in the movies? That would be so much easier than having to actually tell him what's in my head.

'Is everything OK?' he asks. 'You look a little strange.'

'No, I don't look strange!' I almost sound angry I'm in such a state. 'What about you? You're covered in make-up.'

'What?!'

He rushes to a small, framed mirror in his hallway and lets out a yelp.

'Girls! Did you do this when Daddy was sleeping?'

There's a gale of hysterical laughter from the sitting room.

'Girls! This is not funny! Daddy has to go out and where is your

Mum?! Call her, Katie, call her... for goodness' sake. Jennifer,' he turns his attention back to me. 'What's up? Something is up.'

'Look it's OK, really,' I insist, 'now is obviously not a good time.'

And I'm all ready to turn and bolt down those metal stairs just as quickly as I bolted up them.

He holds up his hands, takes a deep breath and says: 'Look, you are one of my oldest friends, no, probably my oldest friend, because Derek from primary school, we fell out some time ago. I mean, who shoots their own dog? Who does that? Even if it... Anyway... so, it is always a good time. Come in,' he ushers me into the hallway. 'I can't go anywhere till Hazel gets here anyway. I'm clearly going to need help on the make-up removal front. So, just tell me... cough, spill the beans.'

And then there it is. That look.

He is looking right at me, smiling slightly, head tilted to one side, eyes fixed firmly on mine. He makes me feel that whatever I need to say, it will be OK. He's got me.

'Rory...' I falter and my voice is all cracked and unreliable. 'Rory... I want... I want...' deep breath, I don't know how to say this... I don't know where to begin. But then I see a way and I manage: 'I want to be your plus one.'

His smile widens out into a grin: 'Really?' he asks.

'Yes.' Tears are welling in my eyes. Does he understand what I really mean?

'What is it?' he asks, taking a step closer.

The credits from *Frozen* are playing. In a moment the girls will tumble out of the sitting room and their Mum will arrive. I can't do this now, but I have to do this now, or maybe I won't ever be brave enough again. But what does he mean by dramatic developments? What if he's met someone else, just right now at the exactly wrong time?

'I want to be your plus one,' I repeat, several tears escaping down my face. He holds out his hands and I put mine into them. Then gathering up all my courage, I add, 'and not just for the party.'

For a moment there's a stunned silence between us. I'm sure I can hear both of our hearts thudding.

Then, close to a whisper, Rory says, 'Jennifer McAndrew.'

He takes a breath, lets go of one of my hands so he can fully close the door to the sitting room, then he looks back at me and takes hold of my other hand again.

I've never been more anxious to know what someone is about to say ever.

'Tonight's plus one, don't worry about that...' he begins, 'Declan said his cousin, over from Ireland, blah blah... it's not a date, more like a nice person who is available for dancing.'

Then Rory shuts up for a moment and just looks and looks at me.

'Right, I'm just going to come out with it,' he begins. 'Nothing to lose. Jennifer McAndrew...' I can feel his hands shake in mine. 'I am absolutely crazy about you, even though you keep on running off... and seeing me as "just a friend" and generally breaking my heart.'

There's another moment of stunned silence, then Rory pulls me gently towards him and, for the second time today, I'm holding tight, tight, tight to someone I wish I'd found my way to much sooner. And I don't want to let go.

But this doesn't feel sad. This feels electrifying.

We hold on.

His warm arms are around my back once again and I feel as if he's holding me together.

And finally, against my ear he whispers: 'Do you think we could try kissing? Or do you think it would be weird?'

I move my head from his shoulder and look at him.

There is a first for everything in life and this will be my first kiss with a man wearing blusher, eye shadow and sparkly nail polish.

We look at one another, eye to eye. And then I put my lips to his. My heartbeat is thudding right alongside his. And then we are kissing.

And kissing Rory quickly becomes smoulderingly hot.

This is quite some kiss going on out here in the corridor. This is rocketing straight up to the top of my best five kisses of all time chart.

The lady-slayer... I keep thinking and sort of want to laugh, but I'm still kissing.

I'm pulled in closer and tighter and the touch paper has been set ablaze.

'Whoah!' he says when we finally pull apart. 'Whoah! That was amazing, Jennifer McAndrew. Can we do it again?'

So we do, even though the little girls are now kicking on the sitting room door, which Rory is holding shut. Even though the doorbell is now ringing and the former Mrs Ferguson is outside.

This second kiss is mind-blowing. No other word. This kiss transforms my lovely man-friend into the man I want, who also wants to make me happy. The man with broad shoulders I can lean on, when needed, and arms that don't just hold me and his beloved girls tight, they also push all of us out there to make our way in the world when needed. All of these things make this kiss unbelievably sexy. I want him. I want to make him just as happy as he could make me.

'Please hold that thought. Hold it right there,' he says. Then he opens the sitting room door to allow Maggie and Katie to come stomping out into the hall.

And the front door has to be opened, too, to let Hazel Rudge/Ferguson into the hallway.

This hallway is tiny and now very overcrowded.

There are hellos to say: 'Yes, I'm Jennifer... hi... yes, in his class at school.' And I come up with something amazingly plausible about making an emergency bow tie delivery.

'I better make sure you get that make-up off as well,' I say a little sternly in Rory's direction.

I don't dare to look at him, because I think I'll give something away, but I can't help looking at him. He's squeeze-hugging his girls goodbye and promising to send them photos from the party.

'Especially of the cake,' says Maggie. 'And the bride.'

'Yes, we would definitely like some cake,' from Katie.

'You have to bring us cake, Daddy, you said,' Katie adds.

'I will bring cake,' he promises.

'Hi, Jennifer!'

'Didn't we make Daddy look lovely?' Cue hysterical giggles.

'Bye, Jennifer!'

Finally they are all out of the door and it is barely closed before we are kissing in the corridor again.

I can't quite understand why I am so turned on by this man.

This is Rory.

We had drinks just a few nights ago and I didn't really have any idea. Except maybe I sort of did... He's so nice. And so solid and muscular. And his hands are on my arse. He tastes so good and I want him so much.

He kisses my ears, my neck, my collarbone. I begin to unbutton his shirt.

Every button I undo, he does up again.

'Jennifer,' he says, 'I have to go. I have to give a speech.'

I unbutton.

He buttons.

'You will come with me, won't you? To this party?'

'Of course.'

'Good, I don't want you to go off and... change your mind.'

'I'm not going to change my mind!'

'Jennifer McAndrew,' he says, putting his hands on my shoulder, looking right at me, as if he can't quite believe it.

I can't quite believe it either.

But it feels real.

It always feels real when I'm with Rory.

He looks happier than I've ever seen him look.

And this very happy man is right next to me. Holding on to me. My happiness feels utterly real too. In fact, I don't think I've ever felt so madly happy in my entire life.

And he kisses me again, holding his hands tenderly against my face, making me feel precious and absolutely cherished.

I undo another shirt button.

'We're going to be late to the party,' I tell him.

'Jennifer McAndrew, if this is too much, too soon, we can go and drink tea. Probably we should go and drink tea. I will make you an awesome pot of tea and woo you over the rim of my teacup. Because, let's face it this is probably too soon.'

In reply to this, I undo another button.

'You scared of me?' I joke.

And another button.

'Jennifer McAndrew,' he repeats.

Kiss.

And more kissing.

And much more kissing.

Until we have to pause for breath.

'Too soon?' he asks again.

'I've known you for about twenty-five years, Rory. It's not soon enough.'

'We're definitely going to be late to the party.'

And after a little while, he asks: 'Bedroom or stay in the corridor? Sometimes moving venue can be bad, you know, the moment goes. I don't want you to be standing in my bedroom feeling awkward.'

'To your bedroom please.'

'My bedroom is pretty messy,' he adds.

'You're definitely scared,' I tell him with a grin, unbuttoning the fly on the dinner suit trousers as an encouragement.

'Oh my god... I'm terrified,' he admits. 'I've been thinking about you... for a very long time.'

'Keep thinking.'

He leads me to his bedroom, which is messy, and we fall onto his bed, which causes the neighbour's cat to flee out of the room in a yowling panic.

'Mrs Morton's bloody cat is going to kill me!' Rory shouts and several minutes have to pass while he chases the cat out of the sitting room, out of the kitchen, then finally out of the front door.

And when he comes back... well, we face each other and there's nowhere to hide, nothing to pretend or to joke away. Here we are. We know each other so well and we're going to take this step. Eyes open. Fully awake and fully aware.

We're going to take our clothes off and do this. We're going to take this risk. And afterwards, nothing can ever be the same again.

And as I'm kissing and helping my friend Rory to undress, I'm almost sad that our friendship is about to end... even if it's to transform into something else.

'Will you still love me tomorrow?' he asks, a little jokily. 'In fact, will you still love me when you've seen me in the buff?'

Rory is solid, but much more muscled than I'd expected. He was selling himself short with all his 'lard boy' gags. He's very male, despite the eye shadow and blusher that have been wiped at but not quite removed.

'I love you in the buff,' I tell him.

Our undressing and falling into bed is not very James Bond. There's no evening dress with a long and slinky zip, instead there's quite the undignified tussle with jeans that refuse to get over my ankles.

But this doesn't make it any less hot.

It turns out that two people who know each other very well and have realised how much they want each other can't really get anything wrong in bed. Everything is quite crazily exciting and goes very breathlessly right.

Plus, we're both givers, so we rock in bed.

He is hairy and hunky and funny and just quite delicious. I only want more of what we've just had.

When I'm gathered up in his arms, pulled close to his chest, I'm in a warm, safe and special place. And all my stupid, stupid bad decisions, and my big mistakes, the bad times and anxious anxieties, they wash over me. I want them to be gone. All spent. All over.

And for Rory, all that pent up longing, all that want... he finally gets me.

And I've found him.

The big man with the biggest heart and he wants only me.

We have found each other.

* * *

Afterwards, although we'd like to stay right here because we're all dazed and love-drugged, we have to think about getting ourselves to the wedding party. Rory pulls the white shirt back on and squeezes himself into the trousers and jacket, that I see now are about two sizes too small. He adds a thin black tie, which may be leather or even plastic, and his neck oozes from the shirt collar.

'Jeeezuz,' he exclaims. 'I can't sit down in this suit. The stress eating, when you were planning your new Argentinian life, you would not believe,' he admits. 'There was hardly anything left to sell in the shop.'

I spy his nails too, bitten to the quick, and feel nothing but a rush of love.

Obviously, I'm not dressed for a wedding reception, so I'm directed to Samantha's cupboard where I find the stretchiest available dress and the fishnets I bought with her. When Rory and I see each other all dressed up. We start kissing and wanting all over again.

So then we're on the bed again, even though we really, really have to go now.

'I can't believe this is happening,' Rory says and he kisses my cheek very tenderly.

'I'm mad about you, Jennifer McAndrew, I totally understand that you might need some time to get round to feeling the same way about me. But I hope you will.'

'I will... I do... for goodness' sake.' And I am crying and laughing in some sort of emotional approximation of the Scottish weather on a summer's day.

Propped up on one elbow, eyes fixed on mine, Rory says: 'I'm going to love you till the day I die and that is a fact, Jennifer McAndrew. So why don't we just get married? Maybe next week... if Angela can find us a slot.'

I sit up and stare at him: 'Rory, we've been together for about one hour. You may be slightly out of your mind.'

He shakes his head and gives me the look.

'No,' he says, 'I'm right back in my mind, where you and I have been together for about twenty-two years. I have been just about insane knowing you always choose the wrong guys and then you were moving to Argentina and then you weren't and every day since, I've expected to hear that you've decided to go after all. I mean no one moves to Argentina, apart from that girl, what's her name?'

'Tricia's daughter?' I offer.

'Yes, how do you know?'

'You need to meet Joan. You two are going to have a lot to talk about.'

'OK, no talking about Tricia's daughter, or anyone else. What we are doing is talking about getting married.'

'*You* were talking about getting married. Personally, I think one hour in is a little early. But that's just me.'

'Funny.'

'And who is Angela, anyway?'

'She's the registrar.'

'Look, it's fine, Rory, just calm down. I'm right here, I'm not going anywhere, I promise. I'm here with you. Calm.' I kiss him again and he is warm and delicious. Then I break off and suggest: 'Why don't we go to the party?'

He looks long and hard at me. I find myself smiling at being so closely scrutinised.

'You promise you're not going anywhere, you're going to stay right here?'

'Yeah.'

'In little ol' St Andrews?'

'Yeah – it's all right little ol' St Andrews.'

'You're going to stay right here in St Andrews with me?'

'St Andrews is much better with you in it. Much better. You put the fun into St Andrews.'

'So...' Rory sits up now, his face serious. 'I've had a vasectomy,' he reminds me.

I look up at Rory, hold his gaze and tell him with tears suddenly spilling: 'But... I didn't think I wanted children...'

'But if you change your mind? You might want to have... options.'

'Would it be OK to worry about that in the future... if we need to?'

We... I notice the '*we*' I've just said. *We...* Rory and me.

'You have three children, my sister has two... there are so many people, young and old, out there in the world to love. We could get that dog...' I add.

'You're amazing,' Rory says, 'I totally love you, Jennifer McAndrew. Now let's go party. *Do a little dance... make a little love... get down tonight.*'

'KC and The Sunshine Band? Very retro.'

'Oh yeah. I'm texting that request through to the DJ right now.'

So Rory stands up and even though his suit is too tight, he wears it awesomely. It clings to his muscular bum and legs and I find I want to pull it right off him all over again. But I resist.

I find high sandals lurking at the bottom of Samantha's wardrobe. I apply full make-up, also borrowed, to go with the clinging-too-tightly velveteen dress I'm wearing which Samantha has not been allowed to wear. The look Rory gives me, practically an audible drool, is worth it.

As we drive to the party in Rory's red pickup truck, I feel, for the first time in my life, like an absolutely cherished princess. All those other boyfriends, I think, they didn't know how to look after me like this. I should have walked away much sooner.

Rory takes me on his arm, walks us into a party well underway with loud music, dancing and drinks, and his face is beaming with pride.

'This is Jennifer McAndrew,' he keeps repeating to anyone who will listen, stealing long glances at me, 'I *love* her.'

And the funniest thing is, there are lots of people we know there, way back from our school days and they just take us in, Rory

Ferguson and Jennifer McAndrew, and act totally nonchalant. As if we were always supposed to happen.

And Rory's speech brings the house down, especially when he says: 'Sometimes you have to wait a really, really quite incredibly long time for the love of your life to find you… but that just makes it all… all the more ah-mazing.' We all hear the break in his voice on that word and he is not the only one wiping a tear from his eye.

And much later on, when I've drunk a lot of Champagne and I'm dancing slow in the arms of my man-bear, I think: yeah, Rory Ferguson and Jennifer McAndrew, why has it taken me *so long* to realise that this was always supposed to happen?

And again much later, when we get back to his place and stay awake together for most of the night, I think it over and over again: yeah, Rory Ferguson and Jennifer McAndrew, why has it taken me so long to realise that *this* was always supposed to happen?

35

When you are riotously happy, it turns out that life becomes incredibly simple. You're happy, so you do things that will make you even happier, and you try to help everyone else become as happy as you are too.

Maybe that's the rule of happy – try to make others as happy as you are.

First of all, there is a Sunday lunch to organise. And so, one beautiful day in early September, gathered round the table set out in Dad's garden – once our family garden – we have me, Dad and Joan, plus Isla, Richard and their three children. Of course, it feels a little momentous, because it's the first time we've all been together since... well... a very long time. But there's enough of a touch of family chaos to make it feel quite amazingly normal too: Dad loses the potato salad; Richard is clearly nervy until one of Dad's monster G&Ts sets him right; Pooky eats so many profiteroles, he is sick in the hedge; and at a quiet moment, Isla and I find ourselves on her old bed, in her old bedroom, looking through the box of Mum's belongings and deciding what each of us wants to keep. And it isn't all sad to do this. Now that our rift is healed, we find ourselves enjoying the memory of past happy times together.

When we sit down to eat, Dad doesn't give a speech, thank goodness. There's a dangerous moment when all the wine glasses are filled and he stands up, holding his aloft, but he just says 'cheers, bless you all' and sits abruptly down again with shiny eyes. I do notice though that over the course of the next three hours, he plays 'Good Golly Miss Molly' five times over and 'Love Me Tender' times three, which shows just how happy he is.

It's me, in fact, that makes just a mini-speech that I wasn't expecting to make. 'Here's to families,' I say, 'gotta love them,' I add, caught off guard by the tightening of my throat. 'And I've got some good news,' I go on. 'I'm going to restart my law degree...' I have to pause, because this gathers a happy little round of applause. 'And I'm moving in with Rory Ferguson,' I announce, 'because... well, he's... the love of my life.'

Yes, I think as my family take turns to hug and to kiss me, *he totally is the love of my life.*

* * *

Within a few days, I have moved out of Dad's place and I have persuaded Joan to move in. Because I think, like Rory and me, they will be very happy.

Yes, it is cramped in Rory's cottage flat when we're all at home, but we install some more cupboards and shelves and we tidy up strictly, in fact, almost quite Scandinavianly. Plus, the three girls are with their mother several nights a week, so on those days we have a little more space. Space to go to bed early, to get to know each other very well, to eat recipes from all those cookbooks I've been reading *in bed* and laugh; we spend a lot of time in each other's company laughing. Rory doing his famous Kate Bush karaoke act (*'Let me in through your window oh oh oh oh*'), then tripping over the coffee table and breaking the one nice mug in his home while I am almost sick with hysterical laughter is just our ordinary kind of evening in.

But when the girls are away, it very quickly gets too quiet and we long for the moment when they all stream through the door again, trailing clothes, lunchboxes, tiaras, boxes of Lego, hair straighteners, toy dogs and tantrums.

Soon after I move in with Rory, I take Hazel Rudge/Ferguson out for a very big swanky afternoon tea with a cocktail or three and assure her that I love her children and her ex-husband to bits and she should always consider me an ally, not any kind of rival. And actually, she has such awesome hair that we have quite the little bond over the best place to get your hair cut and coloured in town and decide that we could really like each other, provided we never, ever discuss Rory, so that makes things straightforward.

* * *

So, here I am on a golden early October evening, half an hour from closing time. The light is dropping low in the sky and setting St Andrews aglow, when elderly Mrs Morton comes into Munro & Partners for her appointment.

'Hello, Mrs Morton,' I greet her, 'how are you doing? Excited?'

'Very excited, thank you and really looking forward to the move,' she tells me. 'How about you? Excited too?'

I can't contain my smile: 'Totally thrilled. And thank you so much for keeping it all so top secret.'

She puts her finger to her lips and smiles.

I pull out all the relevant paperwork and call Mick through so that he can do his lawyerly duties.

'You'll be doing this bit soon,' he tells me with a smile. Because just four weeks ago, I enrolled in the part-time course that starts in

January and is going to give me the law degree I was too heartsick to continue all those years ago. Mick is very supportive and has offered to make Munro & Partners, Munro & McAndrew when I qualify, which is all the motivation I need to crack on. Plus, Munro & McAndrew sounds amazing... like a detective agency.

Twenty minutes and several signatures later, I am the proud new owner of Mrs Morton's downstairs, seafront cottage flat.

It turns out that Mrs Morton really did want to move to be closer to her daughter; she just couldn't face all the hassle of estate agents, viewers and making all the necessary arrangements. So, when I made her an offer and promised to do all the arranging, she was only too happy to accept. My one condition was that she didn't breathe a word to anyone about selling her flat... so that I could spring the surprise on Rory and our family that we now own the downstairs part of the cute little cottage too.

Unfortunately, she can't take her cat to her new place... but there we go, you can't have everything. And the cat always seemed to prefer it upstairs at Rory's anyway.

And somehow this has all come together on October 12th, my (errrrhmmm) big round number birthday. Mrs Morton, who let the removals men in at 2 p.m. this afternoon, so I could be certain Rory wouldn't notice anything, now hands me my best birthday present ever: two sets of keys to the downstairs flat and its pretty cottage garden.

I hold the keys tight in my hand, just about delirious with excitement.

We're going to have a garden! And we can move the kitchen downstairs... and install a proper wood fire... and... all my plans and dreams for the little house are tumbling about in my head. But mainly, I cannot wait to tell Rory.

I want to dangle the keys in front of his face and say: 'Rory, we own downstairs. We have the whole place. It's ours. Mrs Morton has moved to her daughter's. We have a family home, for our whole family.'

As I escort Mrs Morton out of the door and into her daughter's car, promising I'll look after Petal, the cat, and the rosebush and phone her if I need to know how anything works, I see two blurs of sparkle and netting burling down the pavement towards me.

Katie and Maggie often hang out in their Daddy's shop after school and then they run up the road to pick me up from work, especially on a riding night.

'Hi, girls, riding's not on tonight, remember?'

'Yes, we know, SHTOOPID, it's your birthday party,' Katie says.

'Don't call Jennifer shtoopid,' Maggie tells her off.

They stick their tongues out at each other.

'C'mon,' Maggie grabs my hand, 'you have to come to the shop, right now, Daddy has a surprise.'

'Shush,' Katie kicks her sharply on the shin, 'you're not supposed to say anything. Not one word.'

'Owwwwwww! She kicked me.'

'Look come in for a few minutes and calm down. I need to switch off my computer and get my coat and hat. Why don't you two look in the biscuit tin and see if there's something there for you?'

They rush off to the tin, not the McIver Hotel any more. Rory made that tin disappear and replaced it with a smiling and waving Harry & Meghan. I still think *OK!* magazine will sue if they ever walk into his shop and see what he's been up to with their photographs, but I can't worry about that right this moment.

Mick appears in his coat and scarf, ready to head home for the evening.

'Congratulations,' he whispers, because he knows too that the flat purchase is a secret, 'and don't forget to take your birthday flowers home.' He points to the lovely bunch he's given me, in the vase on my desk.

'No! I want them here, where I can see them every day – and thank you again.'

He heads out of the door as I switch off the computer and go over to the coat rack where my sturdily waterproof but absolutely stylish coat (imported from Sweden) awaits. I pull on a woolly hat, yes, but it's cashmere with an alpaca bobble and I tuck my two precious sets of keys into a brand-new handbag. Very chic, reassuringly expensive and sourced from the US, where they've managed to create exquisite leather handbags with a totally waterproof coating. I've also discovered suede boots with a neoprene lining, as I continue in my mission to bring London chic to the east coast of Scotland.

'OK, are we all set?' I ask the girls.

I turn out the lights, lock up and then, one girl on each hand, we walk down the high street towards Rory's shop. Historic flagstones beneath my feet, ornate and ancient spires ahead, silhouetted against the sunset, with a sharp, sea smell in the air. I'm so incredibly lucky to live here.

When we're about twenty metres or so away, Maggie and Katie break free, run the last stretch to the shop, open the door and disappear inside in a flurry of giggles.

So, I'm alone as I walk up to Rory's store and am brought to a halt by the window display.

It's so bright – almost dazzling! Pink and orange tissue paper has been put up as a backdrop and more pink and orange tissue paper has been scrunched up and piled to knee-height to cover the bottom layer of the window. Then there's a huge poster, three-feet high, covered in giant letters... a big heart-shaped photograph and a spotlight shining down on a...

I'm scrambling to take it all in.

OK. I take a deep breath.

The poster, start with the poster.

Amazing
Jennifer McAndrew,
Will you marry me?

Underneath these momentous words is a heart-shaped photo of Rory and me.

And the spotlight is resting on a dazzling ring, perched on a stool right there in the window of a shop in St Andrews high street. In fact, people are slowing down to look, point and comment as I stand there and deal with the onslaught of thoughts rushing through my mind.

We should book the bowling club, of course, for a huge party.

There will be so many bridesmaids: Maggie, Katie, Samantha, Jessie and what about Pooky? Would he want to wear knickerbockers? Maybe he could be a page in denim dungarees.

Rory will need a new suit. Maybe we could go country and western. He can wear boots and a hat... and for me, I like the idea of cleavage and some serious ruffles. I can spend some of the money from my dad's bankbook, to make Dad happy. I'll definitely toss my bouquet in Joan's direction.

And Alison, with her new online bijou travel website job, will be in charge of getting the best possible honeymoon on the best possible deal.

Of course, I know what I'm going to say.

Of course, I'm going to say yes!

Yes!!

YES!!! YES!!! YES!!!!!

The tissue-paper backdrop parts and I see Rory's face, looking anxious. He must be worrying that I'm taking too long, that I'm undecided. Behind him, I can see that the shop is absolutely packed, in fact that may even be a lit birthday cake in the background.

I've not had so many people being happy for me on my birthday for years.

I grin madly at him and say 'of course!' and throw my arms up into the air, which causes the little crowd gathered beside me at the shop window to break into applause. Rory's face beams with a hugely relieved smile and he disappears, so I know he's heading for the door.

I head for the door too.

I know when I was small, I used to have a vision of how my grown-up life would look – it involved a cottage by the sea, a gaggle of noisy children, a wonderful man I'd known for years and work that was clever and useful.

I couldn't have guessed how long it would take to get here, and how twisty and surprising and sometimes just downright sad the journey would be.

But none of that matters any more, because I'm right here now, exactly where I want to be.

A huge cheer erupts from the shop as I open the door and rush forward, tears of happiness slipping from my eyes, because I just can't wait for the rest of my life to begin.

ACKNOWLEDGMENTS

Thank you so much to everyone at the amazing Boldwood Books. All of you absolutely rock, but a special shoutout to my editor, Emily Ruston, and proofreader, Camilla Lloyd, who both always help me to raise my game. Not forgetting my agent, Diana Beaumont, who gets extra kudos for this book, in particular.

Huge thanks and hugs to my immediate family: Thomas, Sam and Claudie. Where would I be without you all?

A special mention goes to the wider Family Quinn, who will reconise shades of the late, great Papa, and Nunholm Park, in Jennifer's Dad and family home. What happy times we had.

Thank you so much to Sarah Smith and her family, who let me spend a day in their company in St Andrews, asking all sorts of daft questions. I hope the good citizens of that beautiful town will forgive all my inevitable mistakes.

MORE FROM CARMEN REID

We hope you enjoyed reading *The Woman Who Ran For The Hills*. If you did, please leave a review.

If you'd like to gift a copy, this book is also available as an ebook, hardback, large print, digital audio download and audiobook CD.

Sign up to Carmen Reid's mailing list for news, competitions and updates on future books.

https://bit.ly/CarmenReidNews

Explore more emotional, laugh-out-loud stories from Carmen Reid, available now.

ABOUT THE AUTHOR

Carmen Reid is the bestselling author of numerous women's fiction titles including the Personal Shopper series starring Annie Valentine. After taking a break from writing she is back, introducing her hallmark feisty women characters to a new generation of readers. She lives in Glasgow with her husband and children.

Visit Carmen's website: www.carmenreid.com

Follow Carmen on social media:

facebook.com/carmenreidwrites

instagram.com/carmenreidwrites

Boldwood

Boldwood Books is an award-winning fiction publishing company seeking out the best stories from around the world.

Find out more at www.boldwoodbooks.com

Join our reader community for brilliant books, competitions and offers!

Follow us
@BoldwoodBooks
@BookandTonic

Sign up to our weekly deals newsletter

https://bit.ly/BoldwoodBNewsletter